DATE			

The Lost Salt
Gift of Blood

THE LOST SALT GIFT OF BLOOD

New & Selected Stories

Alistair MacLeod

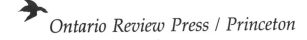 *Ontario Review Press / Princeton*

PT ꓤH

Copyright © 1988 by Ontario Review Press
Published by arrangement with McClelland and Stewart
All rights reserved
Manufactured in the United States of America
First printing 1988

Most of these stories were originally published in Canada by McClelland and
Stewart: in *The Lost Salt Gift of Blood* (1976) and *As Birds Bring Forth the Sun* (1986).

Cover photo by Warren Gordon

Library of Congress Cataloging-in-Publication Data

MacLeod, Alistair.
    The lost salt gift of blood : new & selected stories / Alistair MacLeod.
        p.   cm.
    ISBN 0-86538-063-5 (pbk.) : $10.95
    1. Cape Breton Island (N.S.)—Fiction.   I. Title
PR9199.3.M3342L6   1988
813'.54—dc19   87-36439
                                                                          CIP

Ontario Review Press
in association with Persea Books

Distributed by George Braziller, Inc.
60 Madison Ave., New York, NY 10010

CONTENTS

Preface

A LISTAIR MACLEOD'S brilliantly realized short fiction is set, for the most part, in an area of Canada as remote to most Canadians as it is to most Americans: Cape Breton, Nova Scotia, a Maritime region of particular beauty and isolation. Yet there is nothing foreign or narrowly "regional" about it; one is led to think, in reading MacLeod, of the kindred worlds of Eudora Welty's Mississippi, Frank O'Connor's and Edna O'Brien's Ireland, the Midlands of D. H. Lawrence. One thinks too of those extraordinary watercolors of Winslow Homer that take for their specific subjects the people and seascapes of Prout's Neck, Maine and Cullercoats, England. To suggest that the mythic human drama defines itself by way of such localized and lovingly rendered worlds is in a sense to say what is obvious—"obvious" when one is speaking of art of the highest quality. But in contemplating the work at hand one is likely to forget such high-flown generalizations in the sheer joy of the experience.

For this is an art that conceals itself, an employment of language so refined, yet so marvelously colloquial in its rhythms, that one is apt to forget it *is* art, and not a blunt transcribing of life nearly, at times, too intimate to be borne. (The reader cannot help but assume that everything that has happened in MacLeod's stories is true. If it didn't happen to the author then it happened

—surely!—to someone else.) Because MacLeod is so natural a storyteller, so reminiscent of what might be said to be an "oral tradition," it should be noted that his writerly vision has evolved by way of such masters as Hardy, Lawrence, Joyce, Hemingway, Faulkner. (The young Joyce of *Dubliners*, that is, and the young Hemingway of *Up in Michigan*.) Each paragraph, each sentence, each word has been weighed and *chosen*, not merely used.

When Alistair MacLeod published his first collection of stories, *The Lost Salt Gift of Blood*, in 1976, it was noted that there were seven stories in the book and it took seven years to write them. MacLeod's second collection, *As Birds Bring Forth the Sun*, which consists of seven stories also, was published a decade later. This is to suggest that there is nothing in the volume at hand that has not been deliberated at length; nothing written in haste, or for ephemeral purposes. Virtually all of the stories, one feels, might have been expanded into novels, and, indeed, they give the sense of being part of an imaginative whole, not mere fragments. The voice varies considerably—from the gravely elegiac tone of "The Closing Down of Summer" to the anecdotal ease of "Second Spring"—but it is recognizably the same voice, addressing us from out of the same authorial consciousness. Even in a story so elaborately constructed as "Vision," a small masterpiece of variations on a theme in which tales within tales are spun with admirable boldness and assurance, MacLeod gives us the sense of voices in concert, telling a story that bridges thirteen hundred years.

If there is a single underlying motive for MacLeod's art it is perhaps the sanctification of his subject—a sense both primitive and "modernist" that, if one sets down the right words in the right order, the purely finite (and local) is transcended, and the voiceless is given a voice. For instance, the miner-narrator of "The Closing Down of Summer" thinks:

> I have always wished that my children could see me at my work. That they might journey down with me in the dripping cage to the shaft's bottom or walk the eerie tunnels of the drifts that end in walls of staring stone. And that they might see how articulate we are in the accomplishment of what we

do. That they might appreciate the perfection of our drilling and the calculation of our angles and the measuring of our powder, and that they might understand that what we know through eye and ear and touch is of a finer quality than any information garnered by the most sophisticated of mining engineers with all their elaborate equipment.... I would like to show them how professional we are and how, in spite of the chill and the water and the dark and the danger, there is perhaps a certain eloquent beauty to be found in what we do.

The nameless narrator, his hearing seriously impaired by a quarter-century of mining, his very life running out, will never explain himself to his children: but he explains himself perfectly to us.

More often the narrator is a witness, as in "To Everything There Is a Season" and "As Birds Bring Forth the Sun": the son contemplating the father, the father's impending death, with love, awe, and terror. And in that most appallingly beautiful of stories, "The Boat," the father in his death is memorialized in such incantatory prose—

[It is not an easy thing] to know that your father was found on November twenty-eighth, ten miles to the north [of Port Hawkesbury, Nova Scotia] and wedged between two boulders at the base of the rock-strewn cliffs where he had been hurled and slammed so many many times. His hands were shredded ribbons as were his feet which had lost their boots to the suction of the sea, and his shoulders came apart in our hands when we tried to move him from the rocks. And the fish had eaten his testicles and the gulls had pecked out his eyes and the white-green stubble of his whiskers had continued to grow in death, like the grass on graves, upon the purple, bloated mass that was his face. There was not much left of my father, physically, as he lay there with the brass chains on his wrists and the seaweed in his hair.

—that we are led to understand he is no solitary man; his sacrifice of himself (he who was never suited to be a fisherman, nor ever wanted to be one!) no solitary sacrifice. One is reminded of the old English and Scottish ballads, in which the motive to preserve, to honor, to celebrate, to bear witness took the form of song.

In Alistair MacLeod's short stories one encounters the narrator as son, brother, husband, but above all witness; embarked upon a life's enterprise of forging not the conscience of his race—which MacLeod would probably consider both pretentious and unnecessary—but being the means by which its conscience is expressed. I have always thought the term "regional literature" misleading as well as condescending, for isn't fiction set in our Western capitals (New York City, London, Paris, Toronto) regional literature in the most literal sense?—doesn't it depend for its power, if it has power, on the specifics of streets, neighborhoods, the vagaries of local weather, the contours of an urban landscape its inhabitants take to be permanent, and of enduring significance? In this sense all literature is regional; or conversely, no literature is regional. Alistair MacLeod's Cape Breton is everywhere. And immediately accessible to us.

—JOYCE CAROL OATES

The Boat

THERE ARE TIMES even now when I awake at four o'clock in the morning with the terrible fear that I have overslept, when I imagine that my father is waiting for me in the room below the darkened stairs or that the shorebound men are tossing pebbles against my window while blowing their hands and stomping their feet impatiently on the frozen steadfast earth. There are times when I am half out of bed and fumbling for socks and mumbling for words before I realize that I am foolishly alone, that no one waits at the base of the stairs and no boat rides restlessly in the waters by the pier.

At such times only the gray corpses on the overflowing ashtray beside my bed bear witness to the extinction of the latest spark and silently await the crushing out of the most recent of their fellows. And then because I am afraid to be alone with death, I dress rapidly, make a great to-do about clearing my throat, turn on both faucets in the sink and proceed to make loud splashing ineffectual noises. Later I go out and walk the mile to the all-night restaurant.

In the winter it is a very cold walk and there are often tears in my eyes when I arrive. The waitress usually gives a sympathetic little shiver and says, "Boy, it must be really cold out there; you got tears in your eyes."

"Yes," I say, "it sure is; it really is."

And then the three or four of us who are always in such places at such times make uninteresting little protective chitchat until the dawn reluctantly arrives. Then I swallow the coffee which is always bitter and leave with a great busy rush because by that time I have to worry about being late and whether I have a clean shirt and whether my car will start and about all the other countless things one must worry about when he teaches at a great Midwestern university. And I know then that that day will go by as have all the days of the past ten years, for the call and the voices and the shapes and the boat were not really there in the early morning's darkness and I have all kinds of comforting reality to prove it. They are only shadows and echoes, the animals a child's hands make on the wall by lamplight, and the voices from the rain barrel: the cuttings from an old movie made in the black and white of long ago.

I first became conscious of the boat in the same way and at almost the same time that I became aware of the people it supported. My earliest recollection of my father is a view from the floor of gigantic rubber boots and then of being suddenly elevated and having my face pressed against the stubble of his cheek, and of how it tasted of salt and of how he smelled of salt from his red-soled rubber boots to the shaggy whiteness of his hair.

When I was very small, he took me for my first ride in the boat. I rode the half-mile from our house to the wharf on his shoulders and I remember the sound of his rubber boots galumphing along the gravel beach, the tune of the indecent little song he used to sing, and the odor of the salt.

The floor of the boat was permeated with the same odor and in its constancy I was not aware of change. In the harbor we made our little circle and returned. He tied the boat by its painter, fastened the stern to its permanent anchor and lifted me high over his head to the solidity of the wharf. Then he climbed up the little iron ladder that led to the wharf's cap, placed me once more upon his shoulders and galumphed off again.

When we returned to the house everyone made a great fuss over my precocious excursion and asked, "How did you like the boat?" "Were you afraid in the boat?" "Did you cry in the boat?" They repeated "the boat" at the end of all their questions and I knew it must be very important to everyone.

My earliest recollection of my mother is of being alone with her in the mornings while my father was away in the boat. She seemed to be always repairing clothes that were "torn in the boat," preparing food "to be eaten in the boat" or looking for "the boat" through our kitchen window which faced upon the sea. When my father returned about noon, she would ask, "Well, how did things go in the boat today?" It was the first question I remember asking: "Well, how did things go in the boat today?" "Well, how did things go in the boat today?"

The boat in our lives was registered at Port Hawkesbury. She was what Nova Scotians called a Cape Island boat and was designed for the small inshore fishermen who sought the lobsters of the spring and the mackerel of summer and later the cod and haddock and hake. She was thirty-two feet long and nine wide, and was powered by an engine from a Chevrolet truck. She had a marine clutch and a high-speed reverse gear and was painted light green with the name *Jenny Lynn* stencilled in black letters on her bow and painted on an oblong plate across her stern. Jenny Lynn had been my mother's maiden name and the boat was called after her as another link in the chain of tradition. Most of the boats that berthed at the wharf bore the names of some female member of their owner's household.

I say this now as if I knew it all then. All at once, all about boat dimensions and engines, and as if on the day of my first childish voyage I noticed the difference between a stencilled name and a painted name. But of course it was not that way at all, for I learned it all very slowly and there was not time enough.

I learned first about our house which was one of about fifty which marched around the horseshoe of our harbor and the wharf which was its heart. Some of them were so close to the water that during a storm the sea spray splashed against their windows while others were built farther along the beach as was the case with ours. The houses and their people, like those of the neighboring towns and villages, were the result of Ireland's discontent and Scotland's Highland Clearances and America's

War of Independence. Impulsive emotional Catholic Celts who could not bear to live with England and shrewd determined Protestant Puritans who, in the years after 1776, could not bear to live without.

The most important room in our house was one of those oblong old-fashioned kitchens heated by a wood- and coal-burning stove. Behind the stove was a box of kindling and beside it a coal scuttle. A heavy wooden table with leaves that expanded or reduced its dimensions stood in the middle of the floor. There were five wooden homemade chairs which had been chipped and hacked by a variety of knives. Against the east wall, opposite the stove, there was a couch which sagged in the middle and had a cushion for a pillow, and above it a shelf which contained matches, tobacco, pencils, odd fishhooks, bits of twine, and a tin can filled with bills and receipts. The south wall was dominated by a window which faced the sea and on the north there was a five-foot board which bore a variety of clothes hooks and the burdens of each. Beneath the board there was a jumble of odd footwear, mostly of rubber. There was also, on this wall, a barometer, a map of the marine area and a shelf which held a tiny radio. The kitchen was shared by all of us and was a buffer zone between the immaculate order of ten other rooms and the disruptive chaos of the single room that was my father's.

My mother ran her house as her brothers ran their boats. Everything was clean and spotless and in order. She was tall and dark and powerfully energetic. In later years she reminded me of the women of Thomas Hardy, particularly Eustacia Vye, in a physical way. She fed and clothed a family of seven children, making all of the meals and most of the clothes. She grew miraculous gardens and magnificent flowers and raised broods of hens and ducks. She would walk miles on berry-picking expeditions and hoist her skirts to dig for clams when the tide was low. She was fourteen years younger than my father, whom she had married when she was twenty-six and had been a local beauty for a period of ten years. My mother was of the sea as were all of her people, and her horizons were the very literal ones she scanned with her dark and fearless eyes.

Between the kitchen clothes rack and barometer, a door

opened into my father's bedroom. It was a room of disorder and disarray. It was as if the wind which so often clamored about the house succeeded in entering this single room and after whipping it into turmoil stole quietly away to renew its knowing laughter from without.

My father's bed was against the south wall. It always looked rumpled and unmade because he lay on top of it more than he slept within any folds it might have had. Beside it, there was a little brown table. An archaic goose-necked reading light, a battered table radio, a mound of wooden matches, one or two packages of tobacco, a deck of cigarette papers and an overflowing ashtray cluttered its surface. The brown larvae of tobacco shreds and the gray flecks of ash covered both the table and the floor beneath it. The once-varnished surface of the table was disfigured by numerous black scars and gashes inflicted by the neglected burning cigarettes of many years. They had tumbled from the ashtray unnoticed and branded their statements permanently and quietly into the wood until the odor of their burning caused the snuffing out of their lives. At the bed's foot there was a single window which looked upon the sea.

Against the adjacent wall there was a battered bureau and beside it there was a closet which held his single ill-fitting serge suit, the two or three white shirts that strangled him and the square black shoes that pinched. When he took off his more friendly clothes, the heavy woolen sweaters, mitts and socks which my mother knitted for him and the woolen and doeskin shirts, he dumped them unceremoniously on a single chair. If a visitor entered the room while he was lying on the bed, he would be told to throw the clothes on the floor and take their place upon the chair.

Magazines and books covered the bureau and competed with the clothes for domination of the chair. They further overburdened the heroic little table and lay on top of the radio. They filled a baffling and unknowable cave beneath the bed, and in the corner by the bureau they spilled from the walls and grew up from the floor.

The magazines were the most conventional: *Time, Newsweek, Life, Maclean's Family Herald, Reader's Digest*. They were the result

of various cut-rate subscriptions or of the gift subscriptions associated with Christmas, "the two whole years for only $3.50."

The books were more varied. There were a few hard-cover
magnificents and bygone Book-of-the-Month wonders and some
were Christmas or birthday gifts. The majority of them, however,
were used paperbacks which came from those secondhand book-
stores which advertise in the backs of magazines: "Miscellaneous
Used Paperbacks 10¢ Each." At first he sent for them himself,
although my mother resented the expense, but in later years
they came more and more often from my sisters who had moved
to the cities. Especially at first they were very weird and varied.
Mickey Spillane and Ernest Haycox vied with Dostoyevsky and
Faulkner, and the Penguin Poets edition of Gerard Manley
Hopkins arrived in the same box as a little book on sex technique
called *Getting the Most out of Love.* The former had been assidu-
ously annotated by a very fine hand using a very blue-inked
fountain pen while the latter had been studied by someone with
very large thumbs, the prints of which were still visible in the
margins. At the slightest provocation it would open almost automatically to particularly graphic and well-smudged pages.

When he was not in the boat, my father spent most of his
time lying on the bed in his socks, the top two buttons of his
trousers undone, his discarded shirt on the ever-ready chair and
the sleeves of the woolen Stanfield underwear, which he wore
both summer and winter, drawn halfway up to his elbows. The
pillows propped up the whiteness of his head and the goose-
necked lamp illuminated the pages in his hands. The cigarettes
smoked and smoldered on the ashtray and on the table and the
radio played constantly, sometimes low and sometimes loud.
At midnight and at one, two, three and four, one could sometimes hear the radio, his occasional cough, the rustling thud of
a completed book being tossed to the corner heap, or the movement necessitated by his sitting on the edge of the bed to roll
the thousandth cigarette. He seemed never to sleep, only to
doze, and the light shone constantly from his window to the sea.

My mother despised the room and all it stood for and she had
stopped sleeping in it after I was born. She despised disorder in
rooms and in houses and in hours and in lives, and she had not

had been walking into his room wheel around on one of his rubber-booted heels and look at her with his blue eyes flashing like clearest ice beneath the snow that was his hair. His usually ruddy face was drawn and gray, reflecting the exhaustion of a man of sixty-five who had been working in those rubber boots for eleven hours on an August day, and for a fleeting moment I wondered what I would do if he killed my mother while I stood there in the porch with those three foolish mackerel in my hand. Then he turned and went into his room and the radio blared forth the next day's weather forecast and I retreated under the noise and returned again, stamping my feet and slamming the door too loudly to signal my approach. My mother was busy at the stove when I came in, and did not raise her head when I threw the mackerel in a pan. As I looked into my father's room, I said, "Well how did things go in the boat today?" and he replied, "Oh not too badly, all things considered." He was lying on his back and lighting his first cigarette and the radio was talking about the Virginia coast.

All of my sisters made good money on tips. They bought my father an electric razor which he tried to use for a while and they took out even more magazine subscriptions. They bought my mother a great many clothes of the type she was very fond of, the wide-brimmed hats and the brocaded dresses, but she locked them all in trunks and refused to wear any of them.

On one August day my sisters prevailed upon my father to take some of their restaurant customers for an afternoon ride in the boat. The tourists with their expensive clothes and cameras and sunglasses awkwardly backed down the iron ladder at the wharf's side to where my father waited below, holding the rocking *Jenny Lynn* in snug against the wharf with one hand on the iron ladder and steadying his descending passengers with the other. They tried to look both prim and wind-blown like the girls in the Pepsi-Cola ads and did the best they could, sitting on the thwarts where the newspapers were spread to cover the splattered blood and fish entrails, crowding to one side so that they were in danger of capsizing the boat, taking the inevitable pictures or merely trailing their fingers through the water of their dreams.

All of them liked my father very much and, after he'd brought them back from their circles in the harbor, they invited him to their rented cabins which were located high on a hill overlooking the village to which they were so alien. He proceeded to get very drunk up there with the beautiful view and the strange company and the abundant liquor, and late in the afternoon he began to sing.

I was just approaching the wharf to deliver my mother's summons when he began, and the familiar yet unfamiliar voice that rolled down from the cabins made me feel as I had never felt before in my young life or perhaps as I had always felt without really knowing it, and I was ashamed yet proud, young yet old and saved yet forever lost, and there was nothing I could do to control my legs which trembled nor my eyes which wept for what they could not tell.

The tourists were equipped with tape recorders and my father sang for more than three hours. His voice boomed down the hill and bounced off the surface of the harbor, which was an unearthly blue on that hot August day, and was then reflected to the wharf and the fishing shanties where it was absorbed amidst the men who were baiting their lines for the next day's haul.

He sang all the old sea chanties which had come across from the old world and by which men like him had pulled ropes for generations, and he sang the East Coast sea songs which celebrated the sealing vessels of Northumberland Strait and the long liners of the Grand Banks, and of Anticosti, Sable Island, Grand Manan, Boston Harbor, Nantucket and Block Island. Gradually he shifted to the seemingly unending Gaelic drinking songs with their twenty or more verses and inevitable refrains, and the men in the shanties smiled at the coarseness of some of the verses and at the thought that the singer's immediate audience did not know what they were applauding nor recording to take back to staid old Boston. Later as the sun was setting he switched to the laments and the wild and haunting Gaelic war songs of those spattered Highland ancestors he had never seen, and when his voice ceased, the savage melancholy of three hundred years seemed to hang over the peaceful harbor and the quiet boats and the men leaning in the doorways of their shanties with their cigarettes glowing in the dusk and the women looking to the sea from their open windows with their children in their arms.

When he came home he threw the money he had earned on the kitchen table as he did with all his earnings but my mother refused to touch it and the next day he went with the rest of the men to bait his trawl in the shanties. The tourists came to the door that evening and my mother met them there and told them that her husband was not in although he was lying on the bed only a few feet away with the radio playing and the cigarette upon his lips. She stood in the doorway until they reluctantly went away.

In the winter they sent him a picture which had been taken on the day of the singing. On the back it said, "To Our Ernest Hemingway" and the "Our" was underlined. There was also an accompanying letter telling how much they had enjoyed themselves, how popular the tape was proving and explaining who Ernest Hemingway was. In a way it almost did look like one of those unshaven, taken-in-Cuba pictures of Hemingway. He looked both massive and incongruous in the setting. His bulky fisherman's clothes were too big for the green and white lawn chair in which he sat, and his rubber boots seemed to take up all of the well-clipped grass square. The beach umbrella jarred with his sunburned face and because he had already been singing for some time, his lips which chapped in the winds of spring and burned in the water glare of summer had already cracked in several places, producing tiny flecks of blood at their corners and on the whiteness of his teeth. The bracelets of brass chain which he wore to protect his wrists from chafing seemed abnormally large and his broad leather belt had been slackened and his heavy shirt and underwear were open at the throat revealing an uncultivated wilderness of white chest hair bordering on the semi-controlled stubble of his neck and chin. His blue eyes had looked directly into the camera and his hair was whiter than the two tiny clouds which hung over his left shoulder. The sea was behind him and its immense blue flatness stretched out to touch the arching blueness of the sky. It seemed very far away from him or else he was so much in the foreground that he seemed too big for it.

Each year another of my sisters would read the books and work in the restaurant. Sometimes they would stay out quite late on the hot summer nights and when they came up the stairs my mother would ask them many long and involved questions which they resented and tried to avoid. Before ascending the stairs they would go into my father's room and those of us who waited above could hear them throwing his clothes off the chair before sitting on it or the squeak of the bed as they sat on its edge. Sometimes they would talk to him a long time, the murmur of their voices blending with the music of the radio into a mysterious vapor-like sound which floated softly up the stairs.

I say this again as if it all happened at once and as if all of my sisters were of identical ages and like so many lemmings going into another sea and, again, it was of course not that way at all. Yet go they did, to Boston, to Montreal, to New York with the young men they met during the summers and later married in those faraway cities. The young men were very articulate and handsome and wore fine clothes and drove expensive cars and my sisters, as I said, were very tall and beautiful with their copper-colored hair and were tired of darning socks and baking bread.

One by one they went. My mother had each of her daughters for fifteen years, then lost them for two and finally forever. None married a fisherman. My mother never accepted any of the young men, for in her eyes they seemed always a combination of the lazy, the effeminate, the dishonest and the unknown. They never seemed to do any physical work and she could not comprehend their luxurious vacations and she did not know whence they came nor who they were. And in the end she did not really care, for they were not of her people and they were not of her sea.

I say this now with a sense of wonder at my own stupidity in thinking I was somehow free and would go on doing well in school and playing and helping in the boat and passing into my early teens while streaks of gray began to appear in my mother's dark hair and my father's rubber boots dragged sometimes on the pebbles of the beach as he trudged home from the wharf. And there were but three of us in the house that had at one time been so loud.

Then during the winter that I was fifteen he seemed to grow old and ill at once. Most of January he lay upon the bed, smoking and reading and listening to the radio while the wind howled about the house and the needle-like snow blistered off the ice-covered harbor and the doors flew out of people's hands if they did not cling to them like death.

In February when the men began overhauling their lobster traps he still did not move, and my mother and I began to knit lobster trap headings in the evenings. The twine was as always very sharp and harsh, and blisters formed upon our thumbs and little paths of blood snaked quietly down between our fingers while the seals that had drifted down from distant Labrador wept and moaned like human children on the ice floes of the Gulf.

In the daytime my mother's brother who had been my father's partner as long as I could remember also came to work upon the gear. He was a year older than my mother and was tall and dark and the father of twelve children.

By March we were very far behind and although I began to work very hard in the evenings I knew it was not hard enough and that there were but eight weeks left before the opening of the season on May first. And I knew that my mother worried and my uncle was uneasy and that all of our very lives depended on the boat being ready with her gear and two men, by the date of May the first. And I knew then that *David Copperfield* and *The Tempest* and all of those friends I had dearly come to love must really go forever. So I bade them all good-bye.

The night after my first full day at home and after my mother had gone upstairs he called me into his room where I sat upon the chair beside his bed. "You will go back tomorrow," he said simply.

I refused then, saying I had made my decision and was satisfied.

"That is no way to make a decision," he said, "and if you are satisfied I am not. It is best that you go back." I was almost angry then and told him as all children do that I wished he would leave me alone and stop telling me what to do.

He looked at me a long time then, lying there on the same bed on which he had fathered me those sixteen years before, fathered me his only son, out of who knew what emotions when he was already fifty-six and his hair had turned to snow. Then he swung his legs over the edge of the squeaking bed and sat facing me and looked into my own dark eyes with his of crystal blue and placed his hand upon my knee. "I am not telling you to do anything," he said softly, "only asking you."

The next morning I returned to school. As I left, my mother followed me to the porch and said, "I never thought a son of mine would choose useless books over the parents that gave him life."

In the weeks that followed he got up rather miraculously and the gear was ready and the *Jenny Lynn* was freshly painted by the last two weeks of April when the ice began to break up and the lonely screaming gulls returned to haunt the silver herring as they flashed within the sea.

On the first day of May the boats raced out as they had always done, laden down almost to the gunwales with their heavy cargoes of traps. They were almost like living things as they plunged through the waters of the spring and maneuvered between the still floating icebergs of crystal-white and emerald-green on their way to the traditional grounds that they sought out every May. And those of us who sat that day in the high school on the hill, discussing the water imagery of Tennyson, watched them as they passed back and forth beneath us until by afternoon the piles of traps which had been stacked upon the wharf were no longer visible but were spread about the bottoms of the sea. And the *Jenny Lynn* went too, all day, with my uncle tall and dark, like a latter-day Tashtego standing at the tiller with his legs wide apart and guiding her deftly between the floating pans of ice and my father in the stern standing in the same way with his hands upon the ropes that lashed the cargo to the deck. And at night my mother asked, "Well, how did things go in the boat today?"

And the spring wore on and the summer came and school ended in the third week of June and the lobster season on July first and I wished that the two things I loved so dearly did not exclude each other in a manner that was so blunt and too clear.

At the conclusion of the lobster season my uncle said he had been offered a berth on a deep-sea dragger and had decided to accept. We all knew that he was leaving the *Jenny Lynn* forever and that before the next lobster season he would buy a boat of his own. He was expecting another child and would be supporting fifteen people by the next spring and could not chance my father against the family that he loved.

I joined my father then for the trawling season, and he made no protest and my mother was quite happy. Through the summer we baited the tubs of trawl in the afternoon and set them at sunset and revisited them in the darkness of the early morning. The men would come tramping by our house at 4:00 a.m. and we would join them and walk with them to the wharf and be on our way before the sun rose out of the ocean where it seemed to spend the night. If I was not up they would toss pebbles to my window and I would be very embarrassed and tumble downstairs to where my father lay fully clothed atop his bed, reading his book and listening to his radio and smoking his cigarette. When I appeared he would swing off his bed and put on his boots and be instantly ready and then we would take the lunches my mother had prepared the night before and walk off toward the sea. He would make no attempt to wake me himself.

It was in many ways a good summer. There were few storms and we were out almost every day and we lost a minimum of gear and seemed to land a maximum of fish and I tanned dark and brown after the manner of my uncles.

My father did not tan—he never tanned—because of his reddish complexion, and the salt water irritated his skin as it had for sixty years. He burned and reburned over and over again and his lips still cracked so that they bled when he smiled, and his arms, especially the left, still broke out into the oozing saltwater boils as they had ever since as a child I had first watched him soaking and bathing them in a variety of ineffectual solutions. The chafe-preventing bracelets of brass linked chain that all the men wore about their wrists in early spring were his the full season and he shaved but painfully and only once a week.

And I saw then, that summer, many things that I had seen all my life as if for the first time and I thought that perhaps my father had never been intended for a fisherman either physically or mentally. At least not in the manner of my uncles; he had never really loved it. And I remembered that, one evening in his room when we were talking about *David Copperfield*, he had said that he had always wanted to go to the university and I had dismissed it then in the way one dismisses his father's saying he would like to be a tightrope walker, and we had gone on to talk about the Peggottys and how they loved the sea.

And I thought then to myself that there were many things wrong with all of us and all our lives and I wondered why my father, who was himself an only son, had not married before he was forty and then I wondered why he had. I even thought that perhaps he had had to marry my mother and checked the dates on the flyleaf of the Bible where I learned that my oldest sister had been born a prosaic eleven months after the marriage, and I felt myself then very dirty and debased for my lack of faith and for what I had thought and done.

And then there came into my heart a very great love for my father and I thought it was very much braver to spend a life doing what you really do not want rather than selfishly following forever your own dreams and inclinations. And I knew then that I could never leave him alone to suffer the iron-tipped harpoons which my mother would forever hurl into his soul because he was a failure as a husband and a father who had retained none of his own. And I felt that I had been very small in a little secret place within me and that even the completion of high school was for me a silly shallow selfish dream.

So I told him one night very resolutely and very powerfully that I would remain with him as long as he lived and we would fish the sea together. And he made no protest but only smiled through the cigarette smoke that wreathed his bed and replied, "I hope you will remember what you've said."

The room was now so filled with books as to be almost Dickensian, but he would not allow my mother to move or change them and he continued to read them, sometimes two or three a night. They came with great regularity now, and there were more hard covers, sent by my sisters who had gone so long ago and now seemed so distant and so prosperous, and sent also pictures of small red-haired grandchildren with baseball bats and dolls which he placed upon his bureau and which my mother gazed at wistfully when she thought no one would see. Red-haired grandchildren with baseball bats and dolls who would never know the sea in hatred or in love.

And so we fished through the heat of August and into the cooler days of September when the water was so clear we could almost see the bottom and the white mists rose like delicate ghosts in the early morning dawn. And one day my mother said to me, "You have given added years to his life."

And we fished on into October when it began to roughen and we could no longer risk night sets but took our gear out each morning and returned at the first sign of the squalls; and on into November when we lost three tubs of trawl and the clear blue water turned to a sullen gray and the trochoidal waves rolled rough and high and washed across our bows and decks as we ran within their troughs. We wore heavy sweaters now and the awkward rubber slickers and the heavy woolen mitts which soaked and froze into masses of ice that hung from our wrists like the limbs of gigantic monsters until we thawed them against the exhaust pipe's heat. And almost every day we would leave for home before noon, driven by the blasts of the northwest wind, coating our eyebrows with ice and freezing our eyelids closed as we leaned into a visibility that was hardly there, charting our course from the compass and the sea, running with the waves and between them but never confronting their towering might.

And I stood at the tiller now, on these homeward lunges, stood in the place and in the manner of my uncle, turning to look at my father and to shout over the roar of the engine and the slop of the sea to where he stood in the stern, drenched and dripping with the snow and the salt and the spray and his bushy eyebrows caked in ice. But on November twenty-first, when it seemed we might be making the final run of the season, I turned and he was not there and I knew even in that instant that he would never be again.

On November twenty-first the waves of the gray Atlantic are very very high and the waters are very cold and there are no signposts on the surface of the sea. You cannot tell where you have been five minutes before and in the squalls of snow you cannot see. And it takes longer than you would believe to check a boat that has been running before a gale and turn her ever so carefully in a wide and stupid circle, with timbers creaking and straining, back into the face of storm. And you know that it is useless and that your voice does not carry the length of the boat and that even if you knew the original spot, the relentless waves would carry such a burden perhaps a mile or so by the time you could return. And you know also, the final irony, that your father like your uncles and all the men that form your past, cannot swim a stroke.

The lobster beds off the Cape Breton coast are still very rich and now, from May to July, their offerings are packed in crates of ice, and thundered by the gigantic transport trucks, day and night, through New Glasgow, Amherst, Saint John and Bangor and Portland and into Boston where they are tossed still living into boiling pots of water, their final home.

And though the prices are higher and the competition tighter, the grounds to which the *Jenny Lynn* once went remain untouched and unfished as they have for the last ten years. For if there are no signposts on the sea in storm there are certain ones in calm and the lobster bottoms were distributed in calm before any of us can remember and the grounds my father fished were those his father fished before him and there were others before and before and before. Twice the big boats have come from forty and fifty miles, lured by the promise of the grounds, and strewn the bottom with their traps and twice they have returned to find their buoys cut adrift and their gear lost and destroyed. Twice the Fisheries Officer and the Mounted Police have come and asked many long and involved questions and twice they have received no answers from the men leaning in the doors of their shanties and the women standing at their windows with their children in their arms. Twice they have gone away saying: "There are no legal boundaries in the Marine area"; "No one can own the sea"; "Those grounds don't wait for anyone."

But the men and the women, with my mother dark among them, do not care for what they say, for to them the grounds are sacred and they think they wait for me.

It is not an easy thing to know that your mother lives alone on an inadequate insurance policy and that she is too proud to accept any other aid. And that she looks through her lonely window onto the ice of winter and the hot flat calm of summer and the rolling waves of fall. And that she lies awake in the early morning's darkness when the rubber boots of the men scrunch upon the gravel as they pass beside her house on their way down to the wharf. And she knows that the footsteps never stop, because no man goes from her house, and she alone of all the Lynns has neither son nor son-in-law that walks toward the boat that will take him to the sea. And it is not an easy thing to know that your mother looks upon the sea with love and on you with bitterness because the one has been so constant and the other so untrue.

But neither is it easy to know that your father was found on November twenty-eighth, ten miles to the north and wedged between two boulders at the base of the rock-strewn cliffs where he had been hurled and slammed so many many times. His hands were shredded ribbons as were his feet which had lost their boots to the suction of the sea, and his shoulders came apart in our hands when we tried to move him from the rocks. And the fish had eaten his testicles and the gulls had pecked out his eyes and the white-green stubble of his whiskers had continued to grow in death, like the grass on graves, upon the purple, bloated mass that was his face. There was not much left of my father, physically, as he lay there with the brass chains on his wrists and the seaweed in his hair.

In the Fall

W E'LL JUST HAVE to sell him," I remember my mother saying with finality. "It will be a long winter and I will be alone here with only these children to help me. Besides he eats too much and we will not have enough feed for the cattle as it is."

It is the second Saturday of November and already the sun seems to have vanished for the year. Each day dawns duller and more glowering and the waves of the gray Atlantic are sullen and almost yellow at their peaks as they pound relentlessly against the round smooth boulders that lie scattered as if by a careless giant at the base of the ever-resisting cliffs. At night, when we lie in our beds, we can hear the waves rolling in and smashing, rolling in and smashing, so relentless and regular that it is possible to count rhythmically between the thunder of each: one, two, three, four; one, two, three, four.

It is hard to realize that this is the same ocean that is the crystal blue of summer when only the thin oil slicks left by the fishing boats or the startling whiteness of the riding sea gulls mar its azure sameness. Now it is roiled and angry, and almost anguished, hurling up the brown dirty balls of scudding foam, the sticks of pulpwood from some lonely freighter, the caps of unknown men, buoys from mangled fishing nets and the inevitable bottles that contain no messages. And always also the shreds of blackened and stringy seaweed that it has ripped and torn from its own lower regions, as if this is the season for self-mutilation—the pulling out of the secret, private, unseen hair.

We are in the kitchen of our house and my mother is speaking as she energetically pokes at the wood and coal within her stove. The smoke escapes, billows upward and flattens itself out against the ceiling. Whenever she speaks she does something with her hands. It is as if the private voice within her can only be liberated by some kind of physical action. She is tall and dark with high cheekbones and brown eyes. Her hair which is very long and very black is pulled back severely and coiled in a bun at the base of her neck where it is kept in place by combs of coral.

My father is standing with his back toward us and is looking out the window to where the ocean pounds against the cliffs. His hands are clasped behind his back. He must be squeezing them together very tightly because they are almost white—especially the left. My father's left hand is larger than his right and his left arm is about three inches longer than normal. That is because he holds his stevedore's hook in his left hand when he works upon the waterfront in Halifax. His complexion is lighter than my mother's and his eyes are gray which is also the predominant color of his thinning hair.

We have always lived on the small farm between the ocean and the coal-mining town. My father has always worked on his land in the summer and at one time he would spend his winters working within the caverns of the coal mine. Later when he could bear the underground no longer he had spent the time from November to April as an independent coal-hauler or working in his wood lot where he cut timbers for the mine roof's support. But it must have been a long time ago for I can scarcely remember a time when the mine worked steadily or a winter when he has been with us and I am almost fourteen. Now each winter he goes to Halifax but he is often a long time in going. He will stand as he does now, before the window, for perhaps a week or more and then he will be gone and we will see him only at Christmas and on the odd weekend; for he will be over two hundred miles away and the winter storms will make travelling difficult and uncertain. Once, two years ago, he came home for a weekend and the blizzard came so savagely and with such intensity that he could not return until Thursday. My mother told him he was a fool to make such a journey and that he had lost a week's wages for nothing—a week's wages that she and six children could certainly use. After that he did not come home again until it was almost spring.

"It wouldn't hurt to keep him another winter," he says now, still looking out the window. "We've kept him through all of them before. He doesn't eat much now since his teeth have gone bad."

"He was of some use before," says my mother shortly and rattling the lids of her stove. "When you were home you used him in the woods or to haul coal—not that it ever got us much. These last years he's been worthless. It would be cheaper to rent a horse for the summer or perhaps even hire a tractor. We don't need a horse anymore, not even a young one, let alone one that will probably die in March after we've fed him all that time." She replaces the stove lids—all in their proper places.

They are talking about our old horse Scott who has been with us all of my life. My father had been his driver for two winters in the underground and they had become fond of one another and in the time of the second spring, when he left the mine forever, the man had purchased the horse from the Company so that they might both come out together to see the sun and walk upon the grass. And that the horse might be saved from the blindness that would inevitably come if he remained within the deeps, the darkness that would make him like itself.

At one time he had even looked like coal, when his coat was black and shiny strong, relieved by only a single white star in the center of his forehead; but that too was a long time ago and now he is very gray about the eyes and his legs are stiff when he first begins to walk.

"Oh, he won't die in March," says my father. "He'll be okay. You said the same thing last fall and he came through okay. Once he was on the grass again he was like a two-year-old."

For the past three or four years Scott has had heaves. I guess heaves come to horses from living too near the ocean and its dampness, like asthma comes to people, making them cough and sweat and struggle for breath. Or perhaps from eating dry and dusty hay for too many winters in the prison of a narrow stall. Perhaps from old age too. Perhaps from all of them. I don't know. Someone told my little brother David who is ten that dampening the hay would help, and last winter from early January when Scott began to cough really bad, David would take a dipper of water and sprinkle it on the hay after we'd put it in the manger. Then David would say the coughing was much better and I would say so too.

"He's not a two-year-old," says my mother shortly and begins to put on her coat before going out to feed her chickens. "He's old and useless and we're not running a rest home for retired horses. I am alone here with six children and I have plenty to do."

Long ago when my father was a coal-hauler and before he was married he would sometimes become drunk, perhaps because of his loneliness, and during a short February day and a long February night he had drunk and talked and slept inside the bootlegger's oblivious to the frozen world without until in the next morning's dehydrated despair he had staggered to the door and seen both horse and sleigh where he had left them and where there was no reason for them to be. The coal was glowing black on the sleigh beneath the fine powdered snow that seems to come even when it is coldest, seeming more to form like dew than fall like rain, and the horse was standing like a gray ghostly form in the early morning's darkness. His own black coat was covered with the hoarfrost that had formed of yesterday's sweat, and tiny icicles hung from his nose.

My father could not believe that the horse had waited for him throughout the night of bitter cold, untied and unnecessary, shifting his feet on the squeaking snow, and flickering his muscles beneath the frozen harness. Before that night he had never been waited for by any living thing and he had buried his face in the hoarfrost mane and stood there quietly for a long, long time, his face in the heavy black hair and the ice beading on his cheeks.

He has told us this story many times even though it bores my mother. When he tells it David sits on his lap and says that he would have waited too, no matter how long and no matter how cold. My mother says she hopes David would have more sense.

"Well, I have called MacRae and he is to come for him today," my mother says as she puts on her coat and prepares to feed her chickens. "I wanted to get it over with while you were still here. The next thing I know you'll be gone and we'll be stuck with him for another winter. Grab the pail, James," she says to me. "Come and help me feed the chickens. At least there's some point in feeding them."

"Just a minute," he says. "Just a goddamn minute." He turns quickly from the window and I see his hands turn into fists and his knuckles white and cold. My mother points to the younger children and shakes her head. He is temporarily stymied because she has so often told him he must not swear before them and while he hesitates we take our pails and escape.

As we go to where the chickens are kept, the ocean waves are even higher, and the wind has risen so that we have to use our bodies to shield the pails that we carry. If we do not their contents will be scooped out and scattered wildly to the skies. It is beginning to rain and the drops are so driven by the fierceness of the wind that they ping against the galvanized sides of the pails and sting and then burn upon our cheeks.

Inside the chicken house it is warm and acrid as the chickens press around us. They are really not chickens any more but full-grown capons which my mother has been raising all summer and will soon sell on the Christmas market. Each spring she gets day-old chicks and we feed them ground-up hardboiled eggs and chick-starter. Later we put them into outside pens and then in the fall into this house where they are fattened. They are Light Sussex which is the breed my mother favors because they are hardy and good weight-producers. They are very, very white now with red combs and black and gold glittering eyes and with a ring of startling black at the base of their white, shining necks. It is as if a white fluid had been poured over their heads and cascaded down their necks to where it suddenly and magically changed to black after exposure to the air. The opposite in color but the same in luster. Like piano keys.

My mother moves about them with ease and they are accustomed to her and jostle about her as she fills their troughs with mash and the warm water we have brought. Sometimes I like them and sometimes I do not. The worst part seems to be that it doesn't really matter. Before Christmas they will all be killed and dressed and then in the spring there will be another group and they will always look and act and end in the same way. It is hard to really like what you are planning to kill and almost as hard to feel dislike, and when there are many instead of one they begin to seem almost as the blueberries and strawberries we pick in summer. Just a whole lot of them to be alive in their way for a little while and then to be picked and eaten, except it seems the berries would be there anyway but the capons we are responsible for and encourage them to eat a great deal, and try our best to make them warm and healthy and strong so that we may kill them in the end. My father is always uncomfortable around them and avoids them as much as possible. My friend Henry Van Dyken says that my father feels that way because he is Scottish, and that Scotsmen are never any good at raising poultry or flowers because they think such tasks are for women and that they make a man ashamed. Henry's father is very good at raising both.

As we move about the closeness of the chicken house the door bangs open and David is almost blown in upon us by the force of the wind and the rain. "There's a man with a big truck that's got an old bull on it," he says. "He just went in the house."

When we enter the kitchen MacRae is standing beside the table, just inside the door. My father is still at the window, although now with his back to it. It does not seem that they have said anything.

MacRae, the drover, is in his fifties. He is short and heavyset with a red face and a cigar in the corner of his mouth. His eyes are small and bloodshot. He wears Wellington boots with his trousers tucked inside them, a broad western-style belt, and a brown suede jacket over a flannel shirt which is open at the neck exposing his reddish chest-hair. He carries a heavy stock whip in his hand and taps it against the side of his boot. Because of his short walk in the wind-driven rain his clothes are wet and now in the warmth of the kitchen they give off a steamy, strong odor that mingles uncomfortably with that of his cigar. An odor that comes of his jostling and shoving the countless frightened animals that have been carried on the back of his truck, an odor of manure and sweat and fear.

"I hear you've got an old knacker," he says now around the corner of his cigar. "Might get rid of him for mink-feed if I'm lucky. The price is twenty dollars."

My father says nothing, but his eyes which seem the gray of the ocean behind him remind me of a time when the log which Scott was hauling seemed to ricochet wildly off some half-submerged obstacle, catching the man's legs beneath its onrushing force and dragging and grinding him beneath it until it smashed into a protruding stump, almost uprooting it and knocking Scott back upon his haunches. And his eyes then in their grayness had reflected fear and pain and almost a mute wonder at finding himself so painfully trapped by what seemed all too familiar.

And it seemed now that we had, all of us, conspired against him, his wife and six children and the cigar-smoking MacRae, and that we had almost brought him to bay with his back against the ocean-scarred window so pounded by the driving rain and with all of us ringed before him. But still he says nothing although I think his mind is racing down all the possible avenues of argument, and rejecting all because he knows the devastating truth that awaits him at the end of each: "There is no need of postponing it; the truck is here and there will never be a better opportunity; you will soon be gone; he will never be any younger; the price will never be any higher; he may die this winter and we will get nothing at all; we are not running a rest home for retired horses; I am alone here with six children and I have more than enough to do; the money for his feed could be spent on your children; don't your children mean more to you than a horse; it is unfair to go and leave us here with him to care for."

Then with a nod he moves from the window and starts toward the door. "You're not..." begins David, but he is immediately silenced by his mother. "Be quiet," she says. "Go and finish feeding the chickens," and then, as if she cannot help it, "At least there is some point in feeding them." Almost before my father stops, I know she is sorry about the last part. That she fears that she has reached for too much and perhaps even now has lost

all she had before. It is like when you attempt to climb one of
the almost vertical sea-washed cliffs, edging upward slowly and
groping with blue-tipped fingers from one tiny crevice to the
next and then seeing the tantalizing twig which you cannot resist
seizing, although even as you do, you know it can be grounded
in nothing for there is no vegetation there nor soil to support it
and the twig is but a reject tossed up there by the sea, and even
then you are tensing yourself for the painful, bruising slide that
must inevitably follow. But this time for my mother, it does not.
He only stops and looks at her for a moment before forcing open
the door and going out into the wind. David does not move.

"I think he's going to the barn," says my mother then with
surprising softness in her voice, and telling me with her eyes that
I should go with him. By the time MacRae and I are outside he
is already halfway to the barn; he has no hat nor coat and is
walking sideways and leaning and knifing himself into the wind
which blows his trousers taut against the outlines of his legs.

As MacRae and I pass the truck I cannot help but look at the
bull. He is huge and old and is an Ayrshire. He is mostly white
except for the almost cherry-red markings of his massive shoulders and on his neck and jowls. His heavy head is forced down
almost to the truck's floor by a reinforced chain halter and by a
rope that has been doubled through his nose ring and fastened
to an iron bar bolted to the floor. He has tried to turn his back
into the lashing wind and rain and his bulk is pressed against
the truck's slatted side at an unnatural angle to his grotesquely
fastened head. The floor of the truck is greasy and slippery with
a mixture of the rain and his own excrement, and each time he
attempts to move, his feet slide and threaten to slip from under
him. He is trembling with the strain, and the muscles in his
shoulders give involuntary little twitches and his eyes roll upward in their sockets. The rain mingles with his sweat and
courses down his flanks in rivulets of gray.

"How'd you like to have a pecker on you like that fella,"
shouts MacRae into the wind. "Bet he's had his share and driven
it into them little heifers a good many times. Boy you get hung
like that, you'll have all them horny little girls squealen for you
to take 'em behind the bushes. No time like it with them little

girls, just when the juice starts runnen in 'em and they're finding out what it's for." He runs his tongue over his lips appreciatively and thwacks his whip against the sodden wetness of his boot.

Inside the barn it is still and sheltered from the storm. Scott is in the first stall and then there is a vacant one and then those of the cattle. My father has gone up beside Scott and is stroking his nose but saying nothing. Scott rubs his head up and down against my father's chest. Although he is old he is still strong and the force of his neck as he rubs almost lifts my father off his feet and pushes him against the wall.

"Well, no time like the present," says MacRae, as he unzips his fly and begins to urinate in the alleyway behind the stalls.

The barn is warm and close and silent, and the odor from the animals and from the hay is almost sweet. Only the sound of MacRae's urine and the faint steam that rises from it disturb the silence and the scene. "Ah sweet relief," he says rezipping his trousers and giving his knees a little bend for adjustment as he turns toward us. "Now let's see what we've got here."

He puts his back against Scott's haunches and almost heaves him across the stall before walking up beside him to where my father stands. The inspection does not take long; I suppose because not much is expected of future mink-feed. "You've got a good halter on him there," says MacRae. "I'll throw in a dollar for it, you won't be needing it anyway." My father looks at him for what seems a very long time and then almost imperceptibly nods his head. "Okay," says MacRae, "twenty-one dollars, a deal's a deal." My father takes the money, still without saying anything, opens the barn door and without looking backward walks through the rain toward his house. And I follow him because I do not know what else to do.

Within the house it is almost soundless. My mother goes to the stove and begins rinsing her teapot and moving her kettle about. Outside we hear MacRae starting the engine of his truck and we know he is going to back it against the little hill beside the barn. It will be easier to load his purchase from there. Then it is silent again, except for the hissing of the kettle which is now too hot and which someone should move to the back of the stove; but nobody does.

And then all of us are drawn with a strange fascination to the window, and, yes, the truck is backed against the little hill as we knew and MacRae is going into the barn with his whip still in his hand. In a moment he reappears leading Scott behind him.

As he steps out of the barn the horse almost stumbles but regains his balance quickly. Then the two ascend the little hill, both of them turning their faces from the driving rain. Scott stands quietly while MacRae lets down the tailgate of his truck. When the tailgate is lowered it forms a little ramp from the hill to the truck and MacRae climbs it with the halter-shank in his hand, tugging it impatiently. Scott places one foot on the ramp and we can almost hear, or perhaps I just imagine it, the hollow thump of his hoof upon the wet planking; but then he hesitates, withdraws his foot and stops. MacRae tugs at the rope but it has no effect. He tugs again. He comes halfway down the little ramp, reaches out his hand, grasps the halter itself and pulls; we can see his lips moving and he is either coaxing or cursing or both; he is facing directly into the rain now and it is streaming down his face. Scott does not move. MacRae comes down from the truck and leads Scott in a wide circle through the wet grass. He goes faster and faster, building up speed and soon both man and horse are almost running. Through the grayness of the blurring, slanting rain they look almost like a black-and-white movie that is badly out of focus. Suddenly without changing speed MacRae hurries up the ramp of the truck and the almost trotting horse follows him, until his hoof strikes the tailboard. Then he stops suddenly. As the rope jerks taut, MacRae who is now in the truck and has been carried forward by his own momentum is snapped backward; he bounces off the side of the bull, loses his footing on the slimy planking and falls into the wet filth of the truck box's floor. Almost before we can wonder if he is hurt, he is back upon his feet; his face is livid and his clothes are smeared with manure and running brown rivulets; he brings the whip, which he has somehow never relinquished even in his fall, down savagely between the eyes of Scott, who is still standing rigidly at the tailgate. Scott shakes his head as if dazed and backs off into the wet grass trailing the rope behind him.

It has all happened so rapidly that we in the window do not

really know what to do, and are strangely embarrassed by finding ourselves where we are. It is almost as if we have caught ourselves and each other doing something that is shameful. Then David breaks the spell. "He is not going to go," he says, and then almost shouts, "He is just not going to go—ever. Good for him. Now that he's hit him, it's for sure. He'll never go and he'll have to stay." He rushes toward my father and throws his arms around his legs.

And then the door is jerked open and MacRae is standing there angrily with his whip still in his hand. His clothes are still soggy from his fall and the water trails from them in brown drops upon my mother's floor. His face is almost purple as he says, "Unless I get that fucken horse on the truck in the next five minutes, the deal's off and you'll be a goddamn long time tryen to get anybody else to pay that kinda money for the useless old cocksucker."

It is as if all of the worst things one imagines happening suddenly have. But it is not at all as you expected. And I think I begin to understand for the first time how difficult and perhaps how fearful it is to be an adult and I am suddenly and selfishly afraid not only for myself now but for what it seems I am to be. For I had somehow always thought that if one talked like that before women or small children or perhaps even certain men that the earth would open up or lightning would strike or that at least many people would scream and clap their hands over their ears in horror or that the offender if not turned to stone would certainly be beaten by a noble, clean-limbed hero. But it does not happen that way at all. All that happens is the deepening of the thunder-cloud grayness in my father's eyes and the heightening of the color in my mother's cheeks. And I realize also with a sort of shock that in spite of Scott's refusal to go on the truck nothing has really changed. I mean not really; and that all of the facts remain awfully and simply the same: that Scott is old and that we are poor and that my father must soon go away and that he must leave us either with Scott or without him. And that it is somehow like my mother's shielding her children from "swearing" for so many years, only to find one day that it too is there in its awful reality in spite of everything that she had wished and wanted. And even as I am thinking this my father

goes by MacRae who is still standing in the ever-widening puddles of brown, seeming like some huge growth that is nourished
by the foul-smelling waters that he himself has brought.

David who had released my father's legs with the entrance
of MacRae makes a sort of flying tackle for them now but I
intercept him and find myself saying as if from a great distance
my mother's phrases in something that sounds almost like her
voice, "Let's go and finish feeding the chickens." I tighten my
grip on his arm and we almost have to squeeze past MacRae
whose bulk is blocking the doorway and who has not yet made
a motion to leave.

Out of doors my father is striding directly into the slashing
rain to where Scott is standing in something like puzzlement
with his back to the rain and his halter-shank dangling before
him. When he sees my father approach he cocks his ears and
nickers in recognition. My father who looks surprisingly slight
with his wet clothes plastered to his body takes the rope in his
hand and moves off with the huge horse following him eagerly.
Their movement seems almost that of the small tug docking the
huge ocean freighter, except that they are so individually and
collectively alive. As they approach the truck's ramp, it is my
father who hesitates and seems to flinch, and it is his foot which
seems to recoil as it touches the planking; but on the part of
Scott there is no hesitation at all; his hooves echo firmly and
confidently on the strong wet wood and his head is almost
pressed into the small of my father's back, he is so eager to get
to wherever they are going.

He follows him as I have remembered them all of my life and
imagined them even before. Following wildly through the darkened caverns of the mine in its dryness as his shoes flashed
sparks from the tracks and the stone; and in its wetness with
both of them up to their knees in water, feeling rather than
seeing the landing of their splashing feet and with the coal cars
thundering behind them with such momentum that were the
horse to stumble the very cars he had set in motion would roll
over him, leaving him mangled and grisly to be hauled above
ground only as carrion for the wheeling gulls. And on the surface, following, in the summer's heat with the jolting hay wagon

and the sweat churned to froth between his legs and beneath his collar, fluttering white on the blackness of his glistening coat. And in the winter, following, over the semi-frozen swamps as the snapping, whistling logs snaked behind him, grunting as he broke through the shimmering crystal ice which slashed his fetlocks and caused a scarlet trail of bloodied perforations on the whiteness of the snow. And in the winter, too, with the ton of coal upon the sleigh, following, even over the snowless stretches, driven bare by the wind, leaning low with his under-side parallel and almost touching the ground, grunting, and swinging with violent jolts to the right and then to the left, moving the sleigh forward only by moving it sideways, which he had learned was the only way it would move at all.

Even as my father is knotting the rope, MacRae is hurrying past us and slamming shut the tailgate and dropping down the iron bolts that will hold it in its place. My father climbs over the side of the box and down as MacRae steps onto the running board and up into the cab. The motor roars and the truck lurches forward. It leaves two broad wet tracks in the grass like the trails of two slimy, giant slugs and the smell of its exhaust hangs heavy on the air. As it makes the turn at the bottom of the lane Scott tries to turn his head and look back but the rope has been tied very short and he is unable to do so. The sheets of rain come down like so many slanted, beaded curtains making it impossible to see what we know is there, and then there is only the receding sound of the motor, the wet trails on the grass and the exhaust fumes in the air.

It is only then that I realize that David is no longer with me, but even as the question comes to the surface so also does its answer and I run toward the squawking of the chicken house.

Within the building it is difficult to see and difficult to breathe and difficult to believe that so small a boy could wreak such havoc in so short a time. The air is thick with myriad dust particles from the disturbed floor, and bits of straw and tiny white scarlet-flecked feathers eddy and dip and swirl. The frightened capons, many of them already bloodied and mangled, attempt short and ungainly flights, often colliding with each other in mid-air. Their overfed bodies are too heavy for their weak and unused wings and they are barely able to get off the floor and flounder for a few feet before thumping down to dusty crippled landings. They are screaming with terror and their screams seem as unnatural as their flights, as if they had been terribly miscast in the most unsuitable of roles. Many of them are already lifeless and crumpled and dustied and bloodied on the floor, like sad, gray, wadded newspapers that had been used to wipe up blood. The sheen of their feathers forever gone.

In the midst of it all David moves like a small blood-spattered dervish swinging his axe in all directions and almost unknowingly, as if he were blindfolded. Dust has settled on the dampness of his face and the tears make tiny trails through its grayness, like lonely little rivers that have really nothing to water. A single tiny feather is plastered to his forehead and he is coughing and sobbing, both at the same time.

When my father appears beside me in the doorway he seems to notice for the first time that he is not alone. With a final exhausted heave he throws the axe at my father. "Cocksucker," he says in some kind of small, sad parody of MacRae, and bolts past us through the door almost colliding with my mother who now comes from out of the rain. He has had very little strength with which to throw the axe and it clatters uselessly off the wall and comes to rest against my father's boot, wet and bloodied with feathers and bits of flesh still clinging to its blade.

I am tremendously sorry for the capons, now so ruined and so useless, and for my mother and for all the time and work she has put into them for all of us. But I do not know what to do and I know not what to say.

As we leave the melancholy little building the wind cuts in from the ocean with renewed fury. It threatens to lift you off your feet and blow you to the skies and your crotch is numb and cold as your clothes are flattened hard against the front of your body, even as they tug and snap at your back in insistent, billowing balloons. Unless you turn or lower your head it is impossible to breathe for the air is blown back almost immediately into your lungs and your throat convulses and heaves. The rain is now a stinging sleet which is rapidly becoming the winter's first snow. It is impossible to see into it, and the ocean off which it rushes is lost in the swirling whiteness although it thunders and roars in its invisible nearness like the heavy bass blending with the shrieking tenor of the wind. You hear so much that you can hardly hear at all. And you are almost immobile and breathless and blind and deaf. Almost but not quite. For by turning and leaning your body and your head, you can move and breathe and see and hear a little at a time. You do not gain much but you can hang on to what little you have and your toes curl almost instinctively within your shoes as if they are trying to grasp the earth.

I stop and turn my face from the wind and look back the way I have come. My parents are there, blown together behind me. They are not moving, either, only trying to hold their place. They have turned sideways to the wind and are facing and leaning into each other with their shoulders touching, like the end-timbers of a gabled roof. My father puts his arms around my mother's waist and she does not remove them as I have always seen her do. Instead she reaches up and removes the combs of coral from the heaviness of her hair. I have never seen her hair in all its length before and it stretches out now almost parallel to the earth, its shining blackness whipped by the wind and glistening like the snow that settles and melts upon it. It surrounds and engulfs my father's head and he buries his face within its heavy darkness, and draws my mother closer toward him. I think they will stand there for a long, long time, leaning into each other and into the wind-whipped snow and with the ice freezing to their cheeks. It seems that perhaps they should be left alone so I turn and take one step and then another and move forward a little at a time. I think I will try to find David, that perhaps he may understand.

Second Spring

I T WAS THE SUMMER after the seventh grade that saw me truly smitten with the calf club wish. It was not, of course, a really dazzlingly new idea because, living on a farm, I had always been surrounded by numerous animals. Not a day went by without touching them and the insistence of their presence affected the living of my life and the lives of the other members of my family in very real and tangible ways. Their closeness and the manner of their closeness varied with the time of seasons.

In the winter when they were less plentiful, they crowded together in the shared and dense confinement of their stables, stamping their hooves on the manure-strong planking and tossing their impatient heads and uttering the sounds of their different species. If you ventured into the silent barn at night the wave of their communal warmth rolled out to meet you at the creaking, opened door and the sound of the different rhythms of their breathing rose and fell in the softened darkness. If the flashlight was flicked on, or the carried lantern raised, the luminous eyes of those who were awakened glowed from their stalls and across their mangers, and then various sounds seemed to respond to the presence of the light: the creak of the wooden stanchion posts rubbed by the necks of restless cattle, the murmured grunts of half-asleep pigs, the nickering snorts of horses, the zing of suddenly tightened rope or leather, the jangle of moving halter chains.

By March conditions were even more overcrowded as the females grew awkward and ponderous with the weight of their unborn young. When they lay down in their expanded heaviness the ripples of movement from deep within their wombs were visible against the drum-tight skin of their extended sides. The promise of the future lay warm and heavy within their deep, dark bodies.

Inside the winter house the dogs and cats lay like scattered rugs beneath the kitchen couches and under dining tables or stretched at length behind the wood-filled stoves. At night my dog Laddie lay across my feet, a warm and living comforter whose heartbeat could be felt through the fabric of the bed-clothes. His wet, cold nose was covered by his paws.

By the end of March the birth cycle would begin and would extend sometimes deep into June. First the sheep, then some cattle and later the pigs and finally the wobbly foals with their long, ungainly legs. There would be chickens and kittens and puppies with at-first-unopened eyes. The number of animals would double or almost triple within the allotted weeks and there would be a flurry of activity surrounding the new arrivals and the rapidity of their growth. New pens would be constructed and, amidst squeals of protest, there would be separations, weanings and brandings and the pulling of teeth and the flashing of knives used for the cutting of testicles, the docking of tails and the notching of ears. They would spill out then, according to their kind, to the larger yards and fields or the mountain-high pastures washed by the blue-white sea.

By July first, which always seemed unbelievably soon, the haying season which would ensure their winter's survival would begin. During the summer months while the animals grew sleek and fat and haughty, we, their human owners, would grow thin and burned and irritable, rising often before sunrise and working sometimes until after dark. Only the work horses seemed to share in our drudgery and weight loss, the burns from their collars and the chafings caused by their rubbing traces corresponding to the blisters and calluses upon our hands. Sometimes at night we would rub ourselves with diluted horse liniment to alleviate the sprains and bruises which we accumulated during the day.

Throughout this season, as I said, the animals of summer grew strong and free. Only the milk cows were brought to the barn twice daily for their milking and even they seemed to take on an air of independence that bordered close to arrogance. The others grazed openly and heedlessly through the long days of their summer vacation. From the tops of our hay wagons we could see them, especially on the hottest days, lying on the sandy beaches which separated their pastures from the sea or dangerously close to the rocky edge of the sea cliff's fall. It was always cooler near the sea and there was always a slight breeze and they were not bothered there by the flies that tormented inland animals. Throughout the working days of summer we spent little time ourselves beside or within the turquoise sea.

As the summer progressed and as the season's young became more independent, the mature animals would yearn again to be sexually active. They would demonstrate their needs in various ways, again depending on their species and their sex, and they would continue to do so until they were fulfilled. We, as the humans who depended on them as they did on us, would frequently and of necessity interfere with their needs and desires. We would tether the lusty and often ill-tempered rams to iron stakes driven deep into the earth or isolate them in all-male pens where they frequently took out their frustrations by battering their thick-boned skulls against each other. We would keep them from the ewes until late in the fall, knowing that early matings resulted in the birth of winter lambs who stood little chance of surviving the bitter coldness of the season of their birth. We would keep the young heifers from the heavy bulls, knowing that they were often injured and sometimes permanently maimed in their first sexual encounters and knowing also that even if they did survive the breeding, great difficulty awaited them in such youthful pregnancies and that often they would die attempting to give birth. Another year would make a great difference to them as well as to us. In the same manner we would discourage nesting and maternal hens from bringing forth autumnal chickens who would not be matured enough to meet the demands of cold, rain-lashed November and the harsher months to follow. Like highly protective parents we would hover over such lives, hoping that our attempts at control would result in what was "best" for all. This is for your own good, we would think, as well as for ours, although we would never articulate it in such a manner.

In the fall we would reduce the population that had so flourished through the long, hot summer days. As it had doubled or tripled in the spring, it was reduced by similar numbers in the fall, and reduced in a variety of ways. Livestock buyers came, sometimes walking to the pastures to view their intended victims, offering prices, quoting possibilities, leaving and returning. All of the male lambs would go, and most of the females except a select few singled out to continue the reproductive cycle. When they left, they would be strong and rambunctious, unlike their earlier wobbly-legged selves. They would crowd against one another and jostle as they were ushered up the ramps of the waiting trucks and sometimes they would attempt to leap over the slatted sides of their new confinement. We would hear their indignant bleatings as the trucks took them permanently from the single environment of their one and only summer. Sounds of angered indignation tinged with the very real sound of fear. Later the checks we had exchanged them for would come and we, in our turn, would enter a phase of rejuvenation and hopeful, though temporary, self-confidence.

Sometimes, depending on different factors, it would be more profitable to butcher animals and sell them locally than to trust to the simpler yet more bureaucratic expedient of the truck or train which would take them to more distant killing stations. There was always butchering in the late fall to supply meat for ourselves and our urban relatives, but in some years there would be more than in others. It would always be a melancholy time then, especially if there was a lot of it. The night before we would lay out the ceremonial clothes of death, splattered with bloodstains and bearing the distinctive odor which could never be fully washed away. We would sit on chairs in the kitchen, sharpening the various knives and testing the keenness of the blades with the balls of our calloused thumbs. We would pay attention to the weather and nearly always kill according to the phases of the moon. From the barn we could hear the protesting moans of the unknowing and condemned animals. Unlike condemned prisoners, they would receive neither food nor water before their executions. This was to reduce the bulk of their weight and their body fluids for the day that was to follow, so that their weight, which would so soon become dead, would be less ponderous and easier to handle.

On the day of the actual butchering we would rise early so that we would get a good start. In the late fall the days would be short and since we would normally work by natural light, adjustments would have to be made. The animal would be taken to that part of the barn called the threshing floor and stationed beneath the chain pulleys which would soon be used to elevate its carcass. If it were a huge animal, it would be shot. Sometimes we would draw lines on its trusting head with a crayon, from behind each ear and across its forehead. Generally the point of intersection would be the marksman's target—almost a literal bull's-eye. If the animal were less huge, it would be merely hit between the eyes by a sledgehammer or the blunt side of an axe wielded by the strongest man. Even as its front legs buckled and its eyes glazed, the knife used for the severing of the jugular would be passed handle-first to the waiting hands which had tossed aside the sledgehammer or axe—much as the nurse might pass the scalpel. If done well, it would take but ten or twelve seconds to change life into death. The pigs were always the hardest to kill because their skulls slanted backwards and were more difficult to strike than the flattened foreheads of others. As the blood gushed from the slashed throats, we would gather it in pans so that it might later be used for blood puddings—*maragan*, they were called in Gaelic. One person would hold the pan beneath the neck of the fallen animal while another would raise and steady the convulsing and partly severed head so that the blood would be pumped into the pan and not wasted on the barn-planked floor. Later we would take the hind legs and cut the flesh between the hocks and the main tendons and insert a horizontal stick. To this stick we would fasten the now-descended chain pulleys and we would raise the animal by its widespread legs even as we skinned and disembowelled it. Sometimes the flesh would continue to twitch for a long time after the actual death and even after the hide had been removed. The contents of the body would generally spill into a huge washtub and we would sort them out in their steaming warmth with bloodied slippery hands. We would save at least the heart and the liver and the stomach and the strips of marbled fat, sometimes other portions as well. And if there was time, our father would point out and explain the functions of the mysterious and until-now invisible internal organs. "This is the bladder, and this is the spleen and this is the large intestine. This is the windpipe. These are the lungs. This is the passage that the seed follows from the testicles to the end of the penis." We would listen and watch intently, like those involved in a formal autopsy or like intense medical students about their still cadaver.

Often there would be surprises. Sometimes shingle nails or fence staples or bits of twisted wire would be found imbedded in the stomach, and one time the neck of a beer bottle was found completely surrounded by a strange almost translucent knob of gristle. It seemed to glow like a huge, obscene pearl. We remembered then how more than a year ago the cow had stood for days unable to eat or give milk and for a while barely able to walk. We had no way of knowing then how the sharp-edged amber glass she had so carelessly swallowed in her grazing cut into her stomach's lining, and we did not know when the gristle began to surround it and isolate it, thus allowing her to move and function once again. Another time we found an unborn calf within the womb of a young cow we had considered sterile. We had tried various matings and solutions but she had always failed to conceive. In her fourth year of life her sterility became a luxury we could not afford. "We cannot take her through another winter like that," was the verdict. "She will have to be fattened and killed." When found within the womb of the slaughtered mother, the embryonic calf continued to move for a brief and borrowed time. Its delicate limbs had begun to form and were folded compactly back upon themselves while its eyes seemed large and luminous. Its ears were exquisite and fragile and flatly pressed like the memory of ferns found deep within the darkened earth. No one knew who had fathered the calf, although the time could be roughly estimated. What we had wanted we had found achieved, when it was ironically too late to save the life of either.

Such scenes of selling and butchering would repeat themselves until a rough balance between livestock and available hay was achieved. In dry seasons when the hay crop was less lush there would have to be a corresponding reduction in animal numbers. In years that were more bountiful we could afford to winter individuals who would not have survived the more rigorous selectivity of leaner years. The selection of those who would remain and those who would "go" was always a tight and careful process. Like shrewd and thoughtful managers of athletic teams preparing their lists of protected players, we would go over the strengths and weaknesses of each individual. Age was always a factor, as was general strength; fertility, as I mentioned, another and sometimes even what might be called "personality." Animals who were particularly ill-tempered or high-strung or who had developed bad habits, like leaping fences or raiding summer vegetable gardens, received thoughtful scrutiny as the deadline approached. And as always, if the troublesome individuals had outstanding positive traits, they would be given additional leeway and allowed to make it for another year. Sheep who produced "weighty" lambs or a high proportion of twins were forgiven balancing weaknesses and the cows who were the leading milk producers were generally grudgingly indulged, regardless of how unpleasant they actually might be. They were often the "stars" on not overly strong teams and were catered to accordingly.

I say all of this now so that you might understand the environment in which the calf club wish was born, and also so that you might see the situation in which it existed for a while—wobbly and uncertain but grounded in a kind of realism similar to the animals and the people who were its basic source.

The idea itself, however, came from a new person in our midst. In the late winter and early spring of the seventh grade a new and dynamic agricultural representative began to visit our two-room school. He was young and athletic and brimming with vigor. He was one year away from the completion of his degree and had interrupted his formal studies for a year of "in-the-field" practical experience, and we were to be part of his field. He was almost contagious. We had always had visits from agricultural representatives but they were for the most part men who were older and gave the impression of wishing they were somewhere else. One used to wear a suede jacket and a pair of gray trousers covered with cigarette ashes and other interesting stains. He would sit at the desk in the front of the room and ask if there were any questions. There would seldom be any, so he would ask one: "Well, then what will we talk about?" Then he would look out the window rather longingly, as would we, hoping for, if not a discussion topic, a sort of mutual deliverance. Another used to show slides of "common North American weeds." He seemed to come later in the year, in May or June, and always in the afternoon. Each slide bore the name of the weed which was illustrated, and he would read the label aloud to us in a ritual which we came to call weed parade. "Common Ragwort," he would say, or "Scottish Thistle" or "Wild Onion" or "Broad-leaved Dock." He would always glance surreptitiously at his watch and drink from a thermos bottle of coffee laced with whiskey. In the drowsy hot afternoons as weed followed weed and their names became more slurred and the vapors from the whiskied coffee rose around us, we would find it almost impossible to stay awake. But our new man changed all that.

First he said that in addition to our present vegetable garden clubs we should start a calf club. He had been doing research, he said, and all we needed was a minimum of ten heifer calves produced by a purebred sire. These would be born the following spring so it was not too early to begin thinking of their conception. The mothers could be "any cow of high quality." Such quality would hopefully be transferred to her daughter. We would need a paper signed by the keeper of the purebred sire, indicating the breeding date and the hopeful conception of the desired calf. We were to check our cattle at home and speak with our parents. We were interested in dairy cattle so we should not select a beef-type mother. Neither should we "cross" breeds if we could help it. We should not breed a cow with heavy

Holstein characteristics to an Ayrshire bull, for example, because the breed characteristics would become confused. His research had shown that the predominant strain in the area was Ayrshire and there were two Ayrshire bulls approximately ten miles apart and subsidized by the Department of Agriculture. These bulls, he said, were not being "utilized to their full potential." We copied it all down in our scribblers to refer to at a later time.

On our way home I considered all the cattle that we owned, thinking of their backgrounds and their breeding and when they were due to give birth that spring. I was already a year ahead of myself in searching for my candidate for mother of the year. I settled mentally on a large and consistently gentle cow whom we called Morag. She was basically white with cherry-red markings and long and sweeping elegant Ayrshire horns. She possessed almost all of the "high-quality" requirements which had been mentioned and she would deliver her current "ordinary" calf quite early in the spring. She had always conceived quickly and easily following the births of her other calves, and I could not believe my good fortune.

When I entered our house my father was fixing harness in the kitchen. He was not in a good mood, I realized, but I was so enthusiastic that I told him all about the new agricultural representative and our potential calf club, falling over my words in my excitement.

"Oh," he said with something like vague annoyance, "I've heard all that before. Those agricultural representatives are all the same. They just talk and talk and talk and never do anything. They come in their fancy cars in the middle of the haying season and expect you to drop everything and talk to them. Almost everything they say is common sense anyway: 'Plant early and you will harvest early.' 'Rotate your crops.' 'Use lime.' 'Heavy rainfall results in a high yield.' 'Turkeys are needed for the Thanksgiving market.' Who doesn't know that? What they say is all baloney."

"Well," I said, thinking I had best keep on. "It would just be one cow. I was thinking of Morag after her calf is born. There is a purebred Agricultural Society bull at MacDougall's five miles away. We could breed her there in the summer."

"Not me," he said. "I'm not dragging any more cows on the

end of a rope to one of those bulls. I kept one of those Agricultural
Society bulls here myself about fifteen years ago. More trouble
than he was worth. Took up too much space in the barn. Had
to haul feed and water to him all the time because he was too
dangerous to let out. Then if he didn't get exercise he wouldn't
breed properly. And people always came with cows at the
damndest times. Seven o'clock on Sunday morning. Anytime
there was a wedding or a funeral. Anytime you were leaving
the house you'd be sure to meet someone with a cow and have
to go back in and change your clothes and go to handle the bull
for them. Bull got so he wouldn't let anyone else around him
but me, so I could never leave the house. People would come
with their cows and if I weren't home they'd complain. Not that
they didn't have a right to, I suppose."

He began to gather up his harness from the floor in preparation
for the evening chores. I felt that perhaps I should point out that
all of our best cattle were still descendants of that long-departed
bull but it somehow did not seem a good day for that kind of
logic. After he had gone to the barn, my mother said: "He is
not having a good day but you realize he did not say 'No.' Ask
him something definite and volunteer to do the work yourself.
He is getting tired. You know that if he gives you his word, he
will always keep it."

It was true. Whatever uneven moods my father was prone to,
he possessed a memory which did not permit him to forget anything and he was always true to his word. In retrospect, it does
not seem that we were certain of many things, dwelling in the
realm of fluctuating weather and fickle seasons and aggressive
insects and indifferent soil; but of those traits we were sure, and
we clung to them as the uneasy swimmer to his certain log.

In the barn it was growing dark. My father moved about the
animals with a tired familiarity, leaning against them, pushing
them with his shoulder as he moved towards their mangers,
talking to them in a sort of abbreviated private language, pulling
manure with his fork from beneath them, tightening their halter
chains, distributing their feed so that it was within their reach.

"Okay," he said before I had time to speak. "I didn't say you couldn't, just that I wouldn't. If you raise the fee, you can have the cow."

It was, it seemed, fair enough.

The fee was probably part of the reason we had stopped using the Agricultural Society bull in the first place. Another was that it took valuable time in a period before the widespread use of trucks and artificial insemination. "He," the bull, had gone too far away and it was no longer considered worth it. It was expensive, as I mentioned, and there was also a feeling that paying money for the simple breeding act was a bit too much—as if it were somehow unnatural, a kind of perversion or animal prostitution in which we cared not to be involved, as if there were an uneasy idea that no one should have to "pay for it." There was also the shrewd and pragmatic observation that after a few years of such selective breeding most cattle already contained "good" if not exactly royal blood and further exalted matings were perhaps a waste of time. It was probably a reaction to such spreading ideas that the agricultural representative had come among us in the first place to plant the seeds of the calf club wish.

In any case, I had achieved the first step. Before the birth of Morag's present calf, I had already willed her pregnant once again. I entered my name with the agricultural representative and told my fellow schoolmates that I would "go." The snow had not yet melted, nor had the wild ducks flown north, nor had the first spring lambs and early kittens yet been born, but I was already well into not only this spring but the next as well.

After the birth of Morag's "ordinary" calf, there followed the long period of waiting. If she were to deliver the magic calf by early next spring, she would have to conceive in the middle of summer. It took nine months from conception to birth—"just like people," as we used to say. "Cattle are the only animals that take the same length of time."

As the spring passed and the early summer approached, the hectic pace of our lives increased. School drew to a close and during the last few weeks we attended it irregularly. We were needed at home and whatever we had learned during the year was already in our past. Feverish preparations for the approaching haying season began: the repairing of machinery, the sending away for parts, improvements to the barn and also a myriad of other activities involving gardening, canning and the making of cheese. The short intense summer was upon us and we had no time to lose.

Meanwhile the animals grew sleek and fat and were distant from us most of the time as we prepared to gather in their winter sustenance. In the early weeks of July we began our haying in earnest, cutting the most mature fields and leaving them to dry, then raking and finally pitching onto the wagons, then driving into the barn and pitching off and returning again and then again. Always threatened by broken harness and non-functioning machinery and always fearful of the sudden specter of rain.

On the evening of the fourteenth of July I noticed the signs in Morag when I was bringing the milk cows home from their pasture by the sea. She was coming into her breeding cycle and it caused a restlessness and tension not only within herself but among the other cattle as well. It was late in the evening when I first noticed it and there was nothing I could do that day. That night the radio told us of the approaching rain squalls which were to hit on the following day.

"Goddamn it," said my father, "and us with all that hay out."

We had just recently cut a new field so much of it was still undried. In the morning we were up at 5:00, moving feverishly about our tasks, racing against the weather. At the morning milking Morag's situation was truly obvious, although my father did not notice. He was not around the cattle much but busy harnessing the horses and shouting directions to animals and people alike. The clouds were already bunching, although they still seemed far enough away, hanging over the ocean and visible from a distance.

"Hurry up," he said, coming into the barn where I was milking the cows. "It's going to rain. We haven't got all day."

"I think we should keep Morag in the barn today," I stammered quickly, fearful lest he should get away before I broached the subject.

"What for?" he asked and I could see that he was so harried and preoccupied that he had given my words but little thought.

"She's in heat," I said. "She began last night."

For a moment his eyes seemed to cloud over with noncomprehension, but then they cleared and became filled almost with panic, as he understood the significance of my words. It was as if he were trapped by his memory and his word. Trapped by them at this, his busiest time.

"But there is not time today," he sputtered. "We have other things to do than just worry about this one goddamn cow."

"Okay," I said. "We will just keep her in and see what the day brings. I didn't say I wanted to go with her now."

"Okay," he said, as if he were relieved of an earlier capricious promise. "Take the others down to the shore. We have to get going."

What the day brought was a forenoon of furious activity. First we raked the driest hay and then followed with the groaning wagons. The sun shone erratically but the air was so humid that little actual drying took place. At times the clouds blotted out the sun and once we could actually see the rain falling out to sea, although it had not yet started to fall upon the land. All morning as we raced about, raising new blisters upon the calluses already formed on our hands, Morag moaned and bawled her passion from the barn. When we came in with the loaded wagons, we could hear her threshing about in the frustration of her captivity and her desire.

I would have liked to bring her a pail of water to ease her thirst, although I knew that was not what she really wanted—but there was no time even for that. On one or two occasions I thought I heard an answering call from what seemed like a great distance but I could not really be sure. She was safe in the barn anyway, I thought. Safe for me, if not satisfied for herself. Our work intensified, as did the weather which surrounded us.

When the storm finally broke, it announced itself first in two thunderous cracks and a jagged scar of lightning across the sky and then the rain seemed to hurl itself down as if pressurized forth from the hanging, laden clouds. Everything and everyone became immediately drenched and to save even the half-loaded wagon of imperfectly dried hay we had to shout to the horses and swing the reins over their already steaming backs. They broke into a gallop then, jolting the wagon behind them until they careened into the still, dignified safety of the waiting barn. Within five minutes it was obvious that the day's haying was over and that at a future time we would have to begin again with what was now being so thoroughly soaked. But by then the hay would not be the same but only of the second grade.

The rain poured down all afternoon; rivulets streamed down the windows and the sides of the buildings and cascaded down the laneways, pushing erratic, insistent trenches through the softened earth. Nothing but the water seemed to move. The ocean was still and we were still ourselves after all our desperate activity. Even Morag's passion seemed to lull as if she were cooled and covered by the soothing of the rain. It was late that evening before I could venture down to the shore to bring the milk cows home, and by the next morning Morag was ravenously hungry but otherwise in no way outwardly exceptional. The hope for the mid-April calf was gone and would not come again.

For two days it was overcast and there were sporadic showers and the cut and sodden hay began gradually to turn black. On the third day it cleared in the afternoon and by the forth day the sun shone again and we began to pick up where we had left off prior to the storm. We did not pick up at the same place, for part of our crop was gone or greatly deteriorated. I set my sights on the approximate three-week future and rationalized that a mid-May calf would, after all, not really be so bad.

I was ready in August because I had mentally noted the earlier date. We were still at our haying, although many of the fields had now been cleared. We were all thinner and more irritable and beset by various nagging injuries which bore witness to the activities of our past days and weeks. A thumbnail torn off by a running rope, a back spasm caused by lifting too heavy a pitch, a swollen jaw caused by the unexpected disturbance of a wasp's nest within the deepened grass, a purplish plate-sized bruise on the thigh caused by the kick of a horse irritated by flies.

When I recognized the August signs in Morag, it was in the morning and the day promised to be clear and hot. We were on the home stretch of our summer's haying and things were not as desperate as they had been in the earlier month. I mentioned the situation to my father and he said that I should keep Morag in the barn that day. That evening, after we had done a reasonable day's work, he said, I could be free to go on my five-mile journey. All day as we worked I was intent on my future mission. I was actually a bit afraid as the time drew closer, contemplating the twists and turns of the road I must go, and realizing even then how erratic it might be. From the barn Morag moaned and bawled, her voice sounding like the theme music for the day's production. The answer seemed to come from far away.

In the evening after the other milk cows were stabled, I placed a halter on Morag's head, looped an additional length of rope around her sweeping horns and prepared to set off.

"Don't wrap the rope too tightly around your hand," said my father, "because if she bolts she might pull your shoulder out of its socket." He was on his way to finish the last hay load of the evening.

"Okay," I said, doubling the rope within my hand.

The five-mile journey was a narrow dirt road which followed the erratic indentations of the sea. It was apparently the original path followed by the first settlers in the 1770s when they walked along the shore on their way to their new lands. Now it was almost a private road, rarely used by any automotive traffic because it was so narrow and so dangerous, but used by people on missions such as mine, by people on foot, or those on horseback; sometimes by lovers, sometimes by drunkards or a variety of others who did not appreciate detection. At times it clung to the cliffs and in certain places the edges of it had crumbled and fallen down into the sea some two hundred feet below.

As we began the journey, Morag moved rapidly and I was forced to run to keep by her side. I could feel the strength of her head and shoulders almost surging back along the rope like a current and thought uneasily that if she were to lunge I would not be able to control her. Contrary to what I had been told, I wrapped the rope around my hand, figuring that if she had to drag me, she at least would not escape. We covered the first mile rapidly and both of us were breathing heavily. She will soon tire, I thought, and then she will be easier to handle.

After the first mile the road began to climb steeply and the small rocks rolled beneath our feet but still she did not seem to slacken much.

In one way this is good, I thought. At least we are getting there in a hurry.

I had had an earlier vision of her standing stubbornly in the middle of the road while I tried in vain to urge her on. This was obviously not going to be the case—at least not for the first two miles. After the climb the road passed through a sort of upland plateau for perhaps three hundred yards and then became a series of hairpin turns. Suddenly and unexpectedly it dipped and rose and twisted in such a manner as to make it impossible to see what was ahead. It was in the middle of the second turn that we saw him or perhaps heard him first. There was a low rumble in his throat which he continually repeated as he approached us coming down the hill.

The hill at this spot rose from the cliff edge of the sea which was on our right and ascended steeply before levelling off into another plateau. On that plateau I could now see a herd of cattle in the distance and he was coming from them and rapidly bearing down on us. He weighed perhaps a ton, with immense shoulders and an enormous chest. He was mostly white but his head and neck were a brindled gray which shaded at times almost into blue. He carried his head low as he moved and moaned towards us with strands of bead-like saliva falling from his lower jaw. His horns were thick and yellowed and spiralled downward and outward like those of a mountain sheep. No formal heritage was visible in the way he looked or the way he moved, and there was nothing like him in any book entitled *Standard Breeds of Cattle*.

He was approaching quickly now, coming down the hill towards us, the grade of the hill seeming to give him added momentum. He was walking very rapidly and determinedly with that low moaning rumble in his throat, but he was not running. He was not running at all like those bulls run in the jokes about bulls after cows. None of us, I knew, were in any joke. At the base of the hill beside the road there was a rail fence which formed a separation but I could see that the rails and the posts were rotten and that they represented perhaps more the idea of a fence than the fact of one. I thought that with his size and speed and the downward grade of the hill he would perhaps jump over it, but instead he merely walked through it as if it did not exist at all. The whole section of the fence parted to his progress like the furrow before the breaking plough or the water before the ongoing ship. The edges of the rotted, broken rails seemed to cling to his flanks as he passed through their destruction but they had no effect upon his movement. He continued to bear down upon us rapidly but also unhurriedly, as if he were very certain of everything and very much in control.

In romantic retrospect, I see myself sometimes as one of those "guides" in the Gothic novels, attempting to guard my tremulous female figure from the lascivious, slobbering male who, in the fulfilling of his desires, will cause irrevocable pain. Or by another extension the "concerned father" who will do almost anything to keep his vulnerable daughter from the one he knows to be not right for her. Defense against the figure "with but one thing on his mind."

But in the reality of that evening's dusty road, she swung her head towards him with swift and arching strength. Her sweeping horns seemed almost to whistle through the air and she lifted me, with the rope wrapped tightly around my hand, completely off my feet. As if I were some slight and ridiculous irritant she could no longer tolerate. She swung my body almost into his looming head and I could see, as under a microscope, the dark and deepened liquid of his eyes, the gnarled, yellow rings at the base of his horns, his gray-blue jowls and the strings of beaded saliva trailing from his jaw. I could smell the sweet, heavy hotness of his grass-filled breath as their muzzles touched, and for an instant I thought I might lose my own life if either horned head should swing in the wrong direction. Then with a moan he swung behind her and reared up massively, his heavy shoulders silhouetted and rising into the evening sun which was settling now to the waiting sea. It seemed in that moment as if Morag were approaching her answer even as I was to be denied mine.

"Is that what you want?" came a voice near at hand.

"No," I said or perhaps sobbed, "no," almost before noticing where the voice came from.

"Christ," he said, sliding from the back of the horse almost in one motion.

He too had come upon us suddenly and unexpectedly around

the hairpin turn. He was apparently coming from the village, judging from the two rum bottles which protruded from his faded blue overalls, and it seemed he had not been hurrying because the huge, black horse which immediately began to crop the roadside grass showed no signs of perspiration. He was an old man then, deep into his seventies, and was my grandfather's cousin and therefore also mine. He was a tremendously big man and had lived the kind of reckless life that big men sometimes lead in such communities—perhaps because there was often no one to stop them from doing almost anything they wanted. He was to die at a future time, late at night and in mysterious darkness, falling or pushed from the rickety balcony outside a bootlegger's second-story door. His neck was broken when he was discovered and his money gone and someone had cut the reins of his black horse and its companion as they stood hitched to the steel-wheeled wagon and waiting as on so many other nights. They had galloped home then, wildly through the night, the sparks flashing from the steel of their shoes as they swung the wagon behind them, lifting it off its wheels in the tightest turns and suspending it for seconds over the cliff's edge and above the darkened sea. The people who lived along the road had been awakened by the sound of the rushing horses and had recognized them from the sure-footed terror of their hoofbeats in the same manner that their descendants now recognize the individual motor sounds of different cars. They had heard the sounds before and did not know that on this occasion the black horses were careening through the night, driverless and without a human guide.

When the horses arrived home they were covered with froth, the muscles of their shoulders and flanks trembled and twitched and their eyes were glassy and wild. The people of the house came out then and with lanterns and flashlights began to retrace the journey of the wagon, seeking to find him in the roadside ditch or over the cliff's edge on the boulders touched by the sea, or even perhaps lying sprawled in the middle of the road. But they did not find him at all that night and in the morning someone brought the official, final news. They noticed then that the reins had been cut and wondered why they had not noticed it before.

But that is ahead of my story. For at that meeting on the narrow road and in the presence of the bull, we did not know what future was in store for any of us. Our present seemed too real.

In memory, now, he moved with tremendous speed, although he did not seem to hurry and the illusion was probably due to the length of his legs and the amount of ground he covered in a single step. Without breaking stride, he bent down and with his right hand scooped up a large rock which lay by the roadside. It seemed almost the size of a bowling ball, yet he carried it easily and lightly in his gigantic hand. As he approached the rearing, lunging bull, he extended his left hand up and forward until it grasped one of the mountain-sheep horns and then in one fluid arc of motion and follow-through, he brought the rocky boulder down between the bull's concentrated, widespread eyes. The thud of the rock on skull was like the sound on the butchering days and the bull toppled sideways and to his knees. His eyes, drained of their passion, rolled glassily upwards in their sockets, and two thin streams of saliva now green from regurgitated grass trickled from his nostrils and back into his sagging mouth. His penis, still dripping fluid, collapsed limply within its sheath. His day's breeding or attempted breeding was over.

"Did he get it in?" he said, wiping his hand on his overalls and then reaching for one of the rum bottles.

"I don't know," I said. "I couldn't see."

"If he got it in," he said, "you never can be sure. What are you doing here anyway apart from trying to get yourself killed?"

Briefly and disjointedly I stammered out the nature of my mission.

"Well," he said, "you may as well keep going. I'll go with you partway if you want. Here, you jump on the horse."

Easily and with the same arm he had used for the rock, he lifted me up to the back of the horse and then passed me the reins. He took Morag's rope in his hand and almost automatically she began to move in step with him while I followed behind on the horse. I looked back once at the bull and he was still kneeling and partially lying by the roadside where he had been struck down. His head seemed to loll to one side.

After we had negotiated the remainder of the hairpin turns and had travelled perhaps a mile, he stopped and passed Morag's rope towards me. I dismounted from the horse, exchanging the reins for the proffered rope.

"You should be all right now," he said. "Perhaps you should go back by the other road."

Taking a deep pull from one of his rum bottles, he mounted the black horse and turned him in the direction of his original homeward journey.

Morag and I continued on our way more quietly and more slowly than when we had set out. When we entered the laneway to the MacDougall yard, the sun was almost setting and I could see that they were hurrying to get their last load of hay into the barn before darkness. Mr. MacDougall was on top of the hay wagon, organizing the pitches tossed up by the others, and he was not awfully glad to see us.

"Jesus H. Christ, another goddamn cow," he said, driving his fork deep into the hay before him. I was reminded of my father's earlier remarks.

Nevertheless, he climbed down from the wagon and his place was taken by one of his sons. On the way to the barn, I told him what had happened.

"Did he get it in?" he asked.

"I don't know," I said. "I couldn't see."

"He probably didn't," he said, "if it happened as fast as you say. Perhaps he didn't reach her. Sometimes it takes them a while to get set. Anyway, we'll just have to see."

I stood in the dusky yard, clutching Morag's rope and waiting for the cherry-red and white bull with all the proper characteristics to come moaning forth, guided by a long wooden staff snapped into the ring of his nose. The breeding was almost leisurely and seemed thorough.

"Well, this one is sure as hell in," said MacDougall appreciatively. "No doubt about that. It should be all right."

After the bull was returned to his barn, I paid MacDougall the fee and he went into his house and then returned with a scribbler from which he tore a page. On it he wrote the date and Morag's ownership and the fact that the breeding had occurred. He squinted his eyes in the dusky gloom and his hands were heavy and thick and unaccustomed to holding the stubby, yellow pencil. The funky odor of the bull's perspiration and semen still hung about his hands and about the man himself.

On the return we took a more travelled route and I was afraid as the darkness descended that we might be hit by a passing car or truck, but there was little traffic and we walked steadily and briskly. Although the route was longer, the return journey seemed much shorter than the outgoing one, the way return journeys often do. It was totally dark when we entered our own yard and my father was in the barn where he seemed to be waiting.

"How did you get along?" he asked.

Again, I stated my story.

"Do you think he got it in?" he asked.

"I don't know," I said.

I was so exhausted I could hardly stand. My father took Morag's rope from me and led her into the barn. I went into the house and to bed without eating any supper. The mark from Morag's rope still burned and circled redly about my hand and wrist.

During the weeks that followed I played and replayed the events of the day within the privacy of my mind. I half hoped she had not conceived so that we could perhaps start over again; but I knew that if she had not, valuable time would already be lost and a September mating would at best produce a summer calf instead of a spring one; and that would perhaps be too late for the calf club's organization. When the September dates came, I watched Morag anxiously but there were no signs. She grazed contentedly and lay in the sun by the sea and walked home placidly to be milked. She seemed at ease with everything.

We went into September seriously then with a new round of activities: grain crops had to be harvested and preparations began for the digging of potatoes. School reopened and I was in the eighth grade. There were various fall fairs and exhibitions and our agricultural representative was everywhere. The first truckload of lambs was hauled away, bleating in the autumn sun, and the vines and tendrils of the vegetable gardens turned to russet and then to darker brown.

In October Morag was still quiet and calm when the serious butchering and selling began, and by Halloween when the first snow fell she and the other animals entered the stables for their winter confinement.

All winter I watched her anxiously and nervously, almost as if I were the young expectant father. When she began to grow heavier I moved her to a special stall so she might have more room, and sometimes I would place my hands and arms around her expanded girth, hoping I might feel life. When first I felt it, we were already out of the coldest depths of winter and into the erratic, gale-filled month of March. The calf became even more real then, as I led her through my mind in various elegant postures and positions.

Spring came early that year and although the nights remained cold, during the days the sun shone warmly down upon our backs as we went about repairing fences and replacing sluices and generally rectifying the ravages of winter. By May first the cattle were out during the day busily seeking the first adventurous blades of grass. During the first week the older more mature animals still sought the relative warmth of the stable at night while the younger ones seemed quite willing to give up warmth for the advantages of freedom. I was torn between Morag's giving birth outside where there would be less chance of infection but possible dangers from the cold or keeping her inside where her surroundings would be warmer but more constricted and less sanitary. She was now so heavy that she seemed almost to fall when she lay down and she had great difficulty in getting up.

In the late afternoon of the tenth of May when I went down to the shore for the cows I could not see Morag among them and I knew then that her time had come, apart from any decision that might be mine. I searched for half an hour, knowing that she would not give birth near the sea which was still dotted with the winter's ice floes and the source of chilling winds, so I began to crisscross the wooded hollows and the inland sheltered gatherings of spruce. Finally I found her heavy tracks deep in the wet spring earth. They were already nearly filled with water, indicating that she had passed a considerable time before. I followed them across a small stream which trickled from a marsh and then around the edge of the marsh itself and then up a steep incline and finally to the edge of a considerable grove of spruce and fir.

The trees of the grove were closely crowded together. Parting the branches and still following the heavy tracks in the brown needled floor, I came suddenly into a small clearing which was almost like a room. The edges of it were bordered by wild brambles which had not yet begun to bud and there were also several older heavier trees which had been uprooted and toppled by the winter winds and now lay like heavy barriers along the wooded perimeter. There seemed no way out of it except through the entrance-way that we had used. Morag was lying on her side when I entered. She was already greatly dilated and the mucus discharge had begun. She struggled to her feet when I entered and swung her horns towards me and for a moment I was afraid that she might charge even as the unborn calf began to protrude. But then she became calmer and after pacing several preparatory circles she flopped heavily down upon her side once more.

As in all births, it seemed surprisingly fast once it actually began. After all the months of our waiting, it seemed to take no time at all.

His shoulders were heavy and thick and his chest was large. He was mostly white but his head and neck were a brindled gray that shaded at times almost into blue. No formal heritage was visible in the way he looked and there was nothing like him in any book entitled *Standard Breeds of Cattle*. Morag rose and turned to lick the mucus from his nostrils and nudged him with her nose. Almost immediately he tried to struggle to his feet, clothed in the shimmering curtains of placenta which hung transparently from about his newborn frame.

He tottered and fell and tottered and fell but then seemed to gain control of his wobbly legs even as his mother's nose pushed him firmly but gently towards his first nursing. They seemed very glad to see each other, and if disappointment was mine it obviously was not shared by them.

The calf club wish ended there in the tiny groved room on the tenth of May when the eighth grade was not yet completed.

I do not think I had to work as hard that summer. Perhaps it was just that the weather was better. Or that I was older. Or that my parents were doing more than I realized. Perhaps all of them together. Anyway, there seemed to be more free time, and that was the summer I flung myself into baseball with a passionate enthusiasm.

We played some evenings and on Sunday afternoons and we travelled considerable distances. I found that I could hit the ball naturally and easily but it was the fielding that I loved most of all. I played third base and the shortstop and I divided up our territory and responsibilities.

I would wait then for the bouncers and the line drives and the ground balls with delicious intensity. I would hope that each ball would be hit to me, and I do not recall any of them getting by. I would lunge and leap and bend and fall and pivot and turn and then hope that the next one might once again be mine. In my small area of the earth it seemed that everything was under my control.

The Lost Salt Gift
of Blood

$\smile$

N OW IN THE EARLY evening the sun is flashing everything
in gold. It bathes the blunt gray rocks that loom yearningly
out toward Europe and it touches upon the stunted spruce and
the low-lying lichens and the delicate hardy ferns and the
ganglia-rooted moss and the tiny tough rock cranberries. The
gray and slanting rain squalls have swept in from the sea and
then departed with all the suddenness of surprise marauders.
Everything before them and beneath them has been rapidly,
briefly, and thoroughly drenched and now the clear droplets
catch and hold the sun's infusion in a myriad of rainbow colors.
Far beyond the harbor's mouth more tiny squalls seem to be
forming, moving rapidly across the surface of the sea out there
beyond land's end where the blue ocean turns to gray in rain
and distance and the strain of eyes. Even farther out, somewhere
beyond Cape Spear lies Dublin and the Irish coast, far away but
still the nearest land and closer now than is Toronto or Detroit
to say nothing of North America's more western cities, seeming
almost hazily visible now in imagination's mist.

Overhead the ivory white gulls wheel and cry, flashing also
in the purity of the sun and the clean, freshly washed air. Some-

times they glide to the blue-green surface of the harbor, squawking and garbling, at times almost standing on their pink webbed
feet as if they would walk on water, flapping their wings pomp-
ously against their breasts like over-conditioned he-men who
have successfully passed their body-building courses. At other
times they gather in lazy groups on the rocks above the harbor's
entrance murmuring softly to themselves or looking also quietly
out toward what must be Ireland and the vastness of the sea.

The harbor itself is very small and softly curving, seeming
like a tiny, peaceful womb nurturing the life that now lies within
it but which originated from without, came from without and
through the narrow, rock-tight channel that admits the entering
and withdrawing sea. That sea is entering again now, forcing
itself gently but inevitably through the tightness of the opening
and laving the rocky walls and rising and rolling into the harbor's
inner cove. The dories rise at their moorings and the tide laps
higher on the piles and advances upward toward the high-water
marks upon the land: the running moon-drawn tides of spring.

Around the edges of the harbor brightly colored houses dot
the wet and glistening rocks. In some ways they seem almost
like defiantly optimistic horseshoe nails: yellow and scarlet and
green and pink, buoyantly yet firmly permanent in the gray
unsundered rock.

At the harbor's entrance the small boys are jigging for the
beautifully speckled salmon-pink sea trout. Barefooted they
stand on the tide-wet rocks flicking their wrists and sending
their glistening lines in shimmering golden arcs out into the
rising tide. Their voices mount excitedly as they shout to one
another encouragement, advice, consolation. The trout fleck
dazzlingly on their sides as they are drawn toward the rocks,
turning to seeming silver as they flash within the sea.

It is all of this that I see now, standing at the final road's end
of my twenty-five-hundred-mile journey. The road ends here—
quite literally ends at the door of a now abandoned fishing shanty
some six brief yards in front of where I stand. The shanty is gray
and weather-beaten with two boarded-up windows, vanishing
wind-whipped shingles and a heavy rusted padlock chained fast
to a twisted door. Piled before the twisted door and its equally

twisted frame are some marker buoys, a small pile of rotted rope, a broken oar and an old and rust-flaked anchor.

The option of driving my small rented Volkswagen the remaining six yards and then negotiating a tight many-twists-of-the-steering-wheel turn still exists. I would be then facing toward the west and could simply retrace the manner of my coming. I could easily drive away before anything might begin.

Instead I walk beyond the road's end and the fishing shanty and begin to descend the rocky path that winds tortuously and narrowly along and down the cliff's edge to the sea. The small stones roll and turn and scrape beside and beneath my shoes and after only a few steps the leather is nicked and scratched. My toes press hard against its straining surface.

As I approach the actual water's edge four small boys are jumping excitedly upon the glistening rocks. One of them has made a strike and is attempting to reel in his silver-turning prize. The other three have laid down their rods in their enthusiasm and are shouting encouragement and giving almost physical moral support: "Don't let him get away, John," they say. "Keep the line steady." "Hold the end of the rod up." "Reel in the slack." "Good." "What a dandy!"

Across the harbor's clear water another six or seven shout the same delirious messages. The silver-turning fish is drawn toward the rock. In the shallows he flips and arcs, his flashing body breaking the water's surface as he walks upon his tail. The small fisherman has now his rod almost completely vertical. Its tip sings and vibrates high above his head while at his feet the trout spins and curves. Both of his hands are clenched around the rod and his knuckles strain white through the water-roughened redness of small-boy hands. He does not know whether he should relinquish the rod and grasp at the lurching trout or merely heave the rod backward and flip the fish behind him. Suddenly he decides upon the latter but even as he heaves his bare feet slide out from beneath him on the smooth wetness of the rock and he slips down into the water. With a pirouetting leap the trout turns glisteningly and tears itself free. In a darting flash of darkened greenness it rights itself within the regained water and is gone. "Oh damn!" says the small fisherman, struggling upright onto his rock. He bites his lower lip to hold back the tears welling within his eyes. There is a small trickle of blood coursing down from a tiny scratch on the inside of his wrist and he is wet up to his knees. I reach down to retrieve the rod and return it to him.

Suddenly a shout rises from the opposite shore. Another line zings tautly through the water throwing off fine showers of iridescent droplets. The shouts and contagious excitement spread anew. "Don't let him get away!" "Good for you." "Hang on!" "Hang on!"

I am caught up in it myself and wish also to shout some enthusiastic advice but I do not know what to say. The trout curves up from the water in a wriggling arch and lands behind the boys in the moss and lichen that grow down to the sea-washed rocks. They race to free it from the line and proclaim about its size.

On our side of the harbor the boys begin to talk. "Where do you live?" they ask and is it far away and is it bigger than St. John's? Awkwardly I try to tell them the nature of the North American midwest. In turn I ask them if they go to school. "Yes," they say. Some of them go to St. Bonaventure's which is the Catholic school and others go to Twilling Memorial. They are all in either grade four or grade five. All of them say that they like school and that they like their teachers.

The fishing is good they say and they come here almost every evening. "Yesterday I caught me a nine-pounder," says John. Eagerly they show me all of their simple equipment. The rods are of all varieties as are the lines. At the lines' ends the leaders are thin transparencies terminating in grotesque three-clustered hooks. A foot or so from each hook there is a silver spike knotted into the leader. Some of the boys say the trout are attracted by the flashing of the spike; others say that it acts only as a weight or sinker. No line is without one.

"Here, sir," says John, "have a go. Don't get your shoes wet." Standing on the slippery rocks in my smooth-soled shoes I twice attempt awkward casts. Both times the line loops up too high and the spike splashes down far short of the running, rising life of the channel.

"Just a flick of the wrist, sir," he says. "Just a flick of the wrist. You'll soon get the hang of it." His hair is red and curly and his face is splashed with freckles and his eyes are clear and blue. I attempt three or four more casts and then pass the rod back to the hands where it belongs.

And now it is time for supper. The calls float down from the women standing in the doorways of the multicolored houses and obediently the small fishermen gather up their equipment and their catches and prepare to ascend the narrow upward-winding paths. The sun has descended deeper into the sea and the evening has become quite cool. I recognize this with surprise and a slight shiver. In spite of the advice given to me and my own precautions my feet are wet and chilled within my shoes. No place to be unless barefooted or in rubber boots. Perhaps for me no place at all.

As we lean into the steepness of the path my young companions continue to talk, their accents broad and Irish. One of them used to have a tame sea gull at his house, had it for seven years. His older brother found it on the rocks and brought it home. His grandfather called it Joey. "Because it talked so much," explains John. It died last week and they held a funeral about a mile away from the shore where there was enough soil to dig a grave. Along the shore itself it is almost solid rock and there is no ground for a grave. It's the same with people they say. All week they have been hopefully looking along the base of the cliffs for another sea gull but have not found one. You cannot kill a sea gull they say, the government protects them because they are scavengers and keep the harbors clean.

The path is narrow and we walk in single file. By the time we reach the shanty and my rented car I am wheezing and badly out of breath. So badly out of shape for a man of thirty-three; sauna baths do nothing for your wind. The boys walk easily, laughing and talking beside me. With polite enthusiasm they comment upon my car. Again there exists the possibility of restarting the car's engine and driving back the road that I have come. After all, I have not seen a single adult except for the women calling down the news of supper. I stand and fiddle with my keys.

The appearance of the man and the dog is sudden and unexpected. We have been so casual and unaware in front of the small automobile that we have neither seen nor heard their approach along the rock-worn road. The dog is short, stocky and black and white. White hair floats and feathers freely from his sturdy legs and paws as he trots along the rock looking expectantly out into the harbor. He takes no notice of me. The man is short and stocky as well and he also appears as black and white. His rubber boots are black and his dark heavy worsted trousers are supported by a broadly scarred and blackened belt. The buckle is shaped like a dory with a fisherman standing in the bow. Above the belt there is a dark navy woolen jersey and upon his head a toque of the same material. His hair beneath the toque is white as is the three-or-four-day stubble on his face. His eyes are blue and his hands heavy, gnarled, and misshapen. It is hard to tell from looking at him whether he is in his sixties, seventies, or eighties.

"Well, it is a nice evening tonight," he says, looking first at John and then to me. "The barometer has not dropped so perhaps fair weather will continue for a day or two. It will be good for the fishing."

He picks a piece of gnarled gray driftwood from the roadside and swings it slowly back and forth in his right hand. With desperate anticipation the dog dances back and forth before him, his intense eyes glittering at the stick. When it is thrown into the harbor he barks joyously and disappears, hurling himself down the bank in a scrambling avalanche of small stones. In seconds he reappears with only his head visible, cutting a silent but rapidly advancing *V* through the quiet serenity of the harbor. The boys run to the bank's edge and shout encouragement to him—much as they had been doing earlier for one another. "It's farther out," they cry, "to the right, to the right." Almost totally submerged, he cannot see the stick he swims to find. The boys toss stones in its general direction and he raises himself out of the water to see their landing splashdowns and to change his wide-waked course.

"How have you been?" asks the old man, reaching for a pipe and a pouch of tobacco and then without waiting for an answer, "Perhaps you'll stay for supper. There are just the three of us now."

We begin to walk along the road in the direction that he has come. Before long the boys rejoin us accompanied by the dripping dog with the recovered stick. He waits for the old man to take it from him and then showers us all with a spray of water from his shaggy coat. The man pats and scratches the damp head and the dripping ears. He keeps the returned stick and thwacks it against his rubber boots as we continue to walk along the rocky road I have so recently travelled in my Volkswagen.

Within a few yards the houses begin to appear upon our left. Frame and flat-roofed, they cling to the rocks looking down into the harbor. In storms their windows are splashed by the sea but now their bright colors are buoyantly brave in the shadows of the descending dusk. At the third gate, John, the man, and the dog turn in. I follow them. The remaining boys continue on; they wave and say, "So long."

The path that leads through the narrow whitewashed gate has had its stone worn smooth by the passing of countless feet. On either side there is a row of small, smooth stones, also neatly whitewashed, and seeming like a procession of large white eggs or tiny unbaked loaves of bread. Beyond these stones and also on either side, there are some castoff tires also whitewashed and serving as flower beds. Within each whitened circumference the colorful low-lying flowers nod, some hardy strain of pansies or perhaps marigolds. The path leads on to the square green house, with its white borders and shutters. On one side of the wooden doorstep a skate blade has been nailed, for the wiping off of feet, and beyond the swinging screen door there is a porch which smells saltily of the sea. A variety of sou'westers and rubber boots and mitts and caps hang from the driven nails or lie at the base of the wooden walls.

Beyond the porch there is the kitchen where the woman is at work. All of us enter. The dog walks across the linoleum-covered floor, his nails clicking, and flings himself with a contented sigh beneath the wooden table. Almost instantly he is asleep, his coat still wet from his swim within the sea.

The kitchen is small. It has an iron cookstove, a table against one wall and three or four handmade chairs of wood. There is also a wooden rocking chair covered by a cushion. The rockers are so thin from years of use that it is hard to believe they still function. Close by the table there is a washstand with two pails of water upon it. A washbasin hangs from a driven nail in its side and above it is an old-fashioned mirrored medicine cabinet. There is also a large cupboard, a low-lying couch, and a window facing upon the sea. On the walls a barometer hangs as well as two pictures, one of a rather jaunty young couple taken many years ago. It is yellowed and rather indistinct, the woman in a long dress with her hair done up in ringlets, the man in a serge suit that is slightly too large for him and with a tweed cap pulled rakishly over his right eye. He has an accordion strapped over his shoulders and his hands are fanned out on the buttons and keys. The other picture is of the Christ-child. Beneath it is written, "Sweet Heart of Jesus Pray for Us."

The woman at the stove is tall and fine featured. Her gray hair is combed briskly back from her forehead and neatly coiled with a large pin at the base of her neck. Her eyes are as gray as the storm scud of the sea. Her age, like her husband's, is difficult to guess. She wears a blue print dress, a plain blue apron and low-heeled brown shoes. She is turning fish within a frying pan when we enter.

Her eyes contain only mild surprise as she first regards me. Then with recognition they glow in open hostility which in turn subsides and yields to self-control. She continues at the stove while the rest of us sit upon the chairs.

During the meal that follows we are reserved and shy in our lonely adult ways, groping for and protecting what perhaps may be the only awful dignity we possess. John, unheedingly, talks on and on. He is in the fifth grade and is doing well. They are learning percentages and the mysteries of decimals; to change a percent to a decimal fraction you move the decimal point two places to the left and drop the percent sign. You always, always do so. They are learning the different breeds of domestic animals: the four main breeds of dairy cattle are Holstein, Ayrshire, Guernsey, and Jersey. He can play the mouth organ and will demonstrate after supper. He has twelve lobster traps of his own. They were originally broken ones thrown up on the rocky shore by storms. Ira, he says nodding toward the old man, helped him fix them, nailing on new lathes and knitting new headings. Now they are set along the rocks near the harbor's entrance. He is averaging a pound a trap and the "big" fishermen say that that is better than some of them are doing. He is saving his money in a little imitation keg that was also washed up on the shore. He would like to buy an outboard motor for the small reconditioned skiff he now uses to visit his traps. At present he has only oars.

"John here has the makings of a good fisherman," says the old man. "He's up at five most every morning when I am putting on the fire. He and the dog are already out along the shore and back before I've made tea."

"When I was in Toronto," says John, "no one was ever up before seven. I would make my own tea and wait. It was wonderful sad. There were gulls there though, flying over Toronto harbor. We went to see them on two Sundays."

After the supper we move the chairs back from the table. The woman clears away the dishes and the old man turns on the radio. First he listens to the weather forecast and then turns to shortwave where he picks up the conversations from the offshore fishing boats. They are conversations of catches and winds and tides and of the women left behind on the rocky shores. John appears with his mouth organ, standing at a respectful distance. The old man notices him, nods, and shuts off the radio. Rising, he goes upstairs, the sound of his feet echoing down to us. Returning he carries an old and battered accordion. "My fingers have so much rheumatism," he says, "that I find it hard to play anymore."

Seated, he slips his arms through the straps and begins the squeezing accordion motions. His wife takes off her apron and stands behind him with one hand upon his shoulder. For a moment they take on the essence of the once young people in the photograph. They begin to sing:

Come all ye fair and tender ladies
Take warning how you court your men
They're like the stars on a summer's morning
First they'll appear and then they're gone.

I wish I were a tiny sparrow
And I had wings and I could fly
I'd fly away to my own true lover

And all he'd ask I would deny.

Alas I'm not a tiny sparrow
I have not wings nor can I fly
And on this earth in grief and sorrow
I am bound until I die.

John sits on one of the homemade chairs playing his mouth
organ. He seems as all mouth-organ players the world over: his
right foot tapping out the measures and his small shoulders now
round and hunched above the cupped hand instrument.

"Come now and sing with us, John," says the old man.

Obediently he takes the mouth organ from his mouth and
shakes the moisture drops upon his sleeve. All three of them
begin to sing, spanning easily the half century of time that
touches their extremes. The old and the young singing now their
songs of loss in different comprehensions. Stranded here, alien
of my middle generation, I tap my leather foot self-consciously
upon the linoleum. The words sweep up and swirl about my
head. Fog does not touch like snow yet it is more heavy and
more dense. Oh moisture comes in many forms.

All alone as I strayed by the banks of the river
Watching the moonbeams at evening of day
All alone as I wandered I spied a young stranger
Weeping and wailing with many a sigh.

Weeping for one who is now lying lonely
Weeping for one who no mortal can save
As the foaming dark waters flow silently past him
Onward they flow over young Jenny's grave.

Oh Jenny my darling come tarry here with me
Don't leave me alone, love, distracted in pain
For as death is the dagger that plied us asunder
Wide is the gulf, love, between you and I.

After the singing stops we all sit rather uncomfortably for a
moment. The mood seeming to hang heavily upon our shoul-

ders. Then with my single exception all come suddenly to action. John gets up and takes his battered school books to the kitchen table. The dog jumps up on a chair beside him and watches solemnly in a supervisory manner. The woman takes some navy yarn the color of her husband's jersey and begins to knit. She is making another jersey and is working on the sleeve. The old man rises and beckons me to follow him into the tiny parlor. The stuffed furniture is old and worn. There is a tiny wood-burning heater in the center of the room. It stands on a square of galvanized metal which protects the floor from falling, burning coals. The stovepipe rises and vanishes into the wall on its way to the upstairs. There is an old-fashioned mantelpiece on the wall behind the stove. It is covered with odd shapes of driftwood from the shore and a variety of exotically shaped bottles, blue and green and red, which are from the shore as well. There are pictures here too: of the couple in the other picture, and one of them with their five daughters, and one of the five daughters by themselves. In that far-off picture time all of the daughters seem roughly between the ages of ten and eighteen. The youngest has the reddest hair of all. So red that it seems to triumph over the non-photographic colors of lonely black and white. The pictures are in standard wooden frames.

From behind the ancient chesterfield the old man pulls a collapsible card table and pulls down its warped and shaky legs. Also from behind the chesterfield he takes a faded checkerboard and a large old-fashioned matchbox of rattling wooden checkers. The spine of the board is almost cracked through and is strengthened by layers of adhesive tape. The checkers are circumferences of wood sawed from a length of broom handle. They are about three quarters of an inch thick. Half of them are painted a very bright blue and the other half an equally eye-catching red. "John made these," says the old man. "All of them are not really the same thickness but they are good enough. He gave it a good try."

We begin to play checkers. He takes the blue and I the red. The house is silent with only the click-clack of the knitting needles sounding through the quiet rooms. From time to time the old man lights his pipe, digging out the old ashes with a flattened nail and tamping in the fresh tobacco with the same nail's head. The blue smoke winds lazily and haphazardly toward the low-beamed ceiling. The game is solemn as is the next and then the next. Neither of us loses all of the time.

"It is time for some of us to be in bed," says the old woman after a while. She gathers up her knitting and rises from her chair. In the kitchen John neatly stacks his school books on one corner of the table in anticipation of the morning. He goes outside for a moment and then returns. Saying good-night very formally he goes up the stairs to bed. In a short while the old woman follows, her footsteps travelling the same route.

We continue to play our checkers, wreathed in smoke and only partially aware of the muffled footfalls sounding softly above our heads.

When the old man gets up to go outside I am not really surprised, any more than I am when he returns with the brown, ostensible vinegar jug. Poking at the declining kitchen fire, he moves the kettle about seeking the warmest spot on the cooling stove. He takes two glasses from the cupboard, a sugar bowl and two spoons. The kettle begins to boil.

Even before tasting it, I know the rum to be strong and over-proof. It comes at night and in fog from the French islands of St. Pierre and Miquelon. Coming over in the low-throttled fishing boats, riding in imitation gas cans. He mixes the rum and the sugar first, watching them marry and dissolve. Then to prevent the breakage of glasses he places a teaspoon in each and adds the boiling water. The odor rises richly, its sweetness hung in steam. He brings the glasses to the table, holding them by their tops so that his fingers will not burn.

We do not say anything for some time, sitting upon the chairs, while the sweetened, heated richness moves warmly through and from our stomachs and spreads upward to our brains. Outside the wind begins to blow, moaning and faintly rattling the window's whitened shutters. He rises and brings refills. We are warm within the dark and still within the wind. A clock strikes regularly the strokes of ten.

It is difficult to talk at times with or without liquor, difficult to achieve the actual act of saying. Sitting still we listen further to the rattle of the wind, not knowing where nor how we should begin. Again the glasses are refilled.

"When she married in Toronto," he says at last, "we figured that maybe John should be with her and with her husband. That maybe he would be having more of a chance there in the city. But we would be putting it off and it weren't until nigh on two years ago that he went. Went with a woman from down the cove going to visit her daughter. Well, what was wrong was that we missed him wonderful awful. More fearful than we ever thought. Even the dog. Just pacing the floor and looking out the window and walking along the rocks of the shore. Like us had no moorings, lost in the fog or on the ice floes in a snow squall. Nigh sick unto our hearts we was. Even the grandmother who before that was maybe thinking small to herself that he was trouble in her old age. Ourselves having never had no sons, only daughters."

He pauses, then rising goes upstairs and returns with an envelope. From it he takes a picture which shows two young people standing self-consciously before a half-ton pickup with a wooden extension ladder fastened to its side. They appear to be in their middle twenties. The door of the truck has the information: "Jim Farrell, Toronto: Housepainting, Eavestroughing, Aluminum Siding, Phone 535-3484," lettered on its surface.

"This was in the last letter," he says. "That Farrell I guess was a nice enough fellow, from Heartsick Bay he was.

"Anyway they could have no more peace with John than we could without him. Like I says he was here too long before his going and it all took ahold of us the way it will. They sent word that he was coming on the plane to St. John's with a woman they'd met through a Newfoundland club. I was to go to St. John's to meet him. Well, it was all wrong the night before the going. The signs all bad; the grandmother knocked off the lamp shade and it broke in a hunnerd pieces—the sign of death; and the window blind fell and clattered there on the floor and then lied still. And the dog runned around like he was crazy, moanen and cryen worse than the swiles does out on the ice, and throwen hisself against the walls and jumpen on the table and at the window where the blind fell until we would have to be letten him out. But it be no better for he runned and throwed hisself in the sea and then come back and howled outside the same window and jumped against the wall, splashen the water from his coat all over it. Then he be runnen back to the sea again. All the neighbors heard him and said I should bide at home and not go to St. John's at all. We be all wonderful scared and not know what to do and the next mornen, first thing I drops me knife.

"But still I feels I has to go. It be foggy all the day and everyone be thinken the plane won't come or be able to land. And I says, small to myself, now here in the fog be the bad luck and the death but then there the plane be, almost like a ghost ship comen out the fog with all its lights shinen. I think maybe he won't be on it but soon he comen through the fog, first with the woman and then see'n me and starten to run, closer and closer till I can feel him in me arms and the tears on both our cheeks. Powerful strange how things will take one. That night they be killed."

From the envelope that contained the picture he draws forth a tattered clipping:

Jennifer Farrell of Roncesvalles Avenue was instantly killed early this morning and her husband James died later in emergency at St. Joseph's Hospital. The accident occurred about 2:00 a.m. when the pickup truck in which they were travelling went out of control on Queen St. W. and struck a utility pole. It is thought that bad visibility caused by a heavy fog may have contributed to the accident. The Farrells were originally from Newfoundland.

Again he moves to refill the glasses. "We be all alone," he says. "All our other daughters married and far away in Montreal, Toronto, or the States. Hard for them to come back here, even to visit; they comes only every three years or so for perhaps a week. So we be hav'n only him."

And now my head begins to reel even as I move to the filling of my own glass. Not waiting this time for the courtesy of his offer. Making myself perhaps too much at home with this man's glass and this man's rum and this man's house and all the feelings of his love. Even as I did before. Still locked again for words.

Outside we stand and urinate, turning our backs to the seeming gale so as not to splash our wind-snapped trousers. We are almost driven forward to rock upon our toes and settle on our heels, so blow the gusts. Yet in spite of all, the stars shine clearly down. It will indeed be a good day for the fishing and this wind eventually will calm. The salt hangs heavy in the air and the water booms against the rugged rocks. I take a stone and throw it against the wind into the sea.

Going up the stairs we clutch the wooden bannister unsteadily and say good-night.

The room has changed very little. The window rattles in the wind and the unfinished beams sway and creak. The room is full of sound. Like a foolish Lockwood I approach the window although I hear no voice. There is no Catherine who cries to be let in. Standing unsteadily on one foot when required I manage to undress, draping my trousers across the wooden chair. The bed is clean. It makes no sound. It is plain and wooden, its mattress stuffed with hay or kelp. I feel it with my hand and pull back the heavy patchwork quilts. Still I do not go into it. Instead I go back to the door which has no knob but only an ingenious latch formed from a twisted nail. Turning it, I go out into the hallway. All is dark and the house seems even more inclined to creak where there is no window. Feeling along the wall with my outstretched hand I find the door quite easily. It is closed with the same kind of latch and not difficult to open. But no one waits on the other side. I stand and bend my ear to hear the even sound of my one son's sleeping. He does not beckon any more than the nonexistent voice in the outside wind. I hesitate to touch the latch for fear that I may waken him and disturb his dreams. And if I did what would I say? Yet I would like to see him in his sleep this once and see the room with the quiet bed once more and the wooden chair beside it from off an old wrecked trawler. There is no boiled egg or shaker of salt or glass of water waiting on the chair within this closed room's darkness.

Once though there was a belief held in the outports, that if a girl would see her own true lover she should boil an egg and scoop out half the shell and fill it with salt. Then she should take it to bed with her and eat it, leaving a glass of water by her bedside. In the night her future husband or a vision of him would appear and offer her the glass. But she must only do it once.

It is the type of belief that bright young graduate students were collecting eleven years ago for the theses and archives of North America and also, they hoped, for their own fame. Even as they sought the near-Elizabethan songs and ballads that had sailed from County Kerry and from Devon and Cornwall. All about the wild, wide sea and the flashing silver dagger and the lost and faithless lover. Echoes to and from the lovely, lonely hills and glens of West Virginia and the standing stones of Tennessee.

Across the hall the old people are asleep. The old man's snoring rattles as do the windows, except that now and then there are catching gasps within his breath. In three or four short hours he will be awake and will go down to light his fire. I turn and walk back softly to my room.

Within the bed the warm sweetness of the rum is heavy and intense. The darkness presses down upon me but still it brings no sleep. There are no voices and no shadows that are real. There are only walls of memory touched restlessly by flickers of imagination.

Oh I would like to see my way more clearly. I, who have never understood the mystery of fog. I would perhaps like to capture it in a jar like the beautiful childhood butterflies that always die in spite of the air holes punched with nails in the covers of their captivity—leaving behind the vapors of their lives and deaths; or perhaps as the unknowing child who collects the gray moist condoms from the lovers' lanes only to have them taken from him and to be told to wash his hands. Oh I have collected many things I did not understand.

And perhaps now I should go and say, oh son of my *summa cum laude* loins, come away from the lonely gulls and the silver trout and I will take you to the land of the Tastee Freeze where you may sleep till ten of nine. And I will show you the elevator to the apartment on the sixteenth floor and introduce you to the buzzer system and the yards of the wrought-iron fences where the Doberman pinscher runs silently at night. Or may I offer you the money that is the fruit of my collecting and my most successful life? Or shall I wait to meet you in some known or unknown bitterness like Yeats's Cuchulain by the wind-whipped sea or as Sohrab and Rustum by the future flowing river?

Again I collect dreams. For I do not know enough of the fog

on Toronto's Queen St. West and the grinding crash of the pickup and of lost and misplaced love.

I am up early in the morning as the man kindles the fire from the driftwood splinters. The outside light is breaking and the wind is calm. John tumbles down the stairs. Scarcely stopping to splash his face and pull on his jacket, he is gone, accompanied by the dog. The old man smokes his pipe and waits for the water to boil. When it does he pours some into the teapot then passes the kettle to me. I take it to the washstand and fill the small tin basin in readiness for my shaving. My face looks back from the mirrored cabinet. The woman softly descends the stairs.

"I think I will go back today," I say while looking into the mirror at my face and at those in the room behind me. I try to emphasize the "I." "I just thought I would like to make this trip —again. I think I can leave the car in St. John's and fly back directly." The woman begins to move about the table, setting out the round white plates. The man quietly tamps his pipe.

The door opens and John and the dog return. They have been down along the shore to see what has happened throughout the night. "Well, John," says the old man, "what did you find?"

He opens his hand to reveal a smooth round stone. It is of the deepest green inlaid with veins of darkest ebony. It has been worn and polished by the unrelenting restlessness of the sea and buffed and burnished by the gravelled sand. All of its inadequacies have been removed and it glows with the luster of near perfection.

"It is very beautiful," I say.

"Yes," he says, "I like to collect them." Suddenly he looks up to my eyes and thrusts the stone toward me. "Here," he says, "would you like to have it?"

Even as I reach out my hand I turn my head to the others in the room. They are both looking out through the window to the sea.

"Why, thank you," I say. "Thank you very much. Yes, I would. Thank you. Thanks." I take it from his outstretched hand and place it in my pocket.

We eat our breakfast in near silence. After it is finished the boy and dog go out once more. I prepare to leave.

"Well, I must go," I say, hesitating at the door. "It will take me a while to get to St. John's." I offer my hand to the man. He takes it in his strong fingers and shakes it firmly.

"Thank you," says the woman. "I don't know if you know what I mean but thank you."

"I think I do," I say. I stand and fiddle with the keys. "I would somehow like to help or keep in touch but . . ."

"But there is no phone," he says, "and both of us can hardly write. Perhaps that's why we never told you. John is getting to be a pretty good hand at it though."

"Good-bye," we say again, "good-bye, good-bye."

The sun is shining clearly now and the small boats are putt-putting about the harbor. I enter my unlocked car and start its engine. The gravel turns beneath the wheels. I pass the house and wave to the man and woman standing in the yard.

On a distant cliff the children are shouting. Their voices carol down through the sun-washed air and the dogs are curving and dancing about them in excited circles. They are carrying something that looks like a crippled gull. Perhaps they will make it well. I toot the horn. "Good-bye," they shout and wave, "good-bye, good-bye."

The airport terminal is strangely familiar. A symbol of imper-manence, it is itself glisteningly permanent. Its formica surfaces have been designed to stay. At the counter a middle-aged man in mock exasperation is explaining to the girl that it is Newark he wishes to go to, *not* New York.

There are not many of us and soon we are ticketed and lifting through and above the sun-shot fog. The meals are served in tinfoil and in plastic. We eat above the clouds looking at the tips of wings.

The man beside me is a heavy-equipment salesman who has been trying to make a sale to the developers of Labrador's re-sources. He has been away a week and is returning to his wife and children.

Later in the day we land in the middle of the continent. Be-cause of the changing time zones the distance we have come seems eerily unreal. The heat shimmers in little waves upon the runway. This is the equipment salesman's final destination while for me it is but the place where I must change flights to continue even farther into the heartland. Still we go down the wheeled-up stairs together, donning our sunglasses, and stepping across the heated concrete and through the terminal's electronic doors. The salesman's wife stands waiting along with two small children who are the first to see him. They race toward him with their arms outstretched. "Daddy, Daddy," they cry, "what did you bring me? What did you bring me?"

Island

ALL DAY THE RAIN fell upon the island and she waited. Sometimes it slanted against her window with a pinging sound which meant it was close to hail, and then it was visible as tiny pellets for a moment on the pane before the pellets vanished and rolled quietly down the glass, each drop leaving its own delicate trickle. At other times it fell straight down, hardly touching the window at all, but still there beyond the glass, like a delicate, beaded curtain at the entrance to another room.

She poked the fire within the stove, turning the half-burned lengths of wood so that they would burn more evenly. Some of the wood lengths were old fence posts or timbers which had been hauled from the shore before being cut into sizes which would fit the stove. Some of them contained ancient nails which were bent and twisted deep into the wood's core. When the fire was very hot, they glowed to a cherry red, reminiscent of a blacksmith's shop or, perhaps, their earliest casting. They would glow in the intense heat while the wood was consumed around them and, in the morning, they would be shaken down with the ashes, black and twisted but still there in the grayness of the ashpan. On days when the fire burned with less intensity because the wood was damp or the drafts poor, they remained a rusted brown while the damp wood sputtered and hissed reluctantly before releasing them from the coffins in which they were confined. Today was such a day.

She went to the window and looked out once more. Beneath the table the three black and white dogs followed her with their eyes but made no other movement. They had been outside several times during the day and the wetness of their coats gave off the odor of damp woolen garments which have been hung to dry. When they came in, they shook themselves vigorously beside the stove, causing a further sputtering and hissing, as the water droplets fell against the heated steel.

Through the window and the beaded sheets of rain she could see the gray shape of *tir mòr*, the mainland, more than two miles away. Because of her failing sight and the nature of the weather she was not sure if she could really see it. But she had seen it in all weathers and over so many decades that the image of it was clearly in her mind, and whether she actually saw it or remembered it, now, seemed to make no difference.

The mainland was itself but another large island although most people did not think of it in that way. It was, as many said, larger than the province of Prince Edward Island and even some European countries and it had paved roads and cars and now even shopping centers and a fairly large population.

On rainy or foggy evenings such as this, it was always hard to see and to understand the mainland but when the sun shone it was clearly visible with its white houses and red or gray barns, and with the green lawns and fields surrounding the houses while the rolling mountains of dark green spruce rose behind them. At night the individual houses, and the communities they formed, seemed to be magnified because of the lights. In the daytime if you looked at a certain spot you might see only one house and, perhaps, a barn, but at night there might be several lights shining from the different windows of the house, and perhaps a light at the barn and other lights shining from hydro poles in the yard, or in the driveway or along the road. And there were the moving lights caused by the headlights of the travelling cars. It all seemed more glamorous at night, perhaps because of what you could not see, and conversely a bit more disappointing in the day.

She had been born on the island at a time so long ago that there was now nobody living who could remember it. The event no longer lived in anybody's mind nor was it recorded with accuracy anywhere on paper. She had been born a month prematurely at the beginning of the spring breakup when crossing from the island to the mainland was impossible.

At other times her mother had tried to reach the mainland before her children were born. Sometimes she would cross almost a month before the expected delivery because the weather and the water in all seasons, except summer, could never be depended upon. She had planned to do so this time as well but the ice that covered the channel during the winter months began to decay earlier than usual. It would not bear the weight of a horse and sleigh or even a person on foot and there were visible channels of open water running like eager rivers across what seemed like the gray-white landscape of the rotting ice. It was too late for foot travel and too early for a boat because there was not, as yet, enough open water. And then too she was born a month earlier than expected. All of this she was, of course, told much later. She was also told that when the winter began her parents did not realize that her mother was pregnant. Her father was sixty at the time and her mother close to fifty and they were already grandparents. They had not had any children for five years and had thought their child-bearing years were past and the usual signs were no longer there or at least not recognized until later in the season. So her birth, as her father said, was "unexpected" in more ways than one.

She was the first person ever born on the island as far as anybody knew.

Later she was brought across to the mainland to be christened. And still later when the clergyman was sending his baptismal records to the provincial capitol he included hers along with those of the children who had been born on the mainland. And perhaps to simplify matters he recorded her birthplace as being the same as that of the other children and of her brothers and sisters or if he did not intend to simplify perhaps he had merely forgotten. He also had the birthdate wrong and it was thought that perhaps he had forgotten to ask the parents or had forgotten what they had told him and by the time he was ready to send in his records they had already gone back to the island and he could not contact them. So he seemed to have counted back a number of days before the christening and selected his own date. Her middle name was wrong too. Her parents had called her Agnes but he had somehow copied it down as Angus. Again perhaps he had forgotten or was preoccupied and he was a very old man at the time, as evidenced by his shaky, spidery handwriting. And, it was pointed out, his own middle name was Angus. She did not know any of this until years later when she sent for her official birth certificate in anticipation of her own marriage. Everyone was surprised that a single document could contain so many errors and by that time the old clergyman had died.

Although hers was thought to be the only birth to have occurred on the island there had been a number of deaths. One of them was that of her own grandfather who died one November from "a pain in the side" after pulling up his boat for the winter— thinking there would be no further need for a boat until the spring. He was only forty when it happened, the death occurring only two weeks after his birthday. His widow and children did not know what to do as there was no adequate radio communication and they were not strong enough to get the boat he had so recently hauled up, back into the water. They waited for two days hoping the sullen gray waves would subside, and stretching his body out on the kitchen table and covering it with white sheets—afraid to put too much fire in the kitchen stove lest it might hasten the body's decay.

On the third day they launched a small skiff and tried to row across to the mainland. They did not know if they would be strong enough to make it so they gathered large numbers of dried cattails and reeds from one of the island's marshes and placed them in a metal washtub and doused them with the oil used for the lamp at the lighthouse. They placed the tub in the prow of the skiff and when they rowed out beyond the shape of the island they set the contents of the tub on fire hoping that it might act as a signal and a sign. On the mainland someone saw the rising funnel of gray-black smoke and the shooting flames at its base and then the skiff moving erratically—rowed by the desperate hands of the woman and her children. Most of the mainland boats had already been pulled up for the winter but one was launched and the men went out to what looked like a burning boat and tossed a line to it and towed it in to the wharf after first taking off the woman and her children and comforting them and listening to their story. Later the men went out to the island and brought the man's body over to the mainland so that although he died on the island, he was not buried there. And still later that evening someone went over to light the lamp in the lighthouse so that it might send out its flashing warning to possible travellers on the nighttime sea. Even in the face of her husband's death, the woman, as well as her family, harbored fears that they might lose the job if the Government realized the lightkeeper was dead. They had already purchased their supplies for the winter and there was no other place to go so late in the season, so they decided to say nothing until the spring and returned to the island after the funeral accompanied by the woman's brother.

The original family had gone to the island because of death or rather to aid in death's reduction. The lighthouse was established in the previous century because of the danger the island represented to ships travelling in darkness or in uncertain weather. It was thought that the light would warn sea travellers of the danger of the island or, conversely, that it might represent hope to those already at the sea's mercy and who yearned so much to reach its rocky shore. Before the establishment of the light there had been a number of wrecks which might or might not have been avoided had there been a light. What was known with certainty was that survivors had landed on the island only to die from exposure and starvation because no one knew that they were there. Their skeletons being found, accidently by fishermen in the spring—huddled under trees or outcrops of rock in the positions of their deaths. Some still had the remains of their arms around one another. Some still with tattered, flapping clothes covering their bones although the flesh between the clothing and the bones was no longer there.

When the family first went they were told that their job was to keep the light and to offer salvation to any of those who might come ashore. The Government erected buildings for them which were better than those of their relatives on the mainland and helped them with the purchase of livestock and original supplies. To some it seemed they had a good job—a Government job. In answer to the question of the isolation, they told themselves they would get used to it. They told themselves they were already used to it, coming as they did from a people in the far north of Scotland who had for generations been used to the sea and the sleet and the wind and the rocky outcrops at the edge of their part of Europe. Used to the long nights when no one spoke and to the isolation of islands. Used to seeing their men going to work for the Hudson's Bay Company and the North West Company and not expecting them back for years. Used to seeing their men going to the vast ocean-like tracts of prairie in places like Montana and Wyoming to work as sheepherders. Spending months that sometimes stretched into years, talking only to dogs or to themselves or to imaginary people who blended into ghosts. Startled by the response to their own voices when they appeared, strange and unexpectedly, at the camp or at the store or at the rural trading post. In demand as sheepherders, because it was believed, and because they had been told, that they did not mind the isolation. "Of course I spoke to ghosts," a man was supposed to have said once upon his returning. "Wouldn't you if there was no one else to speak to?"

In the early days on the island, there was no adequate radio communication and if they were in trouble and unable to get across they would light fires on the shore in the hope that such signs would be visible on the mainland. In the hope that they who had gone to the island as part of the business of salvation, might they themselves be saved. And when the Great War was declared, it was said, they did not know of it for weeks, coming ashore to be told the news by their relatives, coming ashore to a world which would be forever changed.

Gradually, with the passage of the years, the family's name as well as their identity became entwined with that of the island. So that although the island had an official name on the marine and nautical charts it became known generally as MacPhedran's Island while they themselves became known less as MacPhedrans than as people "of the island." Being identified as "John the Island," "James the Island," "Mary of the Island," "Theresa of the Island." As if in giving their name to the island they had received its own lonely designation in return.

All of this was already history by the time she was born and she had no choice in any of it. Not choosing, for herself, to be born on the island (although the records said she was not) and not choosing the rather surprised individuals who became her parents after they had already become the grandparents of others. For by the time she was born the intertwined history of her family and the island was already far advanced. And when she was later told the story of the man who died from the pain in his side, it seemed very far away to her although it was not so for her father who had been one of the children in the skiff, rowing with small desperate freezing hands at the bidding of his mother. By the time of her early memories, the Government had already built a wharf at the island which was superior to any on the mainland. The wharf was built "to service" the lighthouse but it also attracted mainland fishermen who were drawn to its superior facilities. Especially during the lobster season months of May and June, men came to live in the shacks and shanties they erected along the shore. Leaving their shanties at four in the morning and returning in the early afternoon to sell their catches to the buyers who came in their big boats from far away. And returning to their mainland homes on Saturday and coming back again on Sunday, late in the afternoon or in the early evening, their weekly supplies of bread and provisions in burlap bags lying at the bottom of their boats. Sometimes lying in the bottoms of the boats there were also yearling calves with trussed feet and eyes bulging with fear who were brought to the island for summer pasturage and would be taken off half-wild in the cold, gray months of fall. Later in the summer the energetic, stifled rams would be brought in the same way, to spend monastic, frustrated months in all-male company before returning to the mainland and the fall fury of the breeding season.

He came to the island the summer she was seventeen. Came before the rams or the young cattle or the buyers' boats. Came at the end of April when there were still white cakes of ice floating in the ocean and when the family's dogs still ran down to the wharf to bark at the approaching boats and to snarl at the men who got out of them. In the time before such boats and men became familiar sights and sounds and odors. Yet even as the boat came into the wharf the dogs seemed to make less fuss than was usual and whatever he said quietened them and caused them to be still. She saw all this from the window of the kitchen. She was drying the dishes for her mother at the time and she wrapped the damp dish towel around her hand as if it were a bandage and then she as quickly unwrapped it again. As he bent to loop the boat's rope to the wharf, his cap fell off and she saw the redness of his hair. It seemed to flash and reflect in the April sun like the sudden and different energy of spring. She and most of her people were dark-haired and had dark eyes as well.

He had come, she learned, to fish for the season with one of the regular men from the mainland. He was the nephew of the man's wife and came from a place located over the mountain. From a distance of some twenty-five miles which was a long distance at the time. He had come early to make preparations for the season. To work on the shanty and repair the winter's damages, to repair the man's lobster traps and to make a few new ones. He told them all of this in the evening when he came up to the lighthouse to borrow oil for his lamp. He brought them bits and scraps of news from the mainland as well although they did not have that many people in common. He spoke in both Gaelic and English although his accent was different from theirs. He seemed about twenty years of age and his eyes were very blue.

They looked at one another often. They were the youngest people in the room.

In the early madness of the lobster season they did not speak to one another although they saw each other almost every day. The men were often up at three in the morning brewing their tea by the flickering lamps, casting their large shadows eerily upon the shanties' walls as they moved about in the semi-darkness. At night they sometimes fell asleep by eight. Sometimes still sitting on their chairs, their heads tilting suddenly forward or backward and their mouths dropping open. She worked with her mother, planting the garden and the potatoes. Sometimes in the evening she would walk down by the shanties but not very often. Not because her parents openly disapproved but because she felt uncomfortable walking so close to so many men. Sometimes they nodded and smiled as all of them knew her name and who she was and some of them were her distant relatives. But at other times she felt uneasy, hearing only bits of the comments and remarks exchanged among them as they stood in their doorways or sat on their homemade chairs or overturned lobster crates. The remarks seemed mainly for themselves, to demonstrate their wit and masculinity to each other. As if they were young school-boys instead of being mostly beyond middle age. Sometimes they reminded her of the late summer rams, playful and friendly and generally grazing contentedly in *achadh nan caoraich*, the field of the sheep, although sometimes given to spontaneous rages against those who would trespass into their territory or some-times unleashing their suppressed fury against one another. Rearing and smashing against one another until their skulls thun-dered and reverberated like the growling icebergs of spring and their pent-up semen ejaculated in spurting jets, leaving them stunned and weak in the knees.

She and her mother were the only women on the island.

One evening she walked to the back of the island, down to the far shore which did not face the mainland but only the open sea. There was a small cove there which was known as *bagh na long bhriseadh*, bay of the shipwreck, because there were timbers found there in the long ago time before the lighthouse was established. She sat on *creig a bhoird*, the table rock which was called so because of its shape, and looked out across the seeming infinity of the sea. And then he was standing beside her. He made no sound in coming and the dog which had accompanied her gave no signal of his approach.

"Oh," she said, on realizing him so unexpectedly close. She stood up quickly.

"Do you come here often?" he said.

"No," she said. "Well yes, sometimes."

The ocean stretched out flat and far before them.

"Were you born here?" he asked.

"Yes," she said. "I guess so."

"Do you stay here all the time? Even in the winter?"

"Yes," she said, "most of the time."

She was defensive, like most of her family, on the subject of the island. Knowing that they were often regarded as slightly eccentric because of how and where they lived. Always anticipating questions about the island's loneliness.

"Some people are lonely no matter where they are," he said as if he were reading her mind.

"Oh," she said. She had never heard anyone say anything quite like that before.

"Would you like to live somewhere else?" he asked.

"I don't know," she said. "Maybe."

"I have to go now," he said. "I'll see you later. I'll come back."

And then he was gone. As suddenly as he had come. Seeming to vanish behind the table rock and the water's edge. She waited for a while, sitting down once more upon the rock to compose herself and then walking up the island's rise towards the lighthouse. Later when she looked down from the kitchen window towards the shanties, she could see him hammering lathes onto a broken lobster trap and readying the bait buckets for the morning. His cap was pushed back upon his head and the evening sun caught the golden highlights of his burnished hair. He looked up once and her hand tightened upon the cloth she was holding. Her mother asked her if she would like some tea.

It was into the next week before she again walked down by the shanties. He was sitting on a lobster crate splicing rope. As she went by she thought she heard him say *Àite na cruinneachadh.* She quickened her step as she felt her color rise, hoping or perhaps imagining that he had said "the meeting place." She went there immediately, down to the bay of shipwrecks and the table rock and waited. She faced out to the sea and sat in such a way that she could not see him *not* coming if that was the way it was supposed to be. The dog sat at her feet and neither of them moved when he came to stand beside them.

"I told you I'd come back," he said.

"Oh," she said. "Oh yes. You did."

In the weeks that followed they went more frequently to the meeting place. Standing and later sitting on the table rock and looking out across the vastness of the sea. Talking more and sometimes laughing and, in retrospect, she could not remember when he asked her to marry him but only that she had burst into tears when she said "Oh yes" and they joined their hands on the flatness of the table rock which was still warm from the retained heat of the descending sun. "Oh yes," she had said. "Oh yes. Oh yes."

He planned to work in a sawmill, he said, after the lobster season was done; and then in the fall or early winter, after the snows began to fall and the ground became frozen, he would go to work in the winter woods of Maine. He would return to fish with the same man the next spring and then in the summer they would marry. They would go then, he said, "to live somewhere else."

"Oh yes," she said. "Oh yes, we will."

It was in the late fall, on the night following a day of cold and slanting rain that she was awakened by the dog pulling at the blankets that lay so heavily upon her bed. She sat up, even as she shivered and pulled the blankets about her shoulders, and tried to adjust her eyes to the darkness of the room. The rain slanted against the window with a pinging sound which meant that it was close to hail and even in the darkness she could see the near-white pellets visible for a moment before they vanished on the pane. The eyes of the dog seemed to glow in the dark and she felt the cold wetness of its nose when she extended her hand beyond the boundary of the bed. She could smell the wetness of its coat and when she moved her hand across its head and down its neck the water filmed upon her palm. She got up then, throwing on what clothes she could find in the darkness of the room, and followed the clacking nails of the dog as it moved down the hallway and past the closed door behind which her parents snored, sometimes snoring regularly and at other times with fitful catches in their sound. She went down through the kitchen and through the tiny puddles caused by the rain slanting through the opened door. Outside it was wet and windy although nothing like a gale and she followed the dog down the darkened path. And then in the revolving cycle of the high lighthouse light the pale beam shone in a straight but moving path. In a single white instant she saw the dark shape of the boat bobbing at the wharf and his straight but dripping form by the corner of the shanties.

The creaky door of the summer shanty yielded easily to his familiar shoulder. Inside it was slightly musty although the wind persisted through some of the unsealed cracks. Their eyes adjusted to the gloom and the few sticks of basic furniture that still remained. The primitive mattresses had been stored away to protect them from mice and the dampness of the sea. They held one another in their urgency and lay upon the floor fumbling with the encumbrances of their clothes. She felt the wet burden of his garments almost heavy upon her although the length of his body seemed light within them.

"Oh," she said, digging her fingers into the dampness of his neck, "when we are married we can do this all the time."

At the moment of explosion their breaths bonded into a single gasp that bordered on a cry.

She thought of this later as she passed the closed door of her parents' room. Thought of how her breath and his had become one and contrasted it with the irregular individual snoring which came from beyond her parents' door. She could not imagine them ever being young.

The same wonder was there the next morning as she watched her father in his undershirt preparing the fire and later going to polish the thick glass of the lighthouse lamp. She watched her mother washing the dishes and then reaching for her knitting needles and the always present ball of yarn.

She went outside and walked down towards the shanties. The door was pulled tight and she had a hard time getting it to move. Inside it all seemed different, probably, she thought, because of the daylight. She looked at the gray boards of the floor thinking she might see the outline of their bodies or even a spot of dampness but there was nothing. She went outside and walked to the wharf, to the spot where the dark boat was moored, but again there was no sign. He had "borrowed" the boat of the man he had fished with and had to have it back before dawn.

The wind was rising as the temperature was dropping. The

hail-like rain had given way to stinging snow and the ground was beginning to freeze. She touched her body to see if it had been a dream.

As the winter began she was alive with the prospect of marriage. She sent for her birth certificate without ever revealing why and helped her mother with the knitting. As the winter deepened she looked at the calendar more often.

When the ice began to rot and break in the spring she looked out the window more frequently. It seemed like a later spring than usual although her father said there was nothing unusual about it. One day the channel would be clear of ice but the next day it would again be solid. The wind shifted and blew from inconsistent directions. On the mainland they could see, or imagined they could see, men moving about and readying their gear for the opening of the season. Because of the ice they were still afraid to launch their boats into the water. They all looked very small and far away.

When the first boats finally came, the dogs ran down to the wharf barking and snarling and her father went down also, calling to the dogs and welcoming the men and telling them not to be afraid. She looked out the window but did not see him in the boats or on the wharf nor moving about the familiar shanties. But neither did she see the mainland man he fished with nor his boat.

When her father came in he was filled with news and carried some fresh supplies and a bundle of newspapers and a bag of mail.

In the midst of all the newness it was a long time before he mentioned the mainland fisherman's name and added, almost as an afterthought, "That young man who fished with him last year was killed in the woods this winter. Went to Maine and was killed on a skidway. He's looking for another man right now."

When her father spoke he was already looking at a marine catalogue and had put on his glasses. He raised his eyes above the rims of his spectacles as he lowered the catalogue and looked towards them. "You remember him," he said without emotion, "the young fellow with the red hair."

"Oh poor fellow," said her mother. "God have mercy on his soul."

"Oh," was all she could say. Her hands tightened so whitely on the metal knitting needles that the point of one pierced and penetrated the ball of her thumb.

"Your hand is bleeding," said her mother. "What happened? You'll have to be more careful or you'll get blood on your knitting and everything will be ruined. What happened?" she asked again. "You'll have to be more careful."

"Nothing," she said, rising quickly and going to the door. "Nothing at all. Yes I'll have to be more careful."

She went outside and looked down towards the shanties where the newly arrived men were busy preparing for the new spring season. The banter of their voices seemed to float on the current of the wind. Sometimes she could hear their actual words but at other times they were lost and unknown. She could not believe the magnitude and suddenness of change. Could not believe the content of the news nor the method of its arrival. Could not believe that news of such outstanding impact could arrive in such a casual manner and mean so little to all of those around her.

She looked down at her bloodied hand. "Why didn't he write?" she asked herself and considered going back in to recheck the contents of the mailbag. But then she thought that both of them were beyond letters and that in the instant of his death it was already too late for that. She did not even know if he could read or write. She had never thought to ask. It had not seemed important at the time. The blood was beginning to darken and dry upon her palm and between her fingers. Suddenly last winter, although it was barely over, seemed like a long, long time ago. She pressed her hand against her stomach and turned her face away from the mainland and the sea.

When it became obvious that she was expecting a child there was great wonder as to how it came to be. She herself was rather surprised that no one had ever seen them together. It was true that she had always walked "over" or "across" the island while he had walked "around": seeming to emerge suddenly and unexpectedly out of the sea by the table rock of their meeting place. Still the island was small and, especially during the fishing season, there was little opportunity for privacy. Perhaps, she thought, they had been more successful, in some ways, than they planned. It was as if he had been invisible to everyone but herself. She was struck by this and tried to relive over and over again their last damp meeting in the dark. Only the single instant of his dark silhouette in the lighthouse beam was recallable to vision. All the rest of it had been touching in the dark. She remembered the lightness of his body in his dark, wet clothes but it was a memory of feeling rather than of sight. She had never seen him with all his clothes off. Had never slept with him in a bed. She had no photograph to emphasize reality. It was as if in vanishing from her future he had also vanished from her past. It was almost as if he had been a ghost, and as she advanced in her pregnancy she found the idea strangely attractive.

"No," she kept saying to the pressure of their questions. "I don't know. I can't say. No, I can't tell you what he looked like."

She wavered only twice. The first time was a week before her delivery at a time when the approximate date of the conception was more than obvious. They were all on the mainland and the late August heat shimmered in layers above the clear deep water. The shape of the island loomed gray and blue and green across the channel and she who had wished to leave it now wished she might return. They were at her aunt's house and she would remain there until her baby would be born. She and her aunt had never liked each other and it bothered her now to be dependent upon her. Before her parents left to return to the island they came into her room accompanied by the aunt who turned to her father and said, "Well go ahead. Tell her what people are saying."

She was shocked to see the pained embarrassment on his face as he twisted his cloth cap and looked out the window in the direction of the island.

"It is just the way we live," he said. "Some say there was no other man."

She remembered the erratic snoring coming from her parents' room and how she could not imagine that they ever had been young.

"Oh," she said. "I'm sorry."

"Is that all you have to say for yourself?" said her aunt.

She wavered a moment. "Yes," she said. "That's all. That's all I have to say."

After the birth of her daughter, with the jet black hair, she received a visit from the clergyman. He was an old man although not as old as she imagined the one who had confused her own birth records, it seemed to her, so very long ago.

At that time it was in the power of clergymen to refuse to christen children unless they knew the identities of both parents. In cases such as hers the identities could be kept as confidential.

"Well," he said. "Can you tell me who the father is?"

"No," she said. "I can't say."

He looked at her as if he had heard it all before. And as if it were an aspect of his job he did not greatly like. He looked at her daughter and back at her. "We wouldn't want innocent people to burn in hell because of the willfulness of others," he said.

She was startled and frightened and looked towards the window.

"Tell me," he said quietly. "Is it your father?"

She thought for a flash of her own unexpected birth and of how her father was surprised again although the situation was so very much different.

"No," she said firmly. "It isn't him."

He seemed vastly relieved. "Good," he said. "I didn't think he would ever do anything like that. I will stop the rumors."

He moved towards the door as if one answer were all answers but then he hesitated with his hand upon the knob. "Tell me then," he said, "one more thing. Do I know him? Is he from around here?"

"No," she said, gaining confidence from seeing his hand upon the knob. "He isn't from around here at all."

That fall she stayed on the mainland until quite late into the season. It seemed as if her daughter were constantly sick and each time the journey was planned a new variation of illness appeared to stifle the departure. Out on the island her parents seemed to grow old all at once or maybe it was just that she saw them in a different light. Of course they had always seemed old to her and she had often thought of having grandparents for parents. But now they seemed for the first time to be almost afraid of the island and the coming of winter. Never since the first year of their marriage had they been there without a child.

When her father fell from the ladder leading up to the lighthouse lamp it was almost as if the fall and the resulting broken arm had been expected.

Ever since her grandfather's death from "a pain in the side," the Government had more or less left them alone. It was as if the officials had been embarrassed by the widow's reluctance to tell them of her husband's death and by her fear that she might lose, in addition to her husband, the only income the family possessed. It was as if the officials had understood that "some MacPhedran" would always be on the island that bore the name and that no further questions ever would be asked. The checks always arrived and the light always shone.

But when her father fell it brought a deeper seriousness. He could neither climb to the light nor navigate the boat across the channel, nor manage, quite, to look after the house and buildings and the animals. It seemed best that they should all try to stay on the mainland for the winter.

Her brother came home from Halifax, reluctantly, and manned the light deep into fall. He was a single man who worked on construction crews and who drank quite heavily at times and was given to moods of deep depression. He was uneasy about the island although he understood it and was regarded as "an excellent man in a boat." At the beginning of the winter he said to his father who stood in the departing boat, "I don't want to stay here. I don't want to stay here at all."

"Oh," said his father, "you'll get used to it," which was what they had always said to one another.

But it seemed he did not get used to it. Deep in the blizzards of February one of the island dogs crossed on the ice to the mainland and came to a familiar door. It was impossible to see or move for three days because of the severe temperatures and the force of the wind-driven snow. Impossible for a man to stand upright in the wind or, as they said, for one "to see the palm of his hand in front of his face." When the storm abated four men started across the vast white landscape of the ice. They could feel parts of their exposed faces freezing and the exhaled moisture of their breath froze upon their eyebrows and they could see their eyelashes drooping heavily with ice. As they neared the island's wharf they could see that it was almost buried under gigantic pans of ice. Some of the pans had been pushed so far up on the shore that they almost tilted against the doors of the summer shanties. There was no smoke from the chimney of the house. The dogs came down snarling and circling at first, but the one who had crossed to the mainland had returned and had a calming effect upon the others. The door of the house was open and the stove was cold. The water in the crockery teapot had frozen causing the teapot itself to split into two delicate halves. There was nobody in any of the rooms and no answer to their calls. Outside, the barn doors were open and swinging in the wind. The animals were all dead, still tied and frozen in their stalls. The frozen flesh of some of them had been gnawed on by the dogs.

It seemed his coat and cap and winter mitts were missing but that was all. A loaded rifle and a shotgun were hanging in the porch. The men started a fire in the stove and made themselves something to eat from the store of winter provisions. Later they went outside again. Some walked across the island and some walked around it. They found no tracks other than their own. They looked at the dogs for a signal or a sign. They even spoke to them and asked them questions but they received nothing in return. He had vanished like his tracks beneath the winter snow.

The men remained for the night and the next day crossed back to the mainland. They told what they had found and not found. The sun shone and although it was a weak February sun it was stronger than it had been a week earlier. It melted the ice upon the window panes and someone pointed out that the days were getting longer and that the winter was more than half way over.

Under the circumstances they decided to go back but to leave the baby behind.

"There seems almost more reason to go back now," said her father, looking through the melting ice on the windows. His broken arm had healed although he knew it would never be the same.

She was often to think of why she went back although at the time there seemed little conscious thought surrounding the decision. While her parents were willing to leave the island to the care of their son they were not willing to abandon it to others. They had found life on the mainland not as attractive as it sometimes seemed when viewed from across the water. They also seemed bothered by complicated shafts of guilt concerning their lost son and their headstrong daughter and while these shafts might persist on the island there would be no people to emphasize and expose them. She, herself, as the child of their advanced years seemed suddenly willing to consider herself old also and to identify with the past now that her future seemed to point in that direction.

She went back with almost a bitter gladness. Glad to leave her carping aunt and her mainland family behind although worried about leaving her sickly daughter in their care. Still, she knew they were right to say that the winter island was no place for a sick child and she felt also that if she did not go her parents could not manage.

"Who will climb up to the light?" asked her father simply. They viewed her youth as their immediate salvation and thought of her as their child rather than as someone else's mother.

It seemed a long time since the red-haired man had asked her to marry him and to share his life in the magical region of "somewhere else." In her persistent refusal to identify him she had pushed him so far back into the recesses of her mind that he seemed even more ghostly than before. She thought sometimes of his body in the dark and of his silhouette by the sea. She was struck by the mystery of his age—if he had an age she thought it had suddenly "stopped" and he had become part of a kind of timelessness—unlike the visible deterioration she witnessed in her father.

In the winter cold of February they returned with a certain sense of relief, each harboring individual reasons. Because of her youth she did most of the work, dressing in her father's heavy, shapeless clothes and following easily the rituals and routines that had become part of her since childhood. More and more her parents remained close to the stove, talking in Gaelic and sometimes playing cards or merely looking at the fire or out the frosted windows.

When March came in with its howling blizzards it seemed

that they had been betrayed by the fickle promise of the February sun and although her father's will was strong his aging body seemed also to contribute to a pattern of betrayal. He was close to eighty and it seemed that each day there was another function which his body refused to perform. It was as if it had suddenly grown tired and was in the process of forgetting.

One day when there was a lull in the storms some of their relatives crossed the ice with a horse and sleigh. They were shocked at the condition and appearance of her father, seeing him changed "suddenly" after an absence of weeks while those who were with him had seen him change but gradually. They insisted that he return with them while the weather was good and the ice still strong. Reluctantly he agreed on the condition that his wife go with him.

After years of isolated permanence he was aware of all the questionable movement.

"Sometimes life is like that," he said to his daughter as he sat bundled in the sleigh at the moment before departure. "It goes on and on at a certain level and then there comes a year when everything changes."

Suddenly a gust of wind passed between them, whipping their faces with fine, sharp granules of snow. And suddenly she knew in that instant that she would never ever see him again. She wanted to tell him, to thank him or perhaps confess now that their time was vanishing between them. The secret of her own loneliness came down upon her and she reached towards his bundled body and his face which was muffled in scarves except for his eyes which were filled with water converting to ice.

"It was," she said, "the red-haired man."

"Oh yes," he said but she did not know with what degree of comprehension he said it. And then the sleigh moved off with its runners squeaking on the winter snow.

Although she was prepared for the death of her father she had not anticipated the loss of her mother who died ten days behind her husband. There was no physical explanation for her death and it seemed not unlike that of certain animals who pine away without their mates or who are unwilling or unable to adjust to new surroundings. As wild birds die in captivity or those who have been caged die from the shock of unexpected freedom or the loss of familiar boundaries.

Because of the spring breakup she was unable to attend either of their funerals and on the respective days she looked across the high gray waves and the grotesque icebergs that rolled between. From the edge of the island she saw the long funeral processions following the horse-drawn coffins along the muddy roads to the graveyard by the mainland church. She turned her face into the wind and climbed up towards the light.

That spring and summer she continued to tend the light although she had little to do with the mainland fishermen and never walked down by the shanties. She began to sign the requisition slips for government supplies with the name "A. Mac-Phedran" because her initial and that of her father were the same. After a while the checks came in the name of "A. MacPhedran" and she had no trouble cashing any of them. No one came to question the keeper of the light, and the sex of A. MacPhedran seemed ambiguously unimportant. After all, she told herself, wryly, her official birth certificate stated that her given name was Angus.

When the fall came she decided to remain on the island for the winter. Some of her relatives approved because they wanted "some MacPhedran" to remain on the island and they cited her youth and the fact that she was "used to it" as part of their reasoning. They were interested in "maintaining tradition" as long as they were not the ones to maintain that specific part of it. Others disapproved and towards them she was, secretly, most defiant. Her aunt and her aunt's family had grown attached to her daughter, had "gotten used to her" as they said and regarded the child as their own. When she visited them she experienced a certain fearful hostility on their part, as if they feared that she might snatch the child and flee while they were busy in another room.

Most of her relatives, however, either willingly or unwillingly, agreed to help her with the island, by assisting her with supplies, by doing some of the heavier autumn work or even by visiting occasionally. She settled into the life with a sort of willful determination tempered by the fact that she was still waiting for something to happen and to bring about the change.

Two years later on a hot summer afternoon, she was in the lighthouse tower when she saw the boat approaching. She had been restless all day and had walked the length and width of the island twice. She had gone to its edge as if testing the boundaries, somewhat as a restless animal might explore the limitations of its cage. She had walked out into the cold salt water feeling it move gradually up and through and under the legs of her father's coveralls which had become, for her, a sort of uniform. She walked farther out feeling the water rise as she felt the rocks turning beneath her feet. She looked downward and saw her coveralled limbs distorted in the green water, shot through by the summer sun. They seemed not to be a part of her but to have become disembodied and convoluted and to be almost floating away from her at a horizontal level. When she closed her eyes she could feel them intensely but when she looked at them they did not appear the way they felt. The dogs lay on the shore, just above the water line, and watched her. They were panting in the summer heat and drops of water fell from the extended redness of their tongues.

She returned to the shore, still dripping, and walked among the shanties. The lobster fishermen had departed at the end of the season leaving very little of themselves behind. She walked among the deserted buildings looking at the few discarded objects, sometimes touching and turning them with her toes: a worn woolen sock, a length of spliced and twisted rope, a rusted knife with a broken blade, tobacco packages with bleached and faded lettering, a rubber boot with a hole in it. It was as if she were walking through the masculine remnants of an abandoned and vanished civilization. She went back to the house to put on dry coveralls and to hang the wet ones on the outside clothesline. As she left to climb to the lighthouse she looked over her shoulder and was startled by the sight of the vertical coveralls. Their dangling legs rasped together with the gentlest of frictions and the moisture had changed their color up to the waist. Droplets dripped from them onto the summer grass which was visibly distorted by their own moving shadow.

There were four men in the approaching boat and she realized that they were mackerel fishing and did not have the island in mind as a specific destination. The boat zigzagged back and forth

across the stillness of the blue-green water stopping frequently
while the men tossed their weighted lines overboard. They
jerked their lines up and down rhythmically hoping to attract
the fish by the movement of the lures. Sometimes they dipped
their hands into pails or tubs of *gruth*, dried cottage cheese, and
flung the white handfuls onto the surface of the water, waiting
and hoping for the unseen fish to strike. She turned her head
and looked towards the back of the island. From her high vantage
point she could see, or thought she could see, pods or schools
of mackerel breaking the surface, beyond the meeting place and
the table rock, and beyond the bay of the shipwreck. They
seemed like moving, floating islands, changing the clear, flat
surface into agitated areas that resembled boiling water.

She hurried down from the lighthouse and shouted and ges-
tured to the men in the boat. They were still far offshore and,
perhaps, saw her before they heard her but were still unable to
comprehend her message. They directed the boat towards the
island. As they approached she realized that the movement of
her arm, which was intended as a pointing gesture to the back
of the island, was also a beckoning gesture, as they might understand it.

When they were within earshot she shouted to them, "The
mackerel. At the back of the island. Go around."

They stopped the boat and leaned forward trying to catch the
meaning of her words. One of the younger men, probably the
one with the best hearing, understood her first and relayed the
message to the others.

"Behind the island?" shouted the oldest man, cupping his
hands to his mouth.

"Yes," she shouted back. "By the bay of the shipwreck."

She almost added, "By the meeting place" before realizing
that the phrase would be meaningless to them.

"Thank you," shouted the oldest man. He took off his cap
and tipped it to her and she could see the whiteness of his hair.
"Thank you," he repeated. "We'll go around."

They changed the course of the boat and began to go around
the island.

She rushed up to the house and changed out of her coveralls

and put on a summer dress which she found in the back of a closet. She walked across the island accompanied by the dogs and went down to the meeting place where she sat on the table rock and waited. The rock was hot from the heat of the day's sun and burned her thighs and the backs of her legs. She could see the floating islands of frenzied mackerel beyond the mouth of the bay. They were deep into their spawning season and she hoped they would still be there when the men in the boat arrived.

"They seem to be taking an awfully long time," she said to no one in particular. And then she saw the prow of the boat rounding the island's end.

She stood up and pointed to the boiling, bubbling mackerel but they had already seen them and even as they waved back they were in the process of readying all their available lines. The boat glided silently towards the fish and by the time the first one struck it was almost completely stilled. The mackerel seemed to surround the boat, changing the water to black by their own density. Their snapping mouths fastened on anything thrown their way and when the men jerked up their lines there were sometimes two or three fish on a single hook. Sometimes they broke the surface as if they would jump into the boat and sometimes their bodies were so densely packed that they became "snagged" as the hooks went into their bellies or their eyes or their backs or their tails. The scent of their own blood spreading within the water spurred them to an even greater frenzy and they fell upon their mutilated fellows, snapping the still living flesh from the moving bones. The men moved in their own frenzy as if to keep pace. Hooks snagged in their thumbs and the singing, sizzling lines burned through the calluses on their hands. The fish filled the bottom of the boat and began to rise in a blue-green, flopping, snapping mass to the level of the men's knees. And then, suddenly, they were gone. The hooks brought back nothing but clear drops of water or shreds of mutilated seaweed. There was no indication of them anywhere either on the surface of the sea or beneath. It was as if they had never been, apart from the heaving weight which caused the boat to ride so low within the water. The men wiped the sweat from their foreheads with swollen hands, sometimes leaving other streaks behind. Some of the streaks contained a mixture of fishblood and their own.

The men looked towards the shore and saw her rise from the table rock and come towards them until she reached the water's edge. They guided the boat across the glass-like sea until its prow grounded heavily on the gravelly shore. They tossed the painter rope to her and she caught it with willing hands.

All afternoon they lay on the table rock. At first they seemed driven by the frenzy of all that had happened and not happened to them. By all the heat and the loneliness and the waiting and all the varied events that had conspired to create their day. The clothes of the men were sprinkled with blackening clots of blood and the golden spawn of the female fish and the milky white semen of the male. She had never seen fully aroused men before, having known only one man at one time, and having experienced in that damp darkness more of feeling than of sight.

She was to remember, for the rest of her life, the oldest man with the white hair. How he took off his cap and then pulled his heavy navy-blue jersey over his shoulders and folded it neatly and placed it on the rock beside her. She was to remember the whiteness of his skin and arms compared with the bronzed redness of his face and neck and that of his bleeding and swollen hands. As if, without clothes, his upper body was still clothed in a costume made of two different materials. The whiteness of his skin and the whiteness of his hair were the same color but totally different as well. After he had folded his jersey he placed his cap neatly upon it. It was as if he were doing it out of long habit and was preparing to lie down with his wife. She almost expected him to brush his teeth.

After the first frenzy they were quieter, lying stretched beneath the sun. Sometimes one of the younger men got up and skipped flat stones across the surface of the sea. The dogs lay above the waterline panting and watching everything. She was later to think how often she had watched them in the fury of their own mating. And how she had seen their surplus young placed in burlap bags, weighted down with rocks, and tossed over the boat's side into the sea.

The sun began to decline and the tide began to fall, the water receding from the heavy boat which was in danger of becoming beached. The men got up and adjusted their clothes. Some walked some distance away to urinate. They came back and all four of them put their shoulders to the prow and prepared to push the boat back into the water.

"One, two, three, heave!" they said, moving in concentrated unison on the last syllable. Their bodies were stretched out almost horizontally as they pushed, the toes of their rubber boots scrabbling in the loose beach gravel. The boat began to move, grudgingly at first, and then more rapidly as the water took its weight. The men scrambled over the prow and over the sides. Most of them were wet up to their waists. They seized their oars to push the boat farther out so there would be room to turn it around and face it towards home.

She watched them leave, standing on the shore. As the boat moved out, she noticed her undergarment crumpled and discarded by the edge of the table rock. The boat moved farther out and farther away and the men waved to her. She felt her arm rising in a similar gesture, almost without her willing it. The man with the white hair tipped his cap. She knew in one of those intuitive flashes that they would never say anything to anyone or scarcely mention the events of the day among themselves. She also knew that they would never be back. As the boat rounded the island's end, she scrunched up her undergarment and threw it into the sea. She began to walk up towards the lighthouse. She touched her body. It was sticky with blood and fishspawn and human seed. "It will have to happen this time," she thought, "because there was so much of it and it went on so long." Comparing the afternoon to her one previous brief encounter in the dark.

When she reached the lighthouse she heard the cries of the scavenging gulls. She looked in the direction of the sound and saw the boat cutting a "v" in the placid water on its way to the mainland. The men were bent double grasping their fishforks and throwing the dead mackerel back into the sea. The gulls swooped and screamed in a whitened noisy cloud.

Two years later she was in a mainland store ordering supplies to take back to the island. Usually she made arrangements with one of her relatives to take the supplies from the store to the water's edge and then ferry them across to the island but on this day she could not find the particular young man. One of the items was a bag of flour. As she stood paying her bill and looking out the door in some agitation, she saw, out of the corner of her eye, the white-haired man in the navy-blue jersey.

"This is too heavy for you," he said. "Let me help," and he bent down and picked up the hundred pound flour sack and threw it easily onto his shoulder. When it landed some of the flour puffed out, sprinkling his blue jersey and his cap and his hair with its fine white powder. She remembered the whiteness of his body beneath the blue jersey and the frenzied afternoon beneath the summer sun. As they were going out the door they met her young relative.

"Here, I'll take that," he said, relieving the man of the bag of flour.

"Thank you," she said to the man.

"My pleasure," he said and tipped his cap towards her. The flour dust fell from his cap onto the floor between them.

"He is a real nice fellow," said her young relative as they moved towards the shore. "But of course you don't know him the way we do."

"No," she said. "Of course I don't." She looked across the channel to the stillness of the island. Her expected child had never arrived.

The years of the next decade passed by in a blur of monotonous sameness. She realized that she was becoming more careless of her appearance and that such carelessness was regarded as further evidence of eccentricity. She came ashore less frequently preferring to try to understand the world through radio. She found her teen-age daughter to be foreign and aloof and embarrassed by her presence. Her aunt's family harbored doubts about their decision to rear the girl and, one day, when she was visiting, suggested that she might want to live on the island with her "real mother." The girl laughed and walked into another room.

Gradually during the next years things changed even more, but so quietly that, in retrospect, she could not link the specific events to the specific years. Many of them had to do with changes on the mainland. The Government built a splendid new wharf and the spring fishermen no longer came to inhabit the shanties which began to fall into disrepair, their doors banging in the wind and the shingles flying from their roofs. Sometimes she looked at the initials carved by the absent men on the shanties' walls but his, as she knew, would never be among them.

Community pastures were established, with regular attendants, and the bound young cattle and the lusty rams no longer came to the summer pasturage. The sweeping headlights of cars became a regular feature of her night vision, mirroring in a myriad manner the beam from her solitary lighthouse. One night after a quarrel with her aunt's family, her daughter left in such a car, and vanished into the mystery of Toronto. She did not know of it until weeks later when she came ashore for the purchase of supplies.

The wharf at the island began to deteriorate and the visitors came less often. She found herself often dealing with members of a newer generation. Many of them were sulky and contributed to the maintaining of island tradition with the utmost reluctance and only because of the badgering of their parents.

Yet the light still shone and the various missives to and from "A. MacPhedran" continued to travel through the mails. The nature of such missives also changed, however gradually. When the first generation of her family went to the island it had been close to the age of sail when captains were at the mercies of the winds. In her own time she had seen the coming of the larger ships and the increasing sophistication of their technology. There had not been a wreck upon the island in all her time of habitation and no freezing, ice-caked travellers had ever knocked upon her midnight door. The "emergency chest" and its store of supplies remained unopened from one inspection to the next.

One summer she realized with a shock that her child-bearing years were over and that that part of her life was past.

Mainland boat operators began to offer "trips around the island," taking tourists on circumnavigational voyages. Very often because of time limitations they did not land but merely circled or anchored briefly offshore. When the boats approached the dogs barked, bringing her to her door or sometimes to the water's edge. At first she was not aware of the image she presented to the tourists with their binoculars or their cameras. Nor was she aware of how she was described by the operators of the boats. Standing at the edge of the sea in her dishevelled men's clothing and surrounded by her snarling dogs, she later realized, she had passed into folklore. She had, without realizing it, become "the mad woman of the island."

It was on a hot summer's day, some years later when, in answer to the barking of the dogs, she looked out the window and saw the big boat approaching. The men wore tan-colored uniforms and the Canadian flag flew from the mast. They tied the boat to the remnants of the wharf and began to climb towards the house as she called off the dogs. The decision had been made, they told her quietly, while sitting in the kitchen, to close the lighthouse officially. The light would still shine but it would be maintained by "modern technology." It would operate automatically and be serviced by supply boats which would come at certain times of the year or, in emergency, they added, by helicopter. It would, however, be maintained in its present state for approximately a year and a half. After that, they said, she would have "to live somewhere else." They got up to leave and thanked her for her decades of fine service.

After they had gone she walked the length and width of the island. She repeated all the place names, many of them in Gaelic, and marvelled that the places would remain but the names would vanish. "Who would know?" she wondered that this spot had once been called *achadh nan caoraich*, or that another was called *creig a bhoird*. And who she thought, with a catch in her heart, would ever know of *Àite na cruinneachadh* and of what had transpired there. She looked across the landscape repeating the phrases of the place-names as if they were those of children about to be abandoned without knowledge of their names. She felt like whispering their names to them so they would not forget.

She realized with a type of shock that in spite of generations of being people "of the island" they had never really owned it in any legal sense. There was nothing physical of it that was, in strict reality, formally theirs.

That autumn and winter her rituals seemed without meaning. There was no need of so many supplies because the future was shorter and she approached each winter task with the knowledge that it would be her last. She approached spring with a longing born of confused emotions. She who had wanted to leave and wanted to return and wanted to stay felt the approaching ache of those who leave the familiar behind. She felt, perhaps, as those who leave bad places or bad situations or bad marriages behind them. As those who must look over their shoulders one last time and who say quietly to themselves, "Oh I have given a lot of my life to this, such as it was, and such was I. And no matter where I go I will never be the same."

That April as the ice broke, for her the final time, she was drying the dishes and looking through the window. Because of her failing eyesight she did not see the boat until it was almost at the remains of the wharf and the dogs did not make their usual sound. She saw the man bending to loop the boat's rope to the wharf and as he did so his cap fell off and she saw the redness of his hair. It seemed to flash and reflect in the April sun like the sudden and different energy of spring. She wrapped the damp dish towel around her hand as if it were a bandage and then she as quickly unwrapped it again.

He started up the path towards the house and the dogs ran happily beside him. She stood in the doorway uncertainly. As he approached she realized that he was talking to the dogs and his accent was slightly unfamiliar. He seemed about twenty years of age and his eyes were very blue. He had an earring in his ear.

"Hello," he said, extending his hand. "I don't know if you recognize me."

It had been so long and so much had happened that she did not know what to say. Her hand tightened on the cloth she was still holding. She stepped aside to let him enter the house and watched as he sat on a chair.

"Do you stay here all the time?" he asked, looking around the kitchen, "even in the winter?"

"Yes," she said. "Most of the time."

"Were you born here?"

"Yes," she said. "I guess so."

"It must be lonely," he said, "but I guess some people are lonely no matter where they are."

She looked at him as if he were a ghost.

"Would you like to live somewhere else?" he asked.

"I don't know," she said. "Maybe."

He raised his hand and touched the earring as if to make certain it was still there. His glance travelled about the kitchen, seeming to rest lightly on each of the familiar objects. She realized that the kitchen had hardly changed since that other April visit so long ago. She could not think of what to say.

"Would you like some tea?" she asked after a moment of awkward silence.

"No thank you," he said. "I'm pressed for time right now but perhaps we'll have it later."

She nodded although she was not certain of his meaning. The dogs lay under the table, now and then thumping the floor with their tails. Through the window she could see the white gulls hanging over the ocean which was still dotted with cakes of floating ice.

He looked at her carefully, as if remembering, and he smiled. Neither of them seemed to know just what to say.

"Well," he said getting up suddenly. "I have to go now. I'll see you later. I'll come back."

"Wait," she said rising as quickly, "please don't go," and she almost added the word "again."

"I'll be back," he said, "in the fall. And then I will take you with me. We will go and live somewhere else."

"Yes," she said and then added almost as an afterthought, "Where have you been?"

"In Toronto," he said. "I was born there. They told me on the mainland that you are my grandmother."

She looked at him as if he were a genetic wonder which indeed he seemed to be.

"Oh," she said.

"I have to go now," he repeated, "but I'll see you later. I'll come back."

"Oh yes," she said. "Oh yes we will."

And then he was gone. She sat transfixed not daring to move. Part of her felt that she should rush and call him back and another fearful part told her she should not know what she might see. Finally she went to the window. Halfway across to the mainland there was a single man in a boat but she could make no clear identification. She did not say anything to anyone about the visit. She could think of no way she could tactfully introduce it. After years of secrecy it seemed a dangerous time to bring up the subject of the red-haired man. Perhaps, again, no one else had seen him? She did not wish to add further evidence to her designation as "the mad woman of the island." She scanned the faces of her relatives carefully but could find nothing. Perhaps he had visited them, she thought, and they had told him not to come. Perhaps they considered themselves in the business of not disturbing the disturbed.

Now as the October rain fell she added yet another stick to the fire. She was no longer bothered by the declining stock of wood because she would not need it for the winter. The rain fell turning more to the consistency of hail and she knew this by its sound as well as by her sight. She looked away from the door as she had so many years ago, the first time at the table rock. Deliberately not looking in the direction of his possible coming so that she could not see him *not* coming if that was the way it was supposed to be. She waited, listening to the regular pattern of the rain, and wondered if she were on the verge of sleep. Suddenly the door blew open and the hail-like rain skittered across the floor. The wet dogs moved from beneath the table and she heard them rather than saw. Perhaps she should mop the wet floor she thought but then she remembered that they planned to tear the house down anyway and its cleanliness seemed like a minor virtue. The water rippled across the floor in rolling little wind-driven waves. The dog came in, its nails clacking across the floor even as little spurts of water rose from beneath its padded paws. It came and lay its head upon her lap. She got up not daring to believe. Outside it was wet and windy and she followed the dog down the darkened path. And then in the revolving cycle of the high lighthouse light she saw in a single white instant the dark shape of the boat bobbing at the wharf and his straight but dripping form by the corner of the shanties.

They moved towards each other.

"Oh," she said, digging her fingers into the dampness of his neck.

"I told you I'd come back," he said.

"Oh," she said. "Oh yes. You did."

She ran her fingers over his face in the darkness and when the light revolved again she saw the blueness of his eyes and his red hair darkened by the dripping water. He was not wearing any earring.

"How old are you?" she asked, embarrassed by the girlish triviality of the question which had bothered her all these years.

"Twenty-one," he said. "I thought I told you."

He took her hands and walked backwards while facing her, down to the darkness of the bobbing boat and the rolling sea.

"Come," he said. "Come with me. It is time we went to live somewhere else."

"Oh yes," she said. "Oh yes we will."

She dug her nails into the palms of his hands as he guided her over the spume-drenched rocks.

"This boat," he said, "has to be back before dawn."

The wind was rising as the temperature was dropping. The hail-like rain had given way to stinging snow and the ground they left behind was beginning to freeze.

A dog barked once. And when the light revolved, its solitary beam found no MacPhedrans on the island or the sea.

To Everything
There Is a Season

I AM SPEAKING HERE *of a time when I was eleven and lived with my family on our small farm on the west coast of Cape Breton. My family had been there for a long, long time and so it seemed had I. And much of that time seems like the proverbial yesterday. Yet when I speak on this Christmas 1977, I am not sure how much I speak with the voice of that time or how much in the voice of what I have since become. And I am not sure how many liberties I may be taking with the boy I think I was. For Christmas is a time of both past and present and often the two are imperfectly blended. As we step into its nowness we often look behind.*

We have been waiting now, it seems, forever. Actually, it has been most intense since Halloween when the first snow fell upon us as we moved like muffled mummers upon darkened country roads. The large flakes were soft and new then and almost generous and the earth to which they fell was still warm and as yet unfrozen. They fell in silence into the puddles and into the sea where they disappeared at the moment of contact. They disappeared, too, upon touching the heated redness of our necks and hands or the faces of those who did not wear masks. We carried our pillowcases from house to house, knocking on doors to become silhouettes in the light thrown out from kitchens (white pillowcases held out by whitened forms). The snow fell between us and the doors and was transformed in shimmering golden beams. When we turned to leave, it fell upon our footprints and as the night wore on obliterated them and all the records of our movements. In the morning everything was soft and still and November had come upon us.

My brother Kenneth, who is two and a half, is unsure of his last Christmas. It is Halloween that looms largest in his memory as an exceptional time of being up late in magic darkness and falling snow. "Who are you going to dress up as at Christmas?" he asks. "I think I'll be a snowman." All of us laugh at that and tell him Santa Claus will find him if he is good and that he need not dress up at all. We go about our appointed tasks waiting for it to happen.

I am troubled myself about the nature of Santa Claus and I am trying to hang on to him in any way that I can. It is true that at my age I no longer *really* believe in him; yet I have hoped in all his possibilities as fiercely as I can, much in the same way, I think, that the drowning man waves desperately to the lights of the passing ship on the high sea's darkness. For without him, as without the man's ship, it seems our fragile lives would be so much more desperate.

My mother has been fairly tolerant of my attempted perpetuation. Perhaps because she has encountered it before. Once I overheard her speaking about my sister Anne to one of her neighbors. "I thought Anne would *believe* forever," she said. "I practically had to tell her." I have somehow always wished I had not heard her say that as I seek sanctuary and reinforcement even in an ignorance I know I dare not trust.

Kenneth, however, believes with an unadulterated fervor, and so do Bruce and Barry who are six-year-old twins. Beyond me there is Anne who is thirteen and Mary who is fifteen, both of whom seem to be leaving childhood at an alarming rate. My mother has told us that she was already married when she was seventeen, which is only two years older than Mary is now. That too seems strange to contemplate and perhaps childhood is shorter for some than it is for others. I think of this sometimes in the evenings when we have finished our chores and the supper dishes have been cleared away and we are supposed to be doing our homework. I glance sideways at my mother, who is always knitting or mending, and at my father, who mostly sits by the stove coughing quietly with his handkerchief at his mouth. He has "not been well" for over two years and has difficulty breathing whenever he moves at more than the slowest pace. He is most sympathetic of all concerning my extended hopes and says we should hang on to the good things in our lives as long as we are able. As I look at him out of the corner of my eye, it does not seem that he has many of them left. He is old, we think, at forty-two.

Yet Christmas, in spite of all the doubts of our different ages, is a fine and splendid time, and now as we pass the midpoint of December our expectations are heightened by the increasing coldness that has settled down upon us. The ocean is flat and calm and along the coast, in the scooped-out coves, has turned to an icy slush. The brook that flows past our house is almost totally frozen and there is only a small channel of rushing water that flows openly at its very center. When we let the cattle out to drink, we chop holes with the axe at the brook's edge so that they can drink without venturing onto the ice.

The sheep move in and out of their lean-to shelter, restlessly stamping their feet or huddling together in tightly packed groups. A conspiracy of wool against the cold. The hens perch high on their roosts with their feathers fluffed out about them, hardly feeling it worthwhile to descend to the floor for their few scant kernels of grain. The pig, who has little time before his butchering, squeals his displeasure to the cold and with his snout tosses his wooden trough high in the icy air. The splendid young horse paws the planking of his stall and gnaws the wooden cribwork of his manger.

We have put a protective barricade of spruce boughs about our kitchen door and banked our house with additional boughs and billows of eel grass. Still, the pail of water we leave standing in the porch is solid in the morning and has to be broken with the hammer. The clothes my mother hangs on the line are frozen almost instantly and sway and creak from their suspending clothespins like sections of dismantled robots: the stiff-legged rasping trousers and the shirts and sweaters with unyielding arms outstretched. In the morning we race from our frigid upstairs bedrooms to finish dressing around the kitchen stove.

We would extend our coldness half a continent away to the Great Lakes of Ontario so that it might hasten the Christmas coming of my oldest brother, Neil. He is nineteen and employed on the "lake boats," the long flat carriers of grain and iron ore whose season ends any day after December tenth, depending on the ice conditions. We wish it to be cold, cold on the Great Lakes of Ontario, so that he may come home to us as soon as possible. Already his cartons have arrived. They come from different places: Cobourg, Toronto, St. Catharines, Welland, Windsor, Sarnia, Sault Ste. Marie. Places that we, with the exception of my father, have never been. We locate them excitedly on the map, tracing their outlines with eager fingers. The cartons bear the lettering of Canada Steamship Lines, and are bound with rope knotted intricately in the fashion of sailors. My mother says they contain his "clothes" and we are not allowed to open them.

For us it is impossible to know the time or manner of his coming. If the lakes freeze early, he may come by train because it is cheaper. If the lakes stay open until December twentieth, he will have to fly because his time will be more precious than his money. He will hitchhike the last sixty or hundred miles from either station or airport. On our part, we can do nothing but listen with straining ears to radio reports of distant ice formations. His coming seems to depend on so many factors which are out there far beyond us and over which we lack control.

The days go by in fevered slowness until finally on the morning of December twenty-third the strange car rolls into our yard. My mother touches her hand to her lips and whispers "Thank God." My father gets up unsteadily from his chair to look through the window. Their longed-for son and our golden older brother is here at last. He is here with his reddish hair and beard and we can hear his hearty laugh. He will be happy and strong and confident for us all.

There are three other young men with him who look much the same as he. They too are from the boats and are trying to get home to Newfoundland. They must still drive a hundred miles to reach the ferry at North Sydney. The car seems very old. They purchased it in Thorold for two hundred dollars because they were too late to make any reservations, and they have driven steadily since they began. In northern New Brunswick their windshield wipers failed but instead of stopping they tied lengths of cord to the wipers' arms and passed them through the front window vents. Since that time, in whatever precipitation, one of them has pulled the cords back and forth to make the wipers function. This information falls tiredly but excitedly from their lips and we greedily gather it in. My father pours them drinks of rum and my mother takes out her mincemeat and the fruitcakes she has been carefully hoarding. We lean on the furniture or look from the safety of sheltered doorways. We would like to hug our brother but are too shy with strangers present. In the kitchen's warmth, the young men begin to nod and doze, their heads dropping suddenly to their chests. They nudge each other with their feet in an attempt to keep awake. They will not stay and rest because they have come so far and tomorrow is Christmas Eve and stretches of mountains and water still lie between them and those they love.

After they leave we pounce upon our brother physically and verbally. He laughs and shouts and lifts us over his head and swings us in his muscular arms. Yet in spite of his happiness he seems surprised at the appearance of his father whom he has not seen since March. My father merely smiles at him while my mother bites her lip.

Now that he is here there is a great flurry of activity. We have left everything we could until the time he might be with us. Eagerly I show him the fir tree on the hill which I have been watching for months and marvel at how easily he fells it and carries it down the hill. We fall over one another in the excitement of decoration.

He promises that on Christmas Eve he will take us to church in the sleigh behind the splendid horse that until his coming we are all afraid to handle. And on the afternoon of Christmas Eve he shoes the horse, lifting each hoof and rasping it fine and hammering the cherry-red horseshoes into shape upon the anvil. Later he drops them hissingly into the steaming tub of water.

My father sits beside him on an overturned pail and tells him what to do. Sometimes we argue with our father, but our brother does everything he says.

That night, bundled in hay and voluminous coats, and with heated stones at our feet, we start upon our journey. Our parents and Kenneth remain at home but all the rest of us go. Before we leave we feed the cattle and sheep and even the pig all that they can possibly eat so that they will be contented on Christmas Eve. Our parents wave to us from the doorway. We go four miles across the mountain road. It is a primitive logging trail and there will be no cars or other vehicles upon it. At first the horse is wild with excitement and lack of exercise and my brother has to stand at the front of the sleigh and lean backwards on the reins. Later he settles down to a trot and still later to a walk as the mountain rises before him. We sing all the Christmas songs we know and watch for the rabbits and foxes scudding across the open patches of snow and listen to the drumming of partridge wings. We are never cold.

When we descend to the country church we tie the horse in a grove of trees where he will be sheltered and not frightened by the many cars. We put a blanket over him and give him oats. At the church door the neighbors shake hands with my brother. "Hello, Neil," they say. "How is your father?"

"Oh," he says, just "Oh."

The church is very beautiful at night with its festooned branches and glowing candles and the booming, joyous sounds that come from the choir loft. We go through the service as if we are mesmerized.

On the way home, although the stones have cooled, we remain happy and warm. We listen to the creak of the leather harness and the hiss of runners on the snow and begin to think of the potentiality of presents. When we are about a mile from home the horse senses his destination and breaks into a trot and then into a confident lope. My brother lets him go and we move across the winter landscape like figures freed from a Christmas card. The snow from the horse's hooves falls about our heads like the whiteness of the stars.

After we have stabled the horse we talk with our parents and eat the meal our mother has prepared. And then I am sleepy and it is time for the younger children to be in bed. But tonight my father says to me, "We would like you to stay up with us a while," and so I stay quietly with the older members of my family.

When all is silent upstairs Neil brings in the cartons that contain his "clothes" and begins to open them. He unties the intricate knots quickly, their whorls falling away before his agile fingers. The boxes are filled with gifts neatly wrapped and bearing tags. The ones for my younger brothers say "from Santa Claus" but mine are not among them anymore, as I know with certainty they will never be again. Yet I am not so much surprised as touched by a pang of loss at being here on the adult side of the world. It is as if I have suddenly moved into another room and heard a door click lastingly behind me. I am jabbed by my own small wound.

But then I look at those before me. I look at my parents drawn together before the Christmas tree. My mother has her hand upon my father's shoulder and he is holding his ever-present handkerchief. I look at my sisters who have crossed this threshold ahead of me and now each day journey farther from the lives they knew as girls. I look at my magic older brother who has come to us this Christmas from half a continent away, bringing everything he has and is. All of them are captured in the tableau of their care.

"Every man moves on," says my father quietly, and I think he speaks of Santa Claus, "but there is no need to grieve. He leaves good things behind."

Winter Dog

I AM WRITING THIS in December. In the period close to Christmas, and three days after the first snowfall in this region of southwestern Ontario. The snow came quietly in the night or in the early morning. When we went to bed near midnight, there was none at all. Then early in the morning we heard the children singing Christmas songs from their rooms across the hall. It was very dark and I rolled over to check the time. It was 4:30 a.m. One of them must have awakened and looked out the window to find the snow and then eagerly awakened the others. They are half crazed by the promise of Christmas, and the discovery of the snow is an unexpected giddy surprise. There was no snow promised for this area, not even yesterday.

"What are you doing?" I call, although it is obvious.

"Singing Christmas songs," they shout back with equal obviousness, "because it snowed."

"Try to be quiet," I say, "or you'll wake the baby."

"She's already awake," they say. "She's listening to our singing. She likes it. Can we go out and make a snowman?"

I roll from my bed and go to the window. The neighboring houses are muffled in snow and silence and there are as yet no lights in any of them. The snow has stopped falling and its whitened quietness reflects the shadows of the night.

"This snow is no good for snowmen," I say. "It is too dry."

"How can snow be dry?" asks a young voice. Then an older one says, "Well, then can we go out and make the first tracks?"

They take my silence for consent and there are great sounds of rustling and giggling as they go downstairs to touch the light switches and rummage and jostle for coats and boots.

"What on earth is happening?" asks my wife from her bed. "What are they doing?"

"They are going outside to make the first tracks in the snow," I say. "It snowed quite heavily last night."

"What time is it?"

"Shortly after 4:30."

"Oh."

We ourselves have been nervous and restless for the past weeks. We have been troubled by illness and uncertainty in those we love far away on Canada's east coast. We have already considered and rejected driving the fifteen hundred miles. Too far, too uncertain, too expensive, fickle weather, the complications of transporting Santa Claus.

Instead, we sleep uncertainly and toss in unbidden dreams. We jump when the phone rings after 10:00 p.m. and are then reassured by the distant voices.

"First of all, there is nothing wrong," they say. "Things are just the same."

Sometimes we make calls ourselves, even to the hospital in Halifax, and are surprised at the voices which answer.

"I just got here this afternoon from Newfoundland. I'm going to try to stay a week. He seems better today. He's sleeping now."

At other times we receive calls from farther west, from Edmonton and Calgary and Vancouver. People hoping to find objectivity in the most subjective of situations. Strung out in uncertainty across the time zones from British Columbia to Newfoundland.

Within our present city, people move and consider possibilities:

If he dies tonight we'll leave right away. Can you come?

We will have to drive as we'll never get air reservations at this time.

I'm not sure if my car is good enough. I'm always afraid of the mountains near Cabano.

If we were stranded in Rivière du Loup we would be worse off than being here. It would be too far for anyone to come and get us.

My car will go but I'm not so sure I can drive it all the way. My eyes are not so good anymore, especially at night in drifting snow.

Perhaps there'll be no drifting snow.

There's always drifting snow.

We'll take my car if you'll drive it. We'll have to drive straight through.

John phoned and said he'll give us his car if we want it or he'll drive—either his own car or someone else's.

He drinks too heavily, especially for long-distance driving, and at this time of year. He's been drinking ever since this news began.

He drinks because he cares. It's just the way he is.

Not everybody drinks.

Not everybody cares, and if he gives you his word, he'll never drink until he gets there. We all know that.

But so far nothing has happened. Things seem to remain the same.

Through the window and out on the white plane of the snow, the silent, laughing children now appear. They move in their muffled clothes like mummers on the whitest of stages. They dance and gesture noiselessly, flopping their arms in parodies of heavy, happy, earthbound birds. They have been warned by the eldest to be aware of the sleeping neighbors so they cavort only in pantomime, sometimes raising mittened hands to their mouths to suppress their joyous laughter. They dance and prance in the moonlight, tossing snow in one another's direction, tracing out various shapes and initials, forming lines which snake across the previously unmarked whiteness. All of it in silence, unknown and unseen and unheard to the neighboring world. They seem unreal even to me, their father, standing at his darkened window. It is almost as if they have danced out of the world of folklore like happy elves who cavort and mimic and caper through the private hours of this whitened dark, only to vanish with the coming of the morning's light and leaving only the signs of their activities behind. I am tempted to check the recently vacated beds to confirm what perhaps I think I know.

Then out of the corner of my eye I see him. The golden

collie-like dog. He appears almost as if from the wings of the stage or as a figure newly noticed in the lower corner of a winter painting. He sits quietly and watches the playful scene before him and then, as if responding to a silent invitation, bounds into its midst. The children chase him in frantic circles, falling and rolling as he doubles back and darts and dodges between their legs and through their outstretched arms. He seizes a mitt loosened from its owner's hand, and tosses it happily in the air and then snatches it back into his jaws an instant before it reaches the ground and seconds before the tumbling bodies fall on the emptiness of its expected destination. He races to the edge of the scene and lies facing them, holding the mitt tantalizingly between his paws, and then as they dash towards him, he leaps forward again, tossing and catching it before him and zigzagging through them as the Sunday football player might return the much sought-after ball. After he has gone through and eluded them all, he looks back over his shoulder and again, like an elated athlete, tosses the mitt high in what seems like an imaginary end zone. Then he seizes it once more and lopes in a wide circle around his pursuers, eventually coming closer and closer to them until once more their stretching hands are able to actually touch his shoulders and back and haunches, although he continues always to wriggle free. He is touched but never captured, which is the nature of the game. Then he is gone. As suddenly as he came. I strain my eyes in the direction of the adjoining street, towards the house where I have often seen him, always within a yard enclosed by woven links of chain. I see the flash of his silhouette, outlined perhaps against the snow or the light cast by the street lamps or the moon. It arcs upwards and seems to hang for an instant high above the top of the fence and then it descends on the other side. He lands on his shoulder in a fluff of snow and with a half roll regains his feet and vanishes within the shadow of his owner's house.

"What are you looking at?" asks my wife.

"That golden collie-like dog from the other street was just playing with the children in the snow."

"But he's always in that fenced-in yard."

"I guess not always. He jumped the fence just now and went

back in. I guess the owners and the rest of us think he's fenced in but he knows he's not. He probably comes out every night and leads an exciting life. I hope they don't see his tracks or they'll probably begin to chain him."

"What are the children doing?"

"They look tired now from chasing the dog. They'll probably soon be back in. I think I'll go downstairs and wait for them and make myself a cup of coffee."

"Okay."

I look once more towards the fenced-in yard but the dog is nowhere to be seen.

I first saw such a dog when I was twelve and he came as a pup of about two months in a crate to the railroad station which was about eight miles from where we lived. Someone must have phoned or dropped in to say: "Your dog's at the station."

He had come to Cape Breton in response to a letter and a check which my father had sent to Morrisburg, Ontario. We had seen the ads for "cattle collie dogs" in the *Family Herald*, which was the farm newspaper of the time, and we were in need of a good young working dog.

His crate was clean and neat and there was still a supply of dog biscuits with him and a can in the corner to hold water. The baggage handlers had looked after him well on the trip east, and he appeared in good spirits. He had a white collar and chest and four rather large white paws and a small white blaze on his forehead. The rest of him was a fluffy, golden brown, although his eyebrows and the tips of his ears as well as the end of his tail were darker, tingeing almost to black. When he grew to his full size the blackish shadings became really black, and although he had the long, heavy coat of a collie, it was in certain areas more gray than gold. He was also taller than the average collie and with a deeper chest. He seemed to be at least part German Shepherd.

It was winter when he came and we kept him in the house where he slept behind the stove in a box lined with an old coat. Our other dogs slept mostly in the stables or outside in the lees of woodpiles or under porches or curled up on the banking of the house. We seemed to care more for him because he was smaller and it was winter and he was somehow like a visitor, and also because more was expected of him and also perhaps because we had paid money for him and thought about his coming for some time—like a "planned" child. Skeptical neighbors and relatives who thought the idea of paying money for a dog was rather exotic or frivolous would ask: "Is that your Ontario dog?" or "Do you think your Ontario dog will be any good?"

He turned out to be no good at all and no one knew why. Perhaps it was because of the suspected German Shepherd blood. But he could not "get the hang of it." Although we worked him and trained him as we had other dogs, he seemed always to bring panic instead of order and to make things worse instead of better. He became a "head dog," which meant that instead of working behind the cattle he lunged at their heads, impeding them from any forward motion and causing them to turn in endless, meaningless bewildered circles. On the few occasions when he did go behind them, he was "rough," which meant that instead of being a floating, nipping, suggestive presence, he actually bit them and caused them to gallop, which was another sin. Sometimes in the summer the milk cows suffering from his misunderstood pursuit would jam pell-mell into the stable, tossing their wide horns in fear, and with their great sides heaving and perspiring while down their legs and tails the wasted milk ran in rivulets mingling with the blood caused by his slashing wounds. He was, it was said, "worse than nothing."

Gradually everyone despaired, although he continued to grow gray and golden and was, as everyone agreed, a "beautiful-looking dog."

He was also tremendously strong and in the winter months I would hitch him to a sleigh which he pulled easily and willingly on almost any kind of surface. When he was harnessed I used to put a collar around his neck and attach a light line to it so that I might have some minimum control over him, but it was hardly ever needed. He would pull home the Christmas tree or the bag of flour or the deer which was shot far back in the woods, and when we visited our winter snares he would pull home the gunnysacks which contained the partridges and rabbits which we gathered. He would also pull us, especially on the flat windswept stretches of land beside the sea. There the snow was never really deep and the water that oozed from a series of fresh-water springs and ponds contributed to a glaze of ice and crisply crusted snow which the sleigh runners seemed to sing over without ever breaking through. He would begin with an easy lope and then increase his swiftness until both he and the sleigh seemed to touch the surface at only irregular intervals. He would stretch out then with his ears flattened against his head and his shoulders bunching and contracting in the rhythm of his speed. Behind him on the sleigh we would cling tenaciously to the wooden slats as the particles of ice and snow dislodged by his nails hurtled towards our faces. We would avert our heads and close our eyes and the wind stung so sharply that the difference between freezing and burning could not be known. He would do that until late in the afternoon when it was time to return home and begin our chores.

On the sunny winter Sunday that I am thinking of, I planned to visit my snares. There seemed no other children around that afternoon and the adults were expecting relatives. I harnessed the dog to the sleigh, opened the door of the house and shouted that I was going to look at my snares. We began to climb the hill behind the house on our way to the woods when we looked back and out towards the sea. The "big ice," which was what we called the major pack of drift ice, was in solidly against the shore and stretched out beyond the range of vision. It had not been "in" yesterday, although for the past weeks we had seen it moving offshore, sometimes close and sometimes distant, depending on the winds and tides. The coming of the big ice marked the official beginning of the coldest part of winter. It was mostly drift ice from the Arctic and Labrador, although some of it was fresh-water ice from the estuary of the St. Lawrence. It drifted down with the dropping temperatures, bringing its own mysterious coldness and stretching for hundreds of miles in craters and pans, sometimes in grotesque shapes and sometimes in dazzling architectural forms. It was blue and white and sometimes gray and at other times a dazzling emerald green.

The dog and I changed our direction towards the sea, to find what the ice might yield. Our land had always been beside the sea and we had always gone towards it to find newness and the extraordinary; and over the years we, as others along the coast, had found quite a lot, although never the pirate chests of gold which were supposed to abound or the reasons for the mysterious lights that our elders still spoke of and persisted in seeing. But kegs of rum had washed up, and sometimes bloated horses and various fishing paraphernalia and valuable timber and furniture from foundered ships. The door of my room was apparently the galley door from a ship called the *Judith Franklin* which was wrecked during the early winter in which my great-grandfather was building his house. My grandfather told of how they had heard the cries and seen the lights as the ship neared the rocks and of how they had run down in the dark and tossed lines to the people while tying themselves to trees on the shore. All were saved, including women clinging to small children. The next day the builders of the new house went down to the shore and salvaged what they could from the wreckage of the vanquished ship. A sort of symbolic marriage of the new and the old: doors and shelving, stairways, hatches, wooden chests and trunks and various glass figurines and lanterns which were miraculously never broken.

People came too. The dead as well as the living. Bodies of men swept overboard and reported lost at sea and the bodies of men still crouched within the shelter of their boats' broken bows. And sometimes in late winter young sealers who had quit their vessels would walk across the ice and come to our doors. They were usually very young—some still in their teens—and had signed on for jobs they could not or no longer wished to handle. They were often disoriented and did not know where they were, only that they had seen land and had decided to walk towards it. They were often frostbitten and with little money and uncertain as to how they might get to Halifax.

The dog and I walked towards the ice upon the sea. Sometimes it was hard to "get on" the ice, which meant that at the point where the pack met the shore there might be open water or irregularities caused by the indentations of the coastline or the workings of the tides and currents, but for us on that day there was no difficulty at all. We were on easily and effortlessly and enthused in our new adventure. For the first mile there was nothing but the vastness of the white expanse. We came to a clear stretch where the ice was as smooth and unruffled as that of an indoor arena and I knelt on the sleigh while the dog loped easily along. Gradually the ice changed to an uneven terrain of pressure ridges and hummocks, making it impossible to ride farther; and then suddenly, upon rounding a hummock, I saw the perfect seal. At first I thought it was alive, as did the dog who stopped so suddenly in his tracks that the sleigh almost collided with his legs. The hackles on the back of his neck rose and he growled in the dangerous way he was beginning to develop. But the seal was dead, yet facing us in a frozen perfection that was difficult to believe. There was a light powder of snow over its darker coat and a delicate rime of frost still formed the outline of its whiskers. Its eyes were wide open and it stared straight ahead towards the land. Even now in memory it seems more real than reality—as if it were transformed by frozen art into something more arresting than life itself. The way the sudden seal in the museum exhibit freezes your eyes with the touch of truth. Immediately I wanted to take it home.

It was frozen solidly in a base of ice so I began to look for something that might serve as a pry. I let the dog out of his harness and hung the sleigh and harness on top of the hummock to mark the place and began my search. Some distance away I found a pole about twelve feet long. It is always surprising to find such things on the ice field but they are, often amazingly, there, almost in the same way that you might find a pole floating in the summer ocean. Unpredictable but possible. I took the pole back and began my work. The dog went off on explorations of his own.

Although it was firmly frozen, the task did not seem impossible and by inserting the end of the pole under first one side and then the other and working from the front to the back, it was possible to cause a gradual loosening. I remember thinking how very warm it was because I was working hard and perspiring heavily. When the dog came back he was uneasy, and I realized it was starting to snow a bit but I was almost done. He sniffed with disinterest at the seal and began to whine a bit, which was something he did not often do. Finally, after another quarter of an hour, I was able to roll my trophy onto the sleigh and with the dog in harness we set off. We had gone perhaps two hundred yards when the seal slid free. I took the dog and the sleigh back and once again managed to roll the seal on. This time I took the line from the dog's collar and tied the seal to the sleigh, reasoning that the dog would go home anyway and there would be no need to guide him. My fingers were numb as I tried to fasten the awkward knots and the dog began to whine and rear. When I gave the command he bolted forward and I clung at the back of the sleigh to the seal. The snow was heavier now and blowing in my face but we were moving rapidly and when we came to the stretch of arena-like ice we skimmed across it almost like an iceboat, the profile of the frozen seal at the front of the sleigh like those figures at the prows of Viking ships. At the very end of the smooth stretch, we went through. From my position at the end of the sleigh I felt him drop almost before I saw him, and rolled backwards seconds before the sleigh and seal followed him into the blackness of the water. He went under once carried by his own momentum but surfaced almost immediately with his head up and his paws scrambling at the icy, jagged edge of the hole; but when the weight and momentum of the sleigh and its burden struck, he went down again, this time out of sight.

I realized we had struck a "seam" and that the stretch of smooth ice had been deceivingly and temporarily joined to the rougher ice near the shore and now was in the process of breaking away. I saw the widening line before me and jumped to the other side just as his head miraculously came up once more. I lay on my stomach and grabbed his collar in both my hands and then in a moment of panic did not know what to do. I could feel myself sliding towards him and the darkness of the water and was aware of the weight that pulled me forward and down. I was also aware of his razor-sharp claws flailing violently before my face and knew that I might lose my eyes. And I was aware that his own eyes were bulging from their sockets and that he might think I was trying to choke him and might lunge and slash my face with his teeth in desperation. I knew all of this but somehow did nothing about it; it seemed almost simpler to hang on and be drawn into the darkness of the gently slopping water, seeming to slop gently in spite of all the agitation. Then

suddenly he was free, scrambling over my shoulder and dragging the sleigh behind him. The seal surfaced again, buoyed up
perhaps by the physics of its frozen body or the nature of its
fur. Still looking more genuine than it could have in life, its
snout and head broke the open water and it seemed to look at
us curiously for an instant before it vanished permanently beneath the ice. The loose and badly tied knots had apparently
not held when the sleigh was in a near-vertical position and we
were saved by the ineptitude of my own numbed fingers. We
had been spared for a future time.

He lay gasping and choking for a moment, coughing up the
icy salt water, and then almost immediately his coat began to
freeze. I realized then how cold I was myself and that even in
the moments I had been lying on the ice, my clothes had begun
to adhere to it. My earlier heated perspiration was now a cold
rime upon my body and I imagined it outlining me there, beneath
my clothes, in a sketch of frosty white. I got on the sleigh once
more and crouched low as he began to race towards home. His
coat was freezing fast, and as he ran the individual ice-coated
hairs began to clack together like rhythmical castanets attuned
to the motion of his body. It was snowing quite heavily in our
faces now and it seemed to be approaching dusk, although I
doubted if it were so on the land which I could now no longer
see. I realized all the obvious things I should have considered
earlier. That if the snow was blowing in our faces, the wind was
off the land, and if it was off the land, it was blowing the ice
pack back out to sea. That was probably one reason why the
seam had opened. And also that the ice had only been in one
night and had not had a chance to set. I realized other things
as well. That it was the time of the late afternoon when the tide
was falling. That no one knew where we were. That I had said
we were going to look at snares, which was not where we had
gone at all. And I remembered now that I had received no answer
even to that misinformation, so perhaps I had not even been
heard. And also if there was drifting snow like this on land, our
tracks would by now have been obliterated.

We came to a rough section of ice: huge slabs on their sides
and others piled one on top of the other as if they were in some

strange form of storage. It was no longer possible to ride the sleigh but as I stood up I lifted it and hung on to it as a means of holding on to the dog. The line usually attached to his collar had sunk with the vanished seal. My knees were stiff when I stood up; and deprived of the windbreak effect which the dog had provided, I felt the snow driving full into my face, particularly my eyes. It did not merely impede my vision, the way distant snow flurries might, but actually entered my eyes, causing them to water and freeze nearly shut. I was aware of the weight of ice on my eyelashes and could see them as they gradually lowered and became heavier. I did not remember ice like this when I got on, although I did not find that terribly surprising. I pressed the soles of my numbed feet firmly down upon it to try to feel if it was moving out, but it was impossible to tell because there was no fixed point of reference. Almost the sensation one gets on a conveyor belt at airports or on escalators; although you are standing still you recognize motion, but should you shut your eyes and be deprived of sight, even that recognition may become ambiguously uncertain.

The dog began to whine and to walk around me in circles, binding my legs with the traces of the harness as I continued to grasp the sleigh. Finally I decided to let him go as there seemed no way to hold him and there was nothing else to do. I unhitched the traces and doubled them up as best I could and tucked them under the backpad of his harness so they would not drag behind him and become snagged on any obstacles. I did not take off my mitts to do so as I was afraid I would not be able to get them back on. He vanished into the snow almost immediately.

The sleigh had been a gift from an uncle, so I hung on to it and carried it with both hands before me like an ineffectual shield against the wind and snow. I lowered my head as much as I could and turned it sideways so the wind would beat against my head instead of directly into my face. Sometimes I would turn and walk backwards for a few steps. Although I knew it was not the wisest thing to do, it seemed at times the only way to breathe. And then I began to feel the water sloshing about my feet.

Sometimes when the tides or currents ran heavily and the ice began to separate, the water that was beneath it would well up and wash over it almost as if it were reflooding it. Sometimes you could see the hard ice clearly beneath the water but at other times a sort of floating slush was formed mingling with snow and "slob" ice which was not yet solid. It was thick and dense and soupy and it was impossible to see what lay beneath it. Experienced men on the ice sometimes carried a slender pole so they could test the consistency of the footing which might or might not lie before them, but I was obviously not one of them, although I had a momentary twinge for the pole I had used to dislodge the seal. Still, there was nothing to do but go forward.

When I went through, the first sensation was almost of relief and relaxation for the water initially made me feel much warmer than I had been on the surface. It was the most dangerous of false sensations for I knew my clothes were becoming heavier by the second. I clung to the sleigh somewhat as a raft and lunged forward with it in a kind of up-and-down swimming motion, hoping that it might strike some sort of solidity before my arms became so weighted and sodden that I could no longer lift them. I cried out then for the first time into the driving snow.

He came almost immediately, although I could see he was afraid and the slobbing slush was up to his knees. Still, he seemed to be on some kind of solid footing for he was not swimming. I splashed towards him and when almost there, desperately threw the sleigh before me and lunged for the edge of what seemed like his footing, but it only gave way as if my hands were closing on icy insubstantial porridge. He moved forward then, although I still could not tell if what supported him would be of any use to me. Finally I grasped the breast strap of his harness. He began to back up then, and as I said, he was tremendously strong. The harness began to slide forward on his shoulders but he continued to pull as I continued to grasp and then I could feel my elbows on what seemed like solid ice and I was able to hook them on the edge and draw myself, dripping and soaking, like another seal out of the black water and onto the whiteness of the slushy ice. Almost at once my clothes began to freeze. My elbows and knees began to creak when I bent them as if I were a robot from the realm of science fiction and then I could see myself clothed in transparent ice as if I had been coated with shellac or finished with clear varnish.

As the fall into the winter sea had at first seemed ironically warm, so now my garments of ice seemed a protection against the biting wind, but I knew it was a deceptive sensation and that I did not have much time before me. The dog faced into the wind and I followed him. This time he stayed in sight, and at times even turned back to wait for me. He was cautious but certain and gradually the slush disappeared, and although we were still in water, the ice was hard and clear beneath it. The frozen heaviness of my clothes began to weigh on me and I could feel myself, ironically, perspiring within my suit of icy armor. I was very tired, which I knew was another dangerous sensation. And then I saw the land. It was very close and a sudden surprise. Almost like coming upon a stalled and unexpected automobile in a highway's winter storm. It was only yards away, and although there was no longer any ice actually touching the shore, there were several pans of it floating in the region between. The dog jumped from one to the other and I followed him, still clutching the sleigh, and missing only the last pan which floated close to the rocky shore. The water came only to my waist and I was able to touch the bottom and splash noisily on land. We had been spared again for a future time and I was never to know whether he had reached the shore himself and come back or whether he had heard my call against the wind.

We began to run towards home and the land lightened and there were touches of evening sun. The wind still blew but no snow was falling. Yet when I looked back, the ice and the ocean were invisible in the swirling squalls. It was like looking at another far and distant country on the screen of a snowy television.

I became obsessed, now that I could afford the luxury, with not being found disobedient or considered a fool. The visitors' vehicles were still in the yard so I imagined most of the family to be in the parlor or living room, and I circled the house and entered through the kitchen, taking the dog with me. I was able to get upstairs unnoticed and get my clothes changed and when I came down I mingled with everybody and tried to appear as normal as I could. My own family was caught up with the visitors and only general comments came my way. The dog, who could not change his clothes, lay under the table with his head on his paws and he was also largely unnoticed. Later as the ice melted from his coat, a puddle formed around him, which I casually mopped up. Still later someone said, "I wonder where that dog has been, his coat is soaking wet." I was never to tell anyone of the afternoon's experience or that he had saved my life.

Two winters later I was sitting at a neighbor's kitchen table when I looked out the window and saw the dog as he was shot. He had followed my father and also me and had been sitting rather regally on a little hill beside the house and I suppose had presented an ideal target. But he had moved at just the right or wrong time and instead of killing him the high-powered bullet smashed into his shoulder. He jumped into the air and turned his snapping teeth upon the wound, trying to bite the cause of the pain he could not see. And then he turned towards home, unsteady but still strong on his three remaining legs. No doubt he felt, as we all do, that if he could get home he might be saved, but he did not make it, as we knew he could not, because of the amount of blood on the snow and the wavering pattern of his three-legged tracks. Yet he was, as I said, tremendously strong and he managed almost three-quarters of a mile. The house he sought must have been within his vision when he died for we could see it quite clearly when we came to his body by the roadside. His eyes were open and his tongue was clenched between his teeth and the little blood he had left dropped red and black on the winter snow. He was not to be saved for a future time anymore.

I learned later that my father had asked the neighbor to shoot him and that we had led him into a kind of ambush. Perhaps my father did so because the neighbor was younger and had a better gun or was a better shot. Perhaps because my father did not want to be involved. It was obvious he had not planned on things turning out so messy.

The dog had become increasingly powerful and protective, to the extent that people were afraid to come into the yard. And he had also bitten two of the neighbor's children and caused them to be frightened of passing our house on their journeys to and from school. And perhaps there was also the feeling in the community that he was getting more than his share of the breeding: that he travelled farther than other dogs on his nightly forays and that he fought off and injured the other smaller dogs who might compete with him for female favors. Perhaps there was fear that his dominance and undesirable characteristics did not bode well for future generations.

This has been the writing down of a memory triggered by the sight of a golden dog at play in the silent snow with my own excited children. After they came in and had their hot chocolate, the wind began to blow; and by the time I left for work, there was no evidence of their early-morning revels or any dog tracks leading to the chain-link fence. The "enclosed" dog looked impassively at me as I brushed the snow from the buried windshield. What does he know? he seemed to say.

The snow continues to drift and to persist as another uncertainty added to those we already have. Should we be forced to drive tonight, it will be a long, tough journey into the wind and the driving snow which is pounding across Ontario and Quebec and New Brunswick and against the granite coast of Nova Scotia. Should we be drawn by death, we might well meet our own. Still, it is only because I am alive that I can even consider such possibilities. Had I not been saved by the golden dog, I would not have these tight concerns or children playing in the snow or of course these memories. It is because of him that I have been able to come this far in time.

It is too bad that I could not have saved him as well and my feelings did him little good as I looked upon his bloodied body there beside the road. It was too late and out of my control and even if I had known the possibilities of the future it would not have been easy.

He was with us only for a while and brought his own changes, and yet he still persists. He persists in my memory and in my life and he persists physically as well. He is there in this winter storm. There in the golden-gray dogs with their black-tipped ears and tails, sleeping in the stables or in the lees of woodpiles or under porches or curled beside the houses which face towards the sea.

As Birds Bring Forth the Sun

O NCE THERE WAS a family with a Highland name who lived beside the sea. And the man had a dog of which he was very fond. She was large and gray, a sort of staghound from another time. And if she jumped up to lick his face, which she loved to do, her paws would jolt against his shoulders with such force that she would come close to knocking him down and he would be forced to take two or three backward steps before he could regain his balance. And he himself was not a small man, being slightly over six feet and perhaps one hundred and eighty pounds.

She had been left, when a pup, at the family's gate in a small handmade box and no one knew where she had come from or that she would eventually grow to such a size. Once, while still a small pup, she had been run over by the steel wheel of a horse-drawn cart which was hauling kelp from the shore to be used as fertilizer. It was in October and the rain had been falling for some weeks and the ground was soft. When the wheel of the cart passed over her, it sunk her body into the wet earth as well as crushing some of her ribs; and apparently the silhouette of her small crushed body was visible in the earth after the man lifted her to his chest while she yelped and screamed. He ran his fingers along her broken bones, ignoring the blood and urine which fell upon his shirt, trying to soothe her bulging eyes and her scrabbling front paws and her desperately licking tongue.

The more practical members of his family, who had seen run-over dogs before, suggested that her neck be broken by his strong hands or that he grasp her by the hind legs and swing her head against a rock, thus putting an end to her misery. But he would not do it.

Instead, he fashioned a small box and lined it with woolen remnants from a sheep's fleece and one of his old and frayed shirts. He placed her within the box and placed the box behind the stove and then he warmed some milk in a small saucepan and sweetened it with sugar. And he held open her small and trembling jaws with his left hand while spooning in the sweetened milk with his right, ignoring the needle-like sharpness of her small teeth. She lay in the box most of the remaining fall and into the early winter, watching everything with her large brown eyes.

Although some members of the family complained about her presence and the odor from the box and the waste of time she involved, they gradually adjusted to her; and as the weeks passed by, it became evident that her ribs were knitting together in some form or other and that she was recovering with the resilience of the young. It also became evident that she would grow to a tremendous size, as she outgrew one box and then another and the gray hair began to feather from her huge front paws. In the spring she was outside almost all of the time and followed the man everywhere; and when she came inside during the following months, she had grown so large that she would no longer fit into her accustomed place behind the stove and was forced to lie beside it. She was never given a name but was referred to in Gaelic as *cù mòr glas*, the big gray dog.

By the time she came into her first heat, she had grown to a tremendous height, and although her signs and her odor attracted many panting and highly aroused suitors, none was big enough to mount her and the frenzy of their disappointment and the longing of her unfulfillment were more than the man could stand. He went, so the story goes, to a place where he knew there was a big dog. A dog not as big as she was, but still a big dog, and he brought him home with him. And at the proper time he took the *cù mòr glas* and the big dog down to the sea where he knew there was a hollow in the rock which appeared only at low tide. He took some sacking to provide footing for the male dog and he placed the *cù mòr glas* in the hollow of the rock and knelt beside her and steadied her with his left arm under her throat and helped position the male dog above her and guided his blood-engorged penis. He was a man used to working with the breeding of animals, with the guiding of rams and bulls and stallions and often with the funky smell of animal semen heavy on his large and gentle hands.

The winter that followed was a cold one and ice formed on the sea and frequent squalls and blizzards obliterated the offshore islands and caused the people to stay near their fires much of the time, mending clothes and nets and harness and waiting for the change in season. The *cù mòr glas* grew heavier and even more large until there was hardly room for her around the stove or even under the table. And then one morning, when it seemed that spring was about to break, she was gone.

The man and even his family, who had become more involved than they cared to admit, waited for her but she did not come. And as the frenzy of spring wore on, they busied themselves with readying their land and their fishing gear and all of the things that so desperately required their attention. And then they were into summer and fall and winter and another spring which saw the birth of the man and his wife's twelfth child. And then it was summer again.

That summer the man and two of his teenaged sons were pulling their herring nets about two miles offshore when the wind began to blow off the land and the water began to roughen. They became afraid that they could not make it safely back to shore, so they pulled in behind one of the offshore islands, knowing that they would be sheltered there and planning to outwait the storm. As the prow of their boat approached the gravelly shore, they heard a sound above them, and looking up they saw the *cù mòr glas* silhouetted on the brow of the hill which was the small island's highest point.

"*M'eudal cù mòr glas*" shouted the man in his happiness—
m'eudal meaning something like dear or darling; and as he
shouted, he jumped over the side of his boat into the waist-deep
water, struggling for footing on the rolling gravel as he waded
eagerly and awkwardly towards her and the shore. At the same
time, the *cù mòr glas* came hurtling down towards him in a
shower of small rocks dislodged by her feet; and just as he was
emerging from the water, she met him as she used to, rearing
up on her hind legs and placing her huge front paws on his
shoulders while extending her eager tongue.

The weight and speed of her momentum met him as he tried
to hold his balance on the sloping angle and the water rolling
gravel beneath his feet, and he staggered backwards and lost
his footing and fell beneath her force. And in that instant again,
as the story goes, there appeared over the brow of the hill six
more huge gray dogs hurtling down towards the gravelled
strand. They had never seen him before; and seeing him
stretched prone beneath their mother, they misunderstood, like
so many armies, the intention of their leader.

They fell upon him in a fury, slashing his face and tearing
aside his lower jaw and ripping out his throat, crazed with bloodlust or duty or perhaps starvation. The *cù mòr glas* turned on
them in her own savagery, slashing and snarling and, it seemed,
crazed by their mistake; driving them bloodied and yelping before her, back over the brow of the hill where they vanished
from sight but could still be heard screaming in the distance. It
all took perhaps little more than a minute.

The man's two sons, who were still in the boat and had witnessed it all, ran sobbing through the salt water to where their
mauled and mangled father lay; but there was little they could
do other than hold his warm and bloodied hands for a few brief
moments. Although his eyes "lived" for a small fraction of time,
he could not speak to them because his face and throat had been
torn away, and of course there was nothing they could do except
to hold and be held tightly until that too slipped away and his
eyes glazed over and they could no longer feel his hands holding
theirs. The storm increased and they could not get home and
so they were forced to spend the night huddled beside their

father's body. They were afraid to try to carry the body to the rocking boat because he was so heavy and they were afraid that they might lose even what little of him remained and they were afraid also, huddled on the rocks, that the dogs might return. But they did not return at all and there was no sound from them, no sound at all, only the moaning of the wind and the washing of the water on the rocks.

In the morning they debated whether they should try to take his body with them or whether they should leave it and return in the company of older and wiser men. But they were afraid to leave it unattended and felt that the time needed to cover it with protective rocks would be better spent in trying to get across to their home shore. For a while they debated as to whether one should go in the boat and the other remain on the island, but each was afraid to be alone and so in the end they managed to drag and carry and almost float him towards the bobbing boat. They lay him face down and covered him with what clothes there were and set off across the still-rolling sea. Those who waited on the shore missed the large presence of the man within the boat and some of them waded into the water and others rowed out in skiffs, attempting to hear the tearful messages called out across the rolling waves.

The *cù mòr glas* and her six young dogs were never seen again, or perhaps I should say they were never seen again in the same way. After some weeks, a group of men circled the island tentatively in their boats but they saw no sign. They went again and then again but found nothing. A year later, and grown much braver, they beached their boats and walked the island carefully, looking into the small sea caves and the hollows at the base of the wind-ripped trees, thinking perhaps that if they did not find the dogs, they might at least find their whitened bones; but again they discovered nothing.

The *cù mòr glas,* though, was supposed to be sighted here and there for a number of years. Seen on a hill in one region or silhouetted on a ridge in another or loping across the valleys or glens in the early morning or the shadowy evening. Always in the area of the half perceived. For a while she became rather like the Loch Ness Monster or the Sasquatch on a smaller scale.

Seen but not recorded. Seen when there were no cameras. Seen but never taken.

The mystery of where she went became entangled with the mystery of whence she came. There was increased speculation about the handmade box in which she had been found and much theorizing as to the individual or individuals who might have left it. People went to look for the box but could not find it. It was felt she might have been part of a *buidseachd* or evil spell cast on the man by some mysterious enemy. But no one could go much farther than that. All of his caring for her was recounted over and over again and nobody missed any of the ironies.

What seemed literally known was that she had crossed the winter ice to have her pups and had been unable to get back. No one could remember ever seeing her swim; and in the early months at least, she could not have taken her young pups with her.

The large and gentle man with the smell of animal semen often heavy on his hands was my great-great-great-grandfather, and it may be argued that he died because he was too good at breeding animals or that he cared too much about their fulfillment and well-being. He was no longer there for his own child of the spring who, in turn, became my great-great-grandfather, and he was perhaps too much there in the memory of his older sons who saw him fall beneath the ambiguous force of the *cù mòr glas*. The youngest boy in the boat was haunted and tormented by the awfulness of what he had seen. He would wake at night screaming that he had seen the *cù mòr glas a' bhàis*, the big gray dog of death, and his screams filled the house and the ears and minds of the listeners, bringing home again and again the consequences of their loss. One morning, after a night in which he saw the *cù mòr glas a' bhàis* so vividly that his sheets were drenched with sweat, he walked to the high cliff which faced the island and there he cut his throat with a fish knife and fell into the sea.

The other brother lived to be forty, but, again so the story goes, he found himself in a Glasgow pub one night, perhaps looking for answers, deep and sodden with the whiskey which had become his anaesthetic. In the half darkness he saw a large, gray-haired man sitting by himself against the wall and mumbled something to him. Some say he saw the *cù mòr glas a' bhàis* or uttered the name. And perhaps the man heard the phrase through ears equally affected by drink and felt he was being called a dog or a son of a bitch or something of that nature. They rose to meet one another and struggled outside into the cobblestoned passageway behind the pub where, most improbably, there were supposed to be six other large, gray-haired men who beat him to death on the cobblestones, smashing his bloodied head into the stone again and again before vanishing and leaving him to die with his face turned to the sky. The *cù mòr glas a' bhàis* had come again, said his family, as they tried to piece the tale together.

This is how the *cù mòr glas a' bhàis* came into our lives, and it is obvious that all of this happened a long, long time ago. Yet with succeeding generations it seemed the specter had somehow come to stay and that it had become *ours*—not in the manner of an unwanted skeleton in the closet from a family's ancient past but more in the manner of something close to a genetic possibility. In the deaths of each generation, the gray dog was seen by some—by women who were to die in childbirth, by soldiers who went forth to the many wars but did not return, by those who went forth to feuds or dangerous love affairs, by those who answered mysterious midnight messages, by those who swerved on the highway to avoid the real or imagined gray dog and ended in masses of crumpled steel. And by one professional athlete who, in addition to his ritualized athletic superstitions, carried another fear or belief as well. Many of the man's descendants moved like careful hemophiliacs, fearing that they carried unwanted possibilities deep within them. And others, while they laughed, were like members of families in which there is a recurrence over the generations of repeated cancer or the diabetes which comes to those beyond middle age. The feeling of those who may say little to others but who may say often and quietly to themselves, "It has not happened to me," while adding always the cautionary "*yet*."

I am thinking all of this now as the October rain falls on the city of Toronto and the pleasant, white-clad nurses pad confidently in and out of my father's room. He lies quietly amidst the whiteness, his head and shoulders elevated so that he is in that hospital position of being neither quite prone nor yet sitting. His hair is white upon his pillow and he breathes softly and sometimes unevenly, although it is difficult ever to be sure.

My five gray-haired brothers and I take turns beside his bedside, holding his heavy hands in ours and feeling their response, hoping ambiguously that he will speak to us, although we know that it may tire him. And trying to read his life and ours into his eyes when they are open. He has been with us for a long time, well into our middle age. Unlike those boys in that boat of so long ago, we did not see him taken from us in our youth. And unlike their youngest brother who, in turn, became our great-great-grandfather, we did not grow into a world in which there was no father's touch. We have been lucky to have this large and gentle man so deep into our lives.

No one in this hospital has mentioned the *cù mòr glas a' bhàis*. Yet as my mother said ten years ago, before slipping into her own death as quietly as a grownup child who leaves or enters her parents' house in the early hours, "It is hard to *not* know what you do know."

Even those who are most skeptical, like my oldest brother who has driven here from Montreal, betray themselves by their nervous actions. "I avoided the Greyhound bus stations in both Montreal and Toronto," he smiled upon his arrival, and then added, "Just in case."

He did not realize how ill our father was and has smiled little since then. I watch him turning the diamond ring upon his finger, knowing that he hopes he will not hear the Gaelic phrase he knows too well. Not having the luxury, as he once said, of some who live in Montreal and are able to pretend they do not understand the "other" language. You cannot *not* know what you do know.

Sitting here, taking turns holding the hands of the man who gave us life, we are afraid for him and for ourselves. We are afraid of what he may see and we are afraid to hear the phrase born of the vision. We are aware that it may become confused with what the doctors call "the will to live" and we are aware that some beliefs are what others would dismiss as "garbage."

We are aware that there are men who believe the earth is flat and that the birds bring forth the sun.

Bound here in our own peculiar mortality, we do not wish to see or see others see that which signifies life's demise. We do not want to hear the voice of our father, as did those other sons, calling down his own particular death upon him.

We would shut our eyes and plug our ears, even as we know such actions to be of no avail. Open still and fearful to the gray hair rising on our necks if and when we hear the scrabble of the paws and the scratching at the door.

Vision

I DON'T REMEMBER when I first heard the story but I remember
the first time that I heard it and remembered it. By that I
mean the first time it made an impression on me and more or
less became *mine*, sort of went into me the way such things do,
went into me in such a way that I knew it would not leave again
but would remain there forever. Something like when you cut
your hand with a knife by accident, and even as you're trying
to staunch the blood flowing out of the wound, you know the
wound will never really heal totally and your hand will never
look quite the same again. You can imagine the scar tissue that
will form and be a different color and texture from the rest of
your skin. You know this even as you are trying to stop the
blood and trying to squeeze the separated edges of skin together
once more. Like trying to squeeze together the separated banks
of a small and newly discovered river so that the stream will be
subterranean once again. It is something like that, although you
know in one case the future scar will be forever on the outside
while the memory will remain forever deep within.

Anyway, on this day we were about a mile and a half offshore
but heading home on the last day of the lobster season. We could
see the trucks of the New Brunswick buyers waiting for us on
the wharf and because it was a sunny day, light reflected and

glinted off the chrome trim and bumpers of the waiting trucks and off their gleaming rooftops as well. It was the last day of June and the time was early afternoon and I was seventeen.

My father was in good spirits because the season was over and we had done reasonably well and we were bringing in most of our gear intact. And there seemed no further need to rush.

The sea was almost calm, although there was a light breeze at our backs and we throttled down our engine because there really was no reason to hurry into the wharf for the last and final time. I was in the stern of the boat steadying the piled lobster traps which we had recently raised from the bottom of the sea. Some of them still gleamed with droplets of salt water and streamers of seaweed dangled from their lathes. In the crates beside my feet the mottled blue-green lobsters moved and rustled quietly, snapping their tails as they slid over one another with that peculiar dry/wet sound of shell and claws over shell and claws. Their hammer claws had been pegged and fastened shut with rubber bands so they would not mutilate each other and so decrease their value.

"Put some of those in a sack for ourselves," said my father, turning his head back over his right shoulder as he spoke. He was standing ahead of me, facing the land and urinating over the side. His water fell into the sea and vanished into the rolling swell of the boat's slow passage.

"Put them in the back there," he said, "behind the bait bucket, and throw our oilers over them. They will want everything we've got, and what they won't see won't hurt them. Put in some markets too, not just canners."

I took a sack and began to pick some lobsters out of the crate, grasping them at the end of their body shells or by the ends of their tails and being careful not to get my fingers snapped. For even with their hammer claws banded shut there was still a certain danger.

"How many do you want?" I asked.

"Oh," he said, turning with a smile and running his hand along the front of his trousers to make sure his fly was closed, "as many as you want. Use your own good judgement."

We did not often take home lobsters for ourselves because

they were so expensive and we needed the money they would bring. And the buyers wanted them with a desperation almost bordering on frenzy. Perhaps even now as I bent over the crate they were watching from the wharf with binoculars to see if any were being concealed. My father stood casually in front of me, once more facing the land and shielding my movements with his body. The boat followed its set course, its keel cutting the blue-green water and turning it temporarily into white.

There was a time long ago when the lobsters were not thought to be so valuable. Probably because the markets of the larger world had not yet been discovered or were so far away. People then ate all they wanted of them and even used them for fertilizer on their fields. And those who did eat them did not consider them to be a delicacy. There is a quoted story from the time which states that in the schools you could always identify the children of the poor because they were the ones with lobster in their sandwiches. The well-to-do were able to afford bologna.

With the establishment of the New England market, things changed. Lobster factories were set up along the coast for the canning of the lobsters at a time before good land transportation and refrigeration became common. In May and June and into July the girls in white caps and smocks packed the lobster meat into burnished cans before they were steam sealed. And the men in the smack boats brought the catches to the rickety piers which were built on piles and jutted out into the sea.

My father's mother was one of the girls, and her job was taking the black vein out of the meat of the lobster's tail before the tail was coiled around the inside of the can. At home they ate the black vein along with the rest of the meat, but the supervisors at the factory said it was unsightly. My father's father was one of the young men standing ready in the smack boat, wearing his cap at a jaunty angle and uttering witty sayings and singing little songs in Gaelic to the girls who stood above him on the wharf. All of this was of course a long time ago and I am just trying to recreate the scene.

On the day of the remembered story, though, the sea was almost serene as I placed the lobsters in the sack and prepared to hide them behind the bait bucket and under our oilers in the stern of the boat. Before we secreted the sack, we leaned over the side and scooped up water in the bailing bucket and soaked the sack to insure the health and life of the lobsters kept within. The wet sack moved and clacked with the shape and sound of the lobsters and it reminded me vaguely of sacks of kittens which were being taken to be drowned. You could see the movement but not the individuals.

My father straightened from his last dip over the side and passed the dripping bucket carefully to me. He steadied himself with his left hand on the gunwale and then seated himself on the thwart and faced towards the north. I gave the lobsters another soaking and moved to place them behind the bait bucket. There was still some bait remaining but we would not have need of it anymore so I threw it over the side. The pieces of blue-gray mackerel turned and revolved before I lost sight of them within the water. The day before yesterday we had taken these same mackerel out of the same sea. We used nets for the spring mackerel because they were blind and could not see to take a baited hook; but in the fall when they returned, the scales had fallen from their eyes and they would lunge at almost anything thrown before them. Even bits of other mackerel ground up and mixed with salt. Mackerel are a windward fish and always swim against the wind. If the wind is off the land, they swim towards the shore and perhaps the waiting nets; but if the wind blows in the opposite direction, they face out to sea and go so far out some years that we miss them altogether.

I put the empty bait bucket in front of the sack of lobsters and placed an empty crate upside down and at an angle over them so that their movements would not be noticeable. And I casually threw our oilers over them as well.

Ahead of us on the land and to the north of the wharf with its waiting trucks was the mile-long sandy beach cut by the river which acted as an erratic boundary between the fishing grounds of ourselves and our neighbors, the MacAllesters. We had traditionally fished to the right of the river and they to the left, and apparently for many years it was constant in its estuary. But in recent years the river mouth, because of the force of storms and tides and the buildup of sand, had become undependable as a visual guide. The shifting was especially affected by the ravages of the winter storms, and some springs the river might empty almost a mile to the north or the south of its previous point of entry. This had caused a tension between ourselves and the MacAllesters because, although we traditionally went to the same grounds, the boundary was no longer fixed and we had fallen into accusations and counteraccusations; sometimes using the actual river when it suited our purpose, and when it did not, using an earlier and imaginary river which we could no longer see.

The MacAllesters' boat was going in ahead of us now and I waved to Kenneth MacAllester, who had become a rather lukewarm friend because of the tension between our families. He was the same age as I and he waved back, although the other two men in the boat did not.

At an earlier time when Kenneth MacAllester and I were friends and in about grade six he told me a story while we were walking home from school in the spring. He told me that his grandmother was descended from a man in Scotland who possessed *Da Shealladh*, two sights or the second sight, and that by looking through a hole in a magical white stone he could see distant contemporary events as well as those of the future. Nearly all of his visions came true. His name was either Munro or MacKenzie and his first name was Kenneth and the eye he placed to the stone for his visions was *cam* or blind in the sense of ordinary sight. He was a favorite of the powerful man for whom he worked but he and the man's wife were jealous and disliked each other. Once when the powerful man was in Paris there was a big party on his estate. In one version "the prophet" commented rather unwisely on the paternity of some of the children present. In another version the man's wife asked him mockingly if he could "see" her husband in Paris but he refused. However, she insisted. Putting the stone to his eye he told her that her husband was enjoying himself rather too much with ladies in Paris and had little thought of her. Enraged and embarrassed, she ordered him to be burned in a barrel of tar into which spikes had been driven from the outside. In one version the execution took place right away but in another it did not take place until some days later. In the second version the man was returning home when he heard the news and saw the black smoke rising. He spurred his horse at utmost speed towards the point where he saw the billowing smoke and called out in an attempt to stop the burning and save his friend; but his horse died beneath him, and though he ran the rest of the way, he arrived too late for any salvation.

Before the prophet died he hurled his white stone as far as he could out into the lake and told the lady that the family would come to an end years hence. And he told her that it would end when there was a deaf-and-dumb father who would outlive his four sons and then all their lands would pass into the hands of strangers. Generations later the deaf-and-dumb father was apparently a fine, good man who was helpless in the face of the prophecy he knew too much about and which he saw unfolding around him with the death of each of his four loved sons. Unable again to offer any salvation.

I thought it was a tremendous story at the time, and Kenneth picked up a white stone from the roadside and held it to his eye to see if "prophecy" would work for him.

"I guess I really wouldn't want it to work," he said with a laugh. "I wouldn't want to be blind," and he threw the stone away. At that time he planned on joining the Air Force and flying towards the sun and being able to see over the tops of mountains and across the sea.

When we got to his house we were still talking about the story and his mother cautioned us not to laugh at such things. She went and found a poem by Sir Walter Scott, which she read aloud to us. We did not pay much attention to it but I remember the lines which referred to the father and his four doomed sons:

> *Thy sons rose around thee in light and in love*
> *All a father could hope, all a friend could approve;*
> *What 'vails it the tale of thy sorrows to tell?*
> *In the springtime of youth and of promise they fell!*

Now, as I said, the MacAllesters' boat was going in ahead of us, loaded down with its final catch and with its stern and washboard piled high with traps. We had no great wish to talk to the MacAllesters at the wharf and there were other boats ahead of us as well. They would unload their catches first and pile their traps upon the wharf and it would be some time before we would find a place to dock. My father cut our engine. There was no need to rush.

"Do you see Canna over there?" he asked, pointing to the north where he was facing. "Do you see the point of Canna?"

"Yes," I said, "I see it. There it is."

There was nothing very unusual about seeing the point of Canna. It was always visible except on the foggiest days or when there was rain or perhaps snow. It was twenty miles away by boat and on the duller days it reached out low and blue like the foot of a giant's boot extended into the sea. On sunny days like this one it sparkled in a distant green. The clearings of the old farms were visible and above them the line of the encroaching trees, the spruce and fir of a darker green. Here and there the white houses stood out and even the gray and weather-beaten barns. It was called after the Hebridean island of Canna, "the green island" where most of its original settlers were born. It was the birthplace of my grandmother who was one of the girls in the white smocks at the Canna lobster factory in that long-ago time.

"It was about this time of year," said my father, "that your Uncle Angus and I went by ourselves to visit our grandmother at the point of Canna. We were eleven at the time and had been asking our parents for weeks to let us go. They seemed reluctant to give us any answer and all they would say was 'We will see' or 'Wait and see.' We wanted to go on the smack boat when it was making its final run of the season. We wanted to go with the men on the smack who were buying lobsters and they would set us ashore at the wharf of Canna point and we would walk the mile to our grandmother's house. We had never gone there by ourselves before. We could hardly remember being there because if you went by land you had to travel by horse and buggy and it was a long way. First you had to go inland to the main road and drive about twenty miles and then come back down towards the shore. It was about twice as far by land as it was by sea and our parents went about once a year. Usually by themselves as there was not enough room for others in the buggy. If we did not get to go on the smack, we were afraid that we would not get to go at all. 'Wait and see' was all they said."

It seemed strange to me, as my father spoke, to think of Canna as far away. By that time it took perhaps three-quarters of an hour by car, even though the final section of the road was often muddy and dangerous enough in the wet months of spring and fall and often blocked by snow in the winter. Still, it was not hard to get there if you really wanted to, and so the old letters from Canna which I discovered in the upstairs attic seemed quite strange and from another distant time. It seemed hard to believe that people only twenty miles away would write letters to one another and only visit once a year. But at that time the distance was hard to negotiate and there were no telephones.

My father and his brother Angus were twins and they had been named after their grandfathers so their names were Angus and Alex. It was common for parents to name their first children after their own parents and it seemed that almost all of the men were called Angus or Alex. In the early years of the century the Syrian and Lebanese pedlars who walked the muddy country roads beneath their heavy backpacks sometimes called themselves Angus or Alex so that they would sound more familiar to their potential customers. The pedlars, like the Gaelic-speaking people in the houses which they visited, had very little English, so anything that aided communication was helpful. Sometimes they unfolded their bolts of cloth and displayed their shining needles before admirers who were unable to afford them, and sometimes sensing the situation they would leave the goods behind. Later, if money became available, the people would say, "Put aside what we owe Angus and Alex in the sugar bowl so that we can pay them when they come."

Sometimes the pedlars would carry letters from one community to the other, to and from the families of the different Anguses and Alexes strung out along the coast. Distinguishing the different families, although their names were much the same, and delivering letters which they could not read.

My father and his brother continued to pester their parents who continued to say "Wait and see," and then one day they went to visit their father's mother who lived in a house quite close to theirs. After they had finished the lunch she had given them, she offered to "read" their teacups and to tell them of the future events revealed in the tea leaves at the bottoms of their cups: "You are going on a journey," she said, peering into the cups as she turned them in her hands. "You are going to cross water. And to take food with you. You will meet a mysterious woman who has dark hair. She will be quite close to you. And . . ." she said, turning the cups in her hands to better see the formation of the leaves, "and . . . oh . . . oh . . . oh."

"What?" they asked. "What?"

"Oh, that's enough for today," she said. "You had better be getting home or they will be worrying about you."

They ran home and burst into their parents' kitchen. "We are going on a trip to Canna," they said. "Grandma told us. She saw it in the tea leaves. She read it in our cups. We are going to take a lunch. We are going across the water. She *said* we were going."

The morning they left they were dressed in their best clothes and waiting at the wharf long before the smack was due, clutching their lunches in their hands. It was sunny when the boat left the wharf but as they proceeded along the coast it became cloudy and then it began to rain. The trip seemed long in the rain and the men told them to go into the boat's cabin where they would be dry and where they could eat their lunch. The first part of the trip seemed to be spoiled by rain.

It was raining heavily when the boat approached the wharf at Canna point. It was almost impossible to see the figures on the wharf or to distinguish them as they moved about in their heavy oil slickers. The lobster buyers were in a hurry, as were the wet men impatiently waiting for them in the rain.

"Do you know where you're going?" said the men in the smack to their young passengers.

"Yes," they said, although they were not quite sure because the rain obscured the landmarks that they thought they would remember.

"Here," said the men in the smack, handing them two men's oil slickers from the boat's cabin. "Wear these to help keep you dry. You can give them back to us sometime."

They climbed up the iron ladder towards the wharf's cap and the busy men reached their hands down to help and pull them up.

Because the men were busy and because of the rain no one on the wharf asked them where they were going and they were too shy and too proud to ask. So they turned the cuffs of the oil slickers back over their wrists and began to walk up the muddy road from the wharf. They were still trying to keep their best clothes clean and pick their spots carefully, placing their good shoes where there were fairly dry spots and avoiding the puddles and little rivulets which rolled the small stones along in their course. The oil slickers were so long that the bottoms of them dragged on the muddy road and sometimes they lifted them up in the way that older ladies might lift the hems of their skirts when stepping over a puddle or some other obstacle in the roadway. When they lifted them, the muddy bottoms rubbed against their good trousers so they let them fall again. Then their shoes were almost invisible and they could hear and feel the tails of the coats dragging behind them as they walked. They were wet and miserable inside the long coats as well as undistinguishable to anyone who might see the small forms in the long coats walking along the road.

After they had walked for half a mile they were overtaken by an old man in a buggy who stopped and offered them a ride. He too was covered in an oil coat and his cap was pulled down almost to his nose. When he stopped to pick them up, the steam rose from his horse as they clambered into the wagon beside him. He spoke to them in Gaelic and asked them their names and where they were from and where they were going.

"To see our grandmother," they said.

"Your grandmother?" he asked.

"Yes," they said. "Our grandmother."

"Oh," he said. "Your grandmother, are your sure?"

"Of course," they said, becoming a bit annoyed. For although they were more uncertain than they cared to admit, they did not want to appear so.

"Oh," he said, "all right then. Would you like some peppermints?" And he reached deeply into a pocket beneath his oil coat and brought out a brown paper bag full of peppermints. Even as he passed the bag to them, the raindrops pelted upon it and it became soggy and began to darken in deterioration.

"Oh," he said, "you may as well keep all of them. I got a whole lot more of them for the store. They just came in on the boat." He motioned to some metal containers in the back of the buggy.

"Are you going to spend the night with your grandmother?" he asked.

"Yes," they said.

"Oh," he answered, pulling on the reins and turning the horse into the laneway of a yard.

He drove them to the door of the house and helped them down from the buggy while his horse stomped its impatient hooves in the mud and tossed its head in the rain.

"Would you like me to go in with you?" he asked.

"No," they said, impatient for him to be gone and out of sight.

"All right," he said and spoke to his uneasy horse which began to trot down the laneway, the buggy wheels throwing hissing jets of mud and water behind them.

They hesitated for a while outside the doorway of the house, waiting for the man to go out of sight and feeling ridiculous for standing in the rain. But halfway down the lane he stopped and looked back. And then he stood up in the buggy and shouted to them and made a "go forward" gesture with his hand towards the house. They opened the door then and went in because they felt embarrassed and did not want to admit that he had brought them to the wrong house.

When they went in, they found themselves in the middle of a combined porch and entranceway which was cluttered with an odd collection of household and farming utensils. Baking pans and jars and sealers and chamber pots and old milk pails and rakes and hoes and hayforks and bits of wire and lengths of chain. There was very little light, and in the gloom something started up from their feet and bounced against their legs and then into a collection of jars and pails, causing a crashing cacophony of sound. It was a half-grown lamb and it bleated as it bounded towards the main door, dropping bits of manure behind it. In the same instant and in response to the sound, the main door opened and the lamb leaped through it and into the house.

Framed in the doorway was a tall old woman clad in layers of clothing, even though it was summer, and wearing wire-framed glasses. On either side of her were two black dogs. They were like collies, although they had no white markings. They growled softly but deep within their throats and the fur on the back of their necks rose and they raised their upper lips to reveal their gleaming teeth. They were poised on the tips of their paws and their eyes seemed to burn in the gloom. She lowered a hand to each of their heads but did not say anything. Everyone seemed to stare straight ahead. The boys would have run away but they were afraid that if they moved, the dogs would be upon them, so they stayed where they were as still as could be. The only sound was the tense growling of the dogs. "*Cò a th'ann?*" she said in Gaelic. "Who's there?"

The boys did not know what to say because all the possible answers seemed so complicated. They moved their feet uneasily, which caused the dogs to each take two steps forward as if they were part of some rehearsed choreography. "*Cò a th'ann?*" she said, repeating the question. "Who's there?"

"We're from Kintail," they said finally. "Our names are Alex and Angus. We're trying to find our grandmother's house. We came on the smack boat."

"Oh," she said. "How old are you?"

"Eleven," they said. "Both of us. We're twins."

"Oh," she said. "Both of you. I have relatives in Kintail. Come in."

They were still afraid and the dogs remained poised, snarling softly with their delicate, dangerous lips flickering above the whiteness of their teeth.

"All right," they said. "We'll come in, but just for a minute. We can't stay long."

Only then did she speak to the dogs. "Go and lie under the table and be quiet," she said. Immediately they relaxed and vanished behind her into the house.

"Did you know these dogs were twins?" she asked.

"No," they said. "We didn't."

"Well," she said. "They are."

Inside the house they sat on the first chairs that they could find and moved them as close to the door as possible. The room that they were in was a primitive kitchen and much of its floor was cluttered with objects not unlike the porch except that the objects were smaller—knives and forks and spoons and the remains of broken cups and saucers. There was a half-completed partition between the kitchen and what might have been a living room or dining room. The upright studs of the partition were firmly in place and someone had nailed wainscotting on either side of them but it only extended halfway to the ceiling. It was difficult to tell if the partition had been left incomplete or if it was gradually being lowered. The space between the walls of the partition was filled with cats. They pulled themselves up by their paws and looked curiously at the visitors and then jumped back down into the space. From the space between the incompleted walls the visitors could hear the mewing of newborn kittens. Other cats were everywhere. They were on the table, licking what dishes there were, and on the backs of the chairs and in and out of a cavern beneath an old couch. Sometimes they leaped over the half-completed partition and vanished into the next room. Sometimes they snarled at one another and feinted with their paws. In one corner a large tiger-striped tomcat was energetically breeding a small gray female flattened out beneath him. Other tentative males circled the breeding pair, growling deeply within their throats. The tiger cat would interrupt his movements from time to time to snarl at them and keep them at bay. The female's nose was pressed against the floor and her ears flattened down against her head. Sometimes he held the fur at the back of her neck within his teeth.

The two black dogs lay under the table and seemed oblivious to the cats. The lamb stood watchfully behind the stove. Everything in the house was extremely dirty—spilled milk and cat hair and unwashed and broken dishes. The old woman wore men's rubber boots upon her feet and her clothing seemed to consist of layers of petticoats and skirts and dresses and sweaters upon sweaters. All of it was very dirty and covered with stains of spilled tea and food remnants and spattered grease. Her hands seemed brown and her fingernails were long and there was a half inch of black grime under each of them. She raised her hands to touch her glasses and they noticed that the outside lenses were smeared and filthy as well. It was then that they realized that she was blind and that the glasses served no useful purpose. They became even more uncertain and frightened than they were before.

"Which one of you is Alex?" she asked, and he raised his hand as if answering a question at school before realizing that she could not see him.

"I am," he answered then, and she turned her face in his direction.

"I have a long association with that name," she said, and they were surprised at her use of a word like "association."

Because of the rain the day seemed to darken early and they could see the fading light through the grimy windows. They wondered for a moment why she did not light a lamp until they realized that there was none and that to her it made no difference.

"I will make you a lunch," she said. "Don't move."

She went to the partial partition and ripped the top board off with her strong brown hands and then she leaned it against the partition and stomped on it with her rubber-booted foot. It splintered and she repeated the action, feeling about the floor for the lengths of splintered wood. She gathered them up and went to the stove and, after removing the lids, began to feed them into the fire. She moved the kettle over the crackling flame.

She began to feel about the cupboards for food, brushing away the insistent cats which crowded about her hands. She found two biscuits in a tin and placed them on plates which she put into the cupboard so the cats would not devour them. She put her hand into a tea tin and took a handful of tea which she placed in the teapot and then she poured the hot water in as well. She found some milk in a dirty pitcher and feeling for the cups she splashed some of it into each.

Then she took the teapot and began to pour the tea. She turned her back to them but as she poured they could see her dipping her long brown finger with the half inch of grimy fingernail quickly into each cup. They realized she was doing it because she had no other way of knowing when the cups were full but their stomachs revolved and they feared they might throw up.

She brought them a cup of tea each and retrieved the biscuits from the cupboard and passed the plates to them. They sat holding the offerings on their laps while she faced them. Although they realized she could not see them, they still felt that she was watching them. They looked at the tea and biscuits with the cat hair and did not know what to do. After a while they began to make slurping sounds with their lips.

"Well, we will have to be on our way," they said. Carefully they bent forward and placed the still-full teacups under their chairs and the biscuits in their pockets.

"Do you know where you are going?" she asked.

"Yes," they said with determination.

"Can you see your way in the dark?"

"Yes," they said again with equal determination.

"We will meet again?" she said, raising her voice to form a question.

"Yes," they said.

"Some are more loyal than others," she said. "Remember that."

They hurried down the laneway, surprised to find that it was not so dark outside as it seemed within the blind woman's house. When they got to the main road, they followed it in the direction that led away from the wharf and it seemed that in a short time they could make out the buildings of their original intended destination.

It was still raining as they entered the laneway to the buildings, and by this time it was indeed quite dark. The laneway ended at the door of the barn and the house was some yards farther. The barn door was open and they stepped inside for a moment to compose themselves. It was very quiet within the barn for all of the animals were away in their summer pastures. They hesitated for a moment in the first stall and then they were aware of a rhythm of sound coming from the next area, the threshing floor. They opened the small connecting door and stepped inside and waited for their eyes to adjust to the gloom. And then in the farthest corner they noticed a lantern turned to its lowest and hanging on a nail. And beyond it they could make out the shape of a man. He was tall and wore rubber boots and bib overalls and had a tweed cap pulled down upon his head. He was facing the south wall of the barn but was sideways to them and presented a profile. He was rhythmically rocking from his heels to the balls of his feet and thrusting his hips back and forth and moaning and talking to himself in Gaelic. But it did not seem that he was talking to himself but to someone of the opposite sex who was not there. The front of his overalls was open and he had a hold of himself in his right hand which he moved to the rhythm of his rocking body.

They did not know what to do. They did not recognize the man and they were terrified that he might turn and see them and they were afraid that if they tried to make a retreat they might cause a sound which would betray their presence. At home they slept upstairs while their parents slept below in a private room ("to keep an eye on the fire," their parents said); and although they were becoming curious about sex, they did not know a great deal about it. They had seen the matings of animals, such as the earlier cats, but they had never seen a fully aroused grown man before, although they recognized some of the words he was moaning to himself and his imaginary partner. Suddenly with a groan he slumped forward as the gray jets of seed spurted onto the south wall of the barn and down to the dry and dusty hay before his feet. He placed his left arm against the wall and rested his forehead against it. They stepped back quietly through the little door and then out of the barn and then they walked rapidly but on their tiptoes through the rain towards the house.

When they entered the porch and the screen door slammed behind them, they heard a voice from within the kitchen. It was harsh and angry and seemed to be cursing, and then the door flew open and they were face to face with their grandmother. At first she did not recognize them in their long coats and her face remained suspicious and angry, but then her expression changed and she came forward to hug them.

"Angus and Alex," she said. "What a surprise!" Looking over their shoulders, she said, "Are you alone? Did you come by your-selves?" And then, "Why didn't you tell us you were coming? We would have gone to meet you."

It had never entered their minds that their arrival would be such a surprise. They had been thinking of the trip with such intensity that in spite of the day's happenings they still somehow assumed that everyone knew they were coming.

"Well, come in, come in," she said, "and take those wet clothes off. How did you say you came again? And are you just arriving now?"

They told her they had come on the smack and of their walk and the ride with the man who had peppermints and of their visit to the blind woman, but they omitted the part about the man in the barn. She listened intently as she moved about the kitchen, hanging up their coats and setting the teapot on the stove. She asked for a description of the man with the peppermints and they told her he said he owned a store, and then she asked them how the blind woman was. They told her of the tea she had served them which they had left and she said, "Poor soul!"

And then the screen door banged again and a heavy foot was heard in the porch, and then in through the kitchen door walked the man they had seen in the barn.

"Your grandchildren are here to see you," she said with an icy edge to her voice. "They came on the smack from Kintail."

He stood blinking and swaying in the light, trying to focus his eyes upon them. They realized then that he was quite drunk and having difficulty comprehending. His eyes were red-rimmed and bloodshot and a white stubble speckled with black indicated that he had not shaved for a number of days. He swayed back and forth, looking at them carefully and trying to see who they really were. They could not help looking at the front of his overalls to see if there were flecks of semen, but he had been out in the rain and all of his clothing was splattered with moisture.

"Oh," he said, as if a veil had been lifted from his eyes. "Oh," he said. "I love you. I love you." And he came forward and hugged each of them and kissed them on the cheek. They could smell the sourness of his breath and feel the rasping scratch of his stubble on their faces.

"Well," he said, turning on his heel, "I am going upstairs to rest for a while. I have been out in the barn and have been busier than you might think. But I will be back down later." And then he kicked off his boots, steadying himself with one hand on a kitchen chair, and swayed upstairs.

The visitors were shocked that they had not recognized their grandfather. When he came to visit them perhaps once a year, he was always splendid and handsome in his blue serge suit, with a gold watch chain linked across the expansiveness of his vest. And with his pockets filled with peppermints. And when they visited in the company of their parents, he had always been gracious and clear-headed and well attired.

When they could no longer hear his footsteps, their grandmother again began to talk to them, asking them questions, inquiring of their parents and of their school work as she busied herself about the stove and began to set the table.

Later he came back downstairs and they all sat around the table. He had changed his clothes and his face was covered with bleeding knicks because he had tried to shave. The meal was uncomfortable as he knocked over his water glass and dropped his food on his lap. The visitors were exhausted as he was and only their grandmother seemed in control. He went back upstairs as soon as the meal was finished, saying, "Tomorrow will be a better day," and their grandmother suggested that they go to bed soon after.

"We are all tired," she said. "He will be all right tomorrow. He tried to shave in honor of your coming. I will talk to him myself. We are glad that you have come."

They slept together under a mountain of quilts and in a room next to their grandparents. Before they went to sleep they could hear them talking in Gaelic, and the next thing they remembered was waking in the morning. Their grandparents were standing near their bed and the sun was shining through the window. Each of their grandparents held a tray containing porridge and sugar and milk and tea and butter. They were both rather formally dressed and like the grandparents they thought they knew. The drunk moaning man in the barn was like a dream they wished they had not had.

When they got up to put on their clothes they discovered bits of the blind woman's biscuits still in their pockets, and when they went outside they threw them behind the barn.

They stayed a week at Canna and all during that time the sun shone and the days were golden. They went visiting with their grandfather in his buggy—visiting women in houses and sometimes standing in barns with men. One day they visited the store and had trouble identifying the man behind the counter with the one who had offered them the ride and the peppermints. He seemed equally surprised when he recognized them and said to their grandfather, "I'm sorry if I made a mistake."

During their week in Canna they noticed small differences in the way of doing things. The people of Canna tied their horses with ropes around their necks instead of with halters. They laid out their gardens in beds instead of rows and they grew a particular type of strawberry whose fruit grew far from the original root. When they drew water from their wells they threw away the first dipperful and the water itself had a slightly different taste. They set their tables for breakfast before retiring for the night. They bowed or curtsied to the new moon and in the Church of St. Columba the women sat on one side of the aisle and the men on the other.

The Church of St. Columba, said their grandfather, was called after the original chapel on the island of Canna. St. Columba or Colum Cille was a brilliant, dedicated missionary in Ireland and he possessed *Da Shealladh*, the second sight, and used a stone to "see" his visions. He was also a lover of beauty and very strong-willed. Once, continued their grandfather, he copied a religious manuscript without permission but believed the copy was rightfully his. The High King of Ireland who was asked to judge the dispute ruled against Colum Cille, saying, "To every cow its calf and to every book its copy." Later the High King of Ireland also executed a young man who had sought sanctuary under the protection of Colum Cille. Enraged at what he perceived as injustice and bad judgement, Colum Cille told the High King he would lead his relations and clansmen against him in battle. On the eve of the battle, as they prayed and fasted, the archangel Michael appeared to Colum Cille in a vision. The angel told him that God would answer his prayers and allow him to win the battle but that He was not pleased with him for praying for such a worldly request and that he should exile himself from Ireland and never see the country anymore or its people or partake of its food and drink except on his outward journey. The forces of Colum Cille won the battle and inflicted losses of three thousand men, and perhaps he could have been the King of Ireland but he obeyed the vision. Some said he left also to do penance for the three thousand lives he had cost. In a small boat and with a few followers who were his relatives, he crossed the sea to the small islands of Scotland and spent the last thirty-four years of his life establishing monasteries and chapels and travelling among the people. Working as a missionary, making predictions, seeing visions and changing forever that region of the world. Leaving Ireland, he said:

There is a gray eye
Looking back on Ireland,
That will never see again
Her men or her women.

Early and late my lamentation,
Alas, the journey I am making;
This will be my secret byname
"Back turned on Ireland."

"Did he ever go back?" they asked.

"Once," said their grandfather, "the poets of Ireland were in danger of being banned and he crossed the sea from Scotland to speak on their behalf. But when he came, he came blindfolded so that he could not see the country or its people."

"Did you know him?" they asked. "Did you ever see him?"

"That was a very long time ago," he laughed. "Over thirteen hundred years ago. But, yes, sometimes I feel I know him and I think I see him as well. This church, as I said, is called after the chapel he established on Canna. That chapel is fallen a long time ago too and all of the people gone, and the well beside the chapel filled up with rocks and the Celtic crosses of their graveyards smashed down and used for the building of roads. But sometimes I imagine I still see them," he said, looking towards the ocean and across it as if he could see the "green island" and its people.

"I see them going about their rituals: riding their horses on Michaelmas and carrying the bodies of their dead round towards the sun. And courting and getting married. Almost all of the people on Canna got married before they were twenty. They considered it unlucky to be either a single man or woman so there were very few single people among them. Perhaps they also found it difficult to wait," he added with a smile, "and that is why their population rose so rapidly. Anyway, all gone."

"You mean dead?" they asked.

"Well, some of them, yes," he said, "but I mean gone from there, scattered all over the world. But some of us are here. That is why this place is called Canna and we carry certain things within us. Sometimes there are things within us which we do not know or fully understand and sometimes it is hard to stamp out what you can't see. It is good that you are here for this while."

Towards the end of the week they learned that there was a government boat checking lighthouses along the coast. It would stop at the point of Canna and later, on its southern journey, also at Kintail. It was an excellent chance for them to get home and it was decided that they should take it. The night before they left, their grandparents served them a splendid dinner with a white tablecloth and candles.

As they prepared to leave on the following morning, the rain began to fall. Their grandmother gave them some packages to deliver to their mother and also a letter and packed a lunch with lobster sandwiches for them. She hugged and kissed them as they were leaving and said, "Thank you for coming. It was good to have you here and it made us feel better about ourselves." She looked at her husband and he nodded.

They climbed into their grandfather's buggy as the rain fell upon them and carefully placed their packages beneath the seat. On the road down to the wharf they passed the lane to the blind woman's house. She was near the roadway with the two black dogs. She was wearing her men's rubber boots and a large kerchief and a heavy rubber raincoat. When she heard the buggy approaching, she called out, "*Cò a th'ann? Cò a th'ann?* Who's there? Who's there?"

But their grandfather said nothing.

"Who's there?" she called. "Who's there? Who's there?"

The rain fell upon her streaked and empty glasses and down her face and along her coat and her strong protruding hands with their grimy fingernails.

"Don't say anything," said their grandfather under his breath. "I don't want her to know you're here."

As the horse approached, she continued to call but none of them said anything. Above the regular hoofbeats of the horse her voice seemed to rise through the falling rain, causing a tension within all of them as they tried to pretend they could not hear her.

"*Cò a th'ann?*" she called. "Who's there? Who's there?"

They lowered their heads as if she could see them. But when they were exactly opposite her, their grandfather could not stand it any longer and suddenly reined in the horse.

"*Cò a th'ann?*" she called. "Who's there?"

"*'Se mi-fhìn,*" he answered quietly. "It's myself!"

She began to curse him in Gaelic and he became embarrassed. "Do you understand what she's saying?" he said to them. They were uncertain. "Some of it," they said.

"Here," he said, "hold the horse," and he passed the reins to them. He took the buggy whip out of its socket as he descended from the buggy and they were uncertain about that too until they realized he was taking it to protect himself from the dogs who came snarling towards him but kept their distance because of the whip. He began to talk to the blind woman in Gaelic and they both walked away from the buggy along the laneway to her house until they were out of earshot. The dogs lay down on the wet roadway and watched and listened carefully.

The visitors could not hear the conversation, only the rising and falling of the two voices through the descending rain. When their grandfather returned, he seemed upset and took the reins from them and spoke to the horse immediately.

"God help me," he said softly and almost to himself, "but I could not pass her by."

There was water running down his face and they thought for a moment he might be crying; but just as when they had looked for the semen on his overalls a week earlier, they could not tell because of the rain.

The blind woman stood in the laneway facing them as they moved off along the road. It was one of those situations which almost automatically calls for waving but even as they began to raise their hands they remembered her blindness and realized it was no use. She stood as if watching them for a long time and then, perhaps when she could no longer hear the sound of the horse and buggy, she turned and walked with the two dogs back towards her house.

"Do you know her well?" they asked.

"Oh," said their grandfather, as if being called back from another time and place, "yes, I do know her quite well and since a long, long time."

Their grandfather waited with them on the wharf for the coming of the government boat, but it was late. When it finally arrived, the men said they would not be long checking the lighthouse and told them to go into the boat to wait. They said their good-byes then and their grandfather turned his wet and impatient horse towards home.

Although the wait was not supposed to be long, it was longer than expected and it was afternoon before the boat left the protection of the wharf and ventured out into the ocean. The rain was still falling and a wind had come up and the sea was choppy. The wind was off the land so they stood with their backs towards Canna and to the wind and the rain. When they were far enough out to sea to have perspective, one of the men said, "It looks like there is a fire back there." And when they looked back they could see the billowing smoke, somehow seeming ironic in the rain. It rose in the distance and was carried by the wind but it was difficult to see its source not only because of the smoke but also because of the driving rain. And because the perspective from the water was different than it was on the land. The government men did not know any of the local people and they were behind schedule and already well out to sea so there was no thought of turning back. They were mildly concerned too about the rising wind and wanted to make as much headway as possible before conditions worsened.

It was that period of the day when the afternoon blends into evening before the boat reached the Kintail wharf. During the last miles the ocean had roughened and within the rocking boat the passengers had become green and seasick and vomited their lobster sandwiches over the side. Canna seemed very far away and the golden week seemed temporarily lost within the reality of the swaying boat and the pelting rain. When the boat docked, they ran to their house as quickly as they could. Their mother gave them soup and dry clothes and they went to bed earlier than usual.

They slept late the next day and when they awoke and went downstairs it was still raining and blowing. And then the Syrian pedlars, Angus and Alex, knocked on the door. They put their heavy wet leather packs upon the kitchen floor and told the boys' mother that there had been a death in Canna. The Canna people were sending word but they had heard the news earlier in the day from another pedlar arriving from that direction and he had asked them to carry the message. The pedlars and the boys' parents talked for a while and the boys were told to "go outside and play" even though it was raining. They went out to the barn.

Almost immediately the boys' parents began to get ready for the journey. The ocean was by this time too rough for a boat and they had already hauled their boat up at the end of the lobster season. They readied their horse and buggy and later in the afternoon they were gone. They were away for five days and when they returned they were drawn and tired.

Through bits and pieces of conversation, the boys learned that it was the blind woman's house which had burned and she within it.

Later, and they were not sure just when, they gathered other details and bits of information. She had been at the stove, it was thought, and her clothes had caught fire. The animals had burned with her. Most of their bones were found before the door to which they had gone to seek escape but she had been unable to open it for them or, it seemed, for herself.

Over the weeks the details blended in with their own experience. They imagined her strong hands pulling down the wainscotting of her own house and placing it in the fire, consuming her own house somehow from within as it was later to consume her. And they could see the fire going up the front of her layers of dirty clothing. Consuming the dirt which she herself had been unable to see. Rising up the front of her clothing, rising up above her shoulders towards her hair, the imaginary orange flames flickering and framing her face and being reflected in the staring lenses of her glasses.

And they imagined the animals too. The savage faithful dogs which were twins snarling at the doorway with their fur in flames, and the lusty cats engaged in their growling copulation in the corner, somehow keeping on, driven by their own heat while the other heat surrounded them, and the bleating lamb with its wool on fire. And in the space between the walls the mewing unseen kittens, dying with their eyes still closed.

And sometimes they imagined her too, in her porch or in her house or standing by the roadside in the rain. *Cò a th'ann?* they heard her call in their imagination and in their dreams. *Cò a th'ann? Cò a th'ann?* Who's there? Who's there? And one night they dreamed they heard themselves answer. *'Se mi-fhìn* they heard themselves say as with one voice. It is myself.

My father and his brother never again spent a week on the green hills of Canna. Perhaps their lives went by too fast or circumstances changed or there were reasons that they did not fully understand themselves.

And one Sunday six years later when they were in church the clergyman gave a rousing sermon on why young men should enlist in World War I. They were very enthusiastic about the idea and told their parents that they were going to Halifax to enlist although they were too young. Their parents were very upset and went to the clergyman in an attempt to convince him it was a mistake. The clergyman was their friend and came to their house and told them it was a general sermon for the day. "I didn't mean *you*," he added, but his first success was better than his second.

They left the next day for Halifax, getting a ride to the nearest railroad station. They had never been on a train before and when they arrived, the city of Halifax was large and awesome. At the induction center their age was easily overlooked but the medical examination was more serious. Although they were young and strong, the routine tests seemed strange and provoked a tension within them. They were unable to urinate in a bottle on request and were asked to wait awhile and then try again. But sitting on two chairs wishing for urine did little good. They drank more and more water and waited and tried but it did not work. On their final attempt, they were discussing their problem in Gaelic while standing in a tiny cubicle with their legs spread apart and their trousers opened. Unexpectedly a voice from the next cubicle responded to them in Gaelic.

The voice belonged to a young man from Canna who had come to enlist as well but who did not have their problem. "Can we 'borrow' some of that?" they asked, looking at his full bottle of urine.

"Sure," he said, "no need to give it back," and he splashed some of his urine into each of their waiting bottles. All of them "passed" the test; and later in the alleyway behind the induction center and standing in the steam of their own urine, they began to talk to the young man from Canna. His grandfather owned the store in Canna, he said, and was opposed to his coming to enlist.

"Do you know Alex?" they asked and mentioned their grandfather's formal name.

He seemed puzzled for a moment and then brightened. "Oh," he said, *"Mac an Amharuis,* sure, everyone knows him. He's my grandfather's friend.

And then, perhaps because they were far from home and more lonely and frightened than they cared to admit, they began to talk in Gaelic. They began with the subject of *Mac an Amharuis,* and the young man told them everything he knew. Surprised perhaps at his own knowledge and at having such attentive listeners. *Mac an Amharuis* translates as "Son of Uncertainty," which meant that he was illegitimate or uncertain as to who his father was. He was supposed to be tremendously talented and clever as a young man but also restless and reluctant to join the other young men of Canna in their fishing boats. Instead he saved his money and purchased a splendid stallion and travelled the country offering the stallion's services. He rode on the stallion's back with only a loose rope around its neck for guidance.

He was also thought to be handsome and to possess a "strong nature" or "too much nature," which meant that he was highly sexed. "Some say," said the young man, "that he sowed almost as much seed as the stallion and who knows who might be descended from him. If we only knew, eh?" he added with a laugh.

Then he became involved with a woman from Canna. She was thought to be "odd" by some because she was given to rages and uncertainty and sometimes she would scream and shout at him in public. At times he would bring back books and sometimes moonshine from wherever he went with the stallion. And sometimes they would read quietly together and talk and at other times they would curse and shout and become physically violent.

And then he became possessed of *Da Shealladh*, the second sight. It seemed he did not want it and some said it came about because of too much reading of the books or perhaps it was inherited from his unknown father. Once he "saw" a storm on the evening of a day which was so calm that no one would believe him. When it came in the evening the boats could not get back and all the men were drowned. And once when he was away with the stallion, he "saw" his mother's house burn down and when he returned he found that it had happened on the very night he saw it and his mother was burned to death.

It became a weight upon him and he could not stop the visions or do anything to interfere with the events. One day after he and the woman had too much to drink they went to visit a well-known clergyman. He told the clergyman he wanted the visions to stop but it did not seem within his power. He and the woman were sitting on two chairs beside each other. The clergyman went for the Bible and prayed over it and then he came and flicked the pages of the Bible before their eyes. He told them the visions would stop but that they would have to give up one another because they were causing a scandal in the community. The woman became enraged and leaped at the clergyman and tried to scratch out his eyes with her long nails. She accused *Mac an Amharuis* of deceiving her and said that he was willing to exchange their stormy relationship for his lack of vision. She spat in his face and cursed him and stormed out the door. *Mac an Amharuis* rose to follow her but the clergyman put his arms around him and wrestled him to the floor. He was far gone in drink and within the clergyman's power.

They stopped appearing with one another and *Mac an*

Amharuis stopped travelling with the stallion and bought himself a boat. He began to visit the woman's younger sister, who was patient and kind. The woman moved out of her parents' house and into an older house nearer the shore. Some thought she moved because she could not stand *Mac an Amharuis* visiting her sister, and others thought that it was planned to allow him to visit her at night without anyone seeing.

Within two months *Mac an Amharuis* and the woman's sister were married. At the wedding the woman cursed the clergyman until he warned her to be careful and told her to leave the building. She cursed her sister too and said, "You will never be able to give him what I can." And as she was going out the door, she said to *Mac an Amharuis* either "I will never forgive you" or "I will never forget you." Her voice was charged with emotion but her back was turned to them and the people were uncertain whether it was a curse or a cry.

The woman did not come near anyone for a long time and people saw her only from a distance, moving about the house and the dilapidated barn, caring for the few animals which her father had given her, and muffled in clothes as autumn turned to winter. At night people watched for a light in her window. Sometimes they saw it and sometimes they did not.

And then one day her father came to the house of his daughter and *Mac an Amharuis* and said that he had not seen a light for three nights and he was worried. The three of them went to the house but it was cold. There was no heat when they put their hands on the stove and the glass of the windowpanes was covered with frost. There was not anybody in any of the rooms.

They went out into the barn and found her lying in a heap. Most of the top part of her body was still covered by layers of clothes, although the lower part was not. She was unconscious or in something like a frozen coma and her eyes were inflamed, with beads of pus at their corners. She had given birth to twin girls and one of them was dead but the other somehow still alive, lying on her breast amidst her layers of clothing. Her father and *Mac an Amharuis* and her sister carried the living into the house and started a fire in the stove and sent for the nearest medical attention, which was some miles away. Later they also carried in the body of the dead baby and placed it in a lobster crate, which was all that they could find. When the doctor came, he said he could not be certain of the baby's exact time of birth but he felt that it would live. He said that the mother had lost a great deal of blood and he thought she might have lacerated her eyes during the birth with her long fingernails and that infection had set in, caused perhaps by the unsanitary conditions within the barn. He was not sure if she would live and, if she did, he feared her sight would never be restored.

Mac an Amharuis and his wife cared for the baby throughout the days that the woman was unconscious, and the baby thrived. The woman herself began to rally and the first time she heard the baby cry she reached out instinctively for it but could not find it in the dark. Gradually, as she recognized, by sound, the people around her, she began to curse them and accused them of having sex when she could not see them. As she grew stronger, she became more resentful of their presence and finally asked them to leave. She began to rise from her bed and walk with her hands before her, sometimes during the day and sometimes during the night because it made no difference to her. And once they saw her with a knife in her hand. They left her then, as she had requested them to do and perhaps because they were afraid. And because there seemed no other choice, they took the baby with them.

They continued to bring her food and to leave it at the door of her porch. Sometimes she cursed at them but at other times she was more quiet. One day while they were talking she extended her hand with the long fingernails to the face of *Mac an Amharuis*. She ran the balls of her fingers and the palm of her hand from his hair down over his eyes and nose and his lips and his chin and down along the buttons of his shirt and below his belt to between his legs, and then her hand closed for an instant and she grasped what she had held before but would never see again.

Mac an Amharuis and his wife had no children of their own. It was thought that it caused a great sadness within her and perhaps a tension because, as people said, "It's sure as hell not *his* fault." Their childlessness was thought also to prey on him and to lead to periodic drinking binges, although he never mentioned it to anyone. For the most part, they were helpful and supportive of each other and no one knew what they talked about when they were alone and together in their bed at night.

This, I guess, is my retelling of the story told by the young man of Canna to my father and his brother at a time when they were all young and on the verge of war. All of the information that spilled out of him came because it was there to be released and he was revealing more than he realized to his attentive listeners. The story was told in Gaelic, and as the people say, "It is not the same in English," although the images are true.

When the war was over, the generous young man from Canna was dead and my father's brother had lost his leg.

My father returned to Kintail and the life that he had left, the boat and the nets and the lobster traps. All of them in the cycle of the seasons. He married before World War II; and when he was asked to go again, he went with the other Highlanders from Cape Breton, leaving his wife pregnant, perhaps without realizing it.

On the beach at Normandy they were emptied into ten feet of water as the rockets and shells exploded around them. And in the mud they fell face down, leaving the imprints of their faces temporarily in the soil, before clawing their way some few feet forward. At the command they rose, as would a wave trying to break farther forward on the shore. And then all of it seemed to happen at once. Before my father's eyes there rose a wall of orange flame and a billowing wave of black smoke. It rose before him even as he felt the power of the strong hand upon his left shoulder. The grip was so powerful that he felt the imprint of the fingers almost as a bruise; and even as he turned his searing eyes, he fell back into his own language. "*Cò a th'ann?*" he said. "*Cò a th'ann?* Who's there?" And in the instant before his blindness, he recognized the long brown fingers on his shoulder with their pointed fingernails caked in dirt. "*'Se mi-fhìn,*" she said quietly. "It is myself."

All of the soldiers in front of my father were killed and in the spot where he stood there was a crater, but this was told to him because he was unable ever to see it for himself.

Later he was told that on the day of his blinding, his grandfather, the man known to some as *Mac an Amharuis*, died. *Mac an*

Amharuis was a man of over a hundred years at the time of his death and his eyes had become covered with the cataracts of age. He did not recognize, either by sight or sound, any of the people around him, and much of his talk was of youth and sex and of the splendid young stallion with the loose rope around its neck. And much of it was of the green island of Canna which he had never literally seen and of the people riding their horses at Michaelmas and carrying the bodies of their dead round towards the sun. And of the strong-willed St. Columba determined to be ascetic with his "back turned on Ireland" and the region of his early love. And of walls of flame and billowing smoke.

When I began this story I was recounting the story which my father told to me as he faced the green hills of Canna on the last day of the lobster season a long time ago. But when I look on it now I realize that all of it did not come from him, exactly as I have told it, on that day. The part about seeing his grandfather in the barn and much of the story of the young man from Canna came instead from his twin brother who participated in most of the events. Perhaps because of the loss of his leg, my father's brother became one of those veterans from World War I who spent a lot of their time in the Legion Hall. When he spoke to me he had none of the embarrassment which my father sometimes showed when discussing certain subjects. Perhaps my father, by omitting certain parts of his story, was merely repeating the custom of his parents who did not reveal to him at once everything there was to be shown.

But perhaps the story also went into me because of other events which happened on that day. After my father had finished, we started our engine and went into the wharf. By the time we arrived, the MacAllesters had gone and many of the other men as well. We hoisted the lobsters to the wharf's cap and I looked at the weight that the scales showed.

Whether the buyers noticed the concealed lobsters behind the crate we were never to know, but they said nothing. We unloaded our traps on the wharf and then climbed up the iron ladder and talked casually to the buyers and received our money. We planned to come back later for the lobsters behind the crate.

There were still other fishermen about and most of them

shared my father's good mood because they were glad that the season had ended and pleased to have the money which was their final payment. Someone offered us a ride in a truck to the Legion and we went.

The Legion Hall was filled with men, most of them fishermen, and the noise was loud and the conversation boisterous. Towards the back of the hall I noticed Kenneth MacAllester with a number of his relatives. Both of us were underage but it did not matter a great deal. If you looked like you were old enough, no one asked any questions. My father's brother and a number of our own relatives were at a table in the middle. They waved to us and I moved towards them. Behind me, my father followed, touching my belt from time to time for guidance. Most of the men pulled in their feet as we approached so that my father would not stumble. The crutch my uncle used in place of his missing leg was propped up across a chair and he removed it as we approached and leaned it against the table so that he could offer the chair to my father. We sat down and my uncle gave me some money to go to the bar for beer. Coming back, I passed another table of MacAllesters. They were relatives of our neighbors and although I recognized them I did not know them very well. One of them said something as I passed but I did not hear what he said and it seemed best not to stop. The afternoon grew more boisterous and bottles and glasses began to shatter on the cement floor. And then there was a shower of droplets over our head.

"What's that?" said my father.

Two of the MacAllesters from the table I had passed were throwing quarts of beer to their relatives at the back of the hall. They were standing up like quarterbacks and spiralling the open quarts off the palms of their hands and I saw Kenneth reach up and catch one as if he were a wide receiver. The quarts, for the most part, stayed upright; but as they revolved and spun, their foaming contents sprinkled or drenched those seated beneath them.

"Those bastards," said my uncle.

The two of them came over to the table. They were about thirty and strong and heavily muscled.

"Who are you talking to?" one of them said.

"Never mind," said my uncle. "Go and sit down."

"I asked you a question," he said. And then turning to me he added, "I asked you a question before too. What's the matter, can't some of your hear? I just thought that some of you couldn't see."

There was a silence then that began to spread to the neighboring tables and the conversations slowed and the men took their hands off their bottles and their glasses.

"I asked you your age," he said, still looking at me. "Are you the oldest or the youngest?"

"He's the only one," said the other man. "Since the war, his father is so blind he can't find his way into his wife's cunt to make any more."

I remember my uncle reaching for the bottom of his crutch, and he swung it like a baseball bat from his sitting position. And I remember the way he planted his one leg onto the floor even as he swung. And I remember the crutch exploding into the nose and mouth of the man and his blood splashing down upon us and then the overturning of tables and chairs and the crashing of broken glass. And I remember also two of the MacAllesters who were our neighbors reaching our table with amazing speed. Each of them went to a side of my father's chair and they lifted it up with him still sitting upon it. And they carried him as carefully as if he were eggs or perhaps an object of religious veneration, and the men who were smashing their fists into one another's mouths moved out of their way when they saw them coming. They deposited him with great gentleness against the far wall where they felt no harm could come to him, bending their knees in unison as they lowered his chair to the floor. And then each of them placed a hand upon his shoulder as one might comfort a frightened child. And then one of them picked up a chair and smashed it over the head of my cousin who had his brother by the throat.

Someone grabbed me and spun me around but I could see by his eyes that he was intent on someone across the hall and that I was merely in his way. And then I saw Kenneth coming towards me, as I half expected him to. It was like the bench-clearing brawls at the hockey games when the goalies seek each other out because they have the most in common.

I saw him coming with his eyes intent upon me and because

I knew him well I believed that he would leap from a spot about three strides ahead of him and that the force of his momentum would carry us backwards and I would be on the bottom with my head on the cement floor. It all took perhaps a fraction of a second, his leap and my bending and moving forward and side-ways, either to go towards him or to get out of the way, and my shoulder grazing his hip as he was airborne with his hands stretched out before him and his body parallel to the floor. He came crashing down on top of the table, knocking it over and forward and beneath him to the cement.

He lay face down and still for a moment and I thought he was unconscious and then I saw the blood spreading from beneath his face and reddening the shards of different colored glass.

"Are you all right?" I said, placing my hand upon his shoulder.

"It's okay," he said. "It's just my eye."

He sat up then with his hands over his face and the blood streaming down between his fingers. I was aware of a pair of rubber boots beside us and then a man's voice. "Stop," he shouted to the brawling hall. "For Christ's sake, stop, someone's been hurt."

In retrospect, and even then, it seemed like a strange thing to say because when one looked at the bloodied men it seemed that almost everyone had been hurt in some way, although not to the same degree. But given the circumstances, he said exactly the right thing and everyone stopped and unclenched his fist and released his grip on his opponent's throat.

In the rush to the doctor and to the hospital, everyone's origi-nal plans went awry. No one thought of the lobsters we had hidden and saved for our end-of-the-season feast; and when we discovered them days later, it was with something like surprise. They were dead and had to be thrown back into the sea, perhaps to serve as food for the spring mackerel with the scales upon their eyes.

That night two cars of MacAllesters came to our house. They told us that Kenneth's eye was lost; and Mr. MacAllester, who was about my father's age, began to cry. The two young men who were throwing the beer held their caps in their hands and their knuckles were still raw and bleeding. Both of them apologized to my father. "We didn't see it getting that out of hand," one of them said. My uncle came in from another room and said that he shouldn't have swung the crutch.

Mr. MacAllester said that if my father would agree, all of us should stop using the fickle river as the boundary between our fishing grounds and take our sightings instead from the two rocky promontories on either side of the beach. One family would fish off the beach one year and the other the next. My father agreed. "I can't see the boundary anyway," he said with a smile. It all seemed so simple in hindsight.

This has been the telling of a story about a story but like most stories it has spun off into others and relied on others and perhaps no story ever really stands alone. This began as the story of two children who long ago went to visit their grandparents but who, because of circumstances, did not recognize them when they saw them. As their grandparents did not see them. And this is a story related by a man who is a descendant of those people. The son of a father who never saw his son but knew him only through sound or by the running of his fingers across the features of his face.

As I write this, my own small daughter comes in from kindergarten. She is at the age where each day she asks a riddle and I am not supposed to know the answer. Today's question is, "What has eyes but cannot see?" Under the circumstances, the question seems overwhelmingly profound. "I don't know," I say and I feel I really mean it.

"A potato," she shouts and flings herself into my arms, enthused and impressed by her own cleverness and by my lack of understanding.

She is the great-great-granddaughter of the blind woman who died in flames and of the man called *Mac an Amharuis*; and both of us, in spite of our age and comprehension, are indeed the children of uncertainty.

Most of the major characters in this story are, as the man called *Mac an Amharuis* once said of others, "all gone" in the literal sense. There remains only Kenneth MacAllester, who works as a janitor for a soap company in Toronto. Unable ever to join the Air Force and fly towards the sun and see over the tops of mountains and across the ocean because of what happened to his eye on that afternoon so long ago. Now he has an artificial eye and, as he says, "Only a few people know the difference."

When we were boys we would try to catch the slippery spring mackerel in our hands and look into the blindness of their eyes, hoping to see our own reflections. And when the wet ropes of the lobster traps came out of the sea, we would pick out a single strand and then try to identify it some few feet farther on. It was difficult to do because of the twisting and turning of the different strands within the rope. Difficult to be ever certain in our judgements or to fully see or understand. Difficult then to see and understand the twisted strands within the rope. And forever difficult to see and understand the tangled twisted strands of love.

The Road to
Rankin's Point

I AM SPEAKING NOW of a July in the early 1970s and it is in the morning just after the sun has risen following a night of heavy rains. My car moves through the quiet village which is yet asleep except for those few houses which have sent fishermen to their nets and trawls some hours before. From such houses the smoke whisks and curls lazily before slanting off at the insistence of the almost imperceptible southeast wind. Upon my right the Gulf of St. Lawrence is flat and blue, dotted here and there with the white fishing boats intent on their quiet work. It has been a bad year for lobsters because of the late ice and then the early storms which destroyed so much of the precious gear. During the last week of the lobster season many of the fishermen did not even visit their traps, preferring to remain drunk and discouraged on the beach or within the dampened privacy of their little shanties.

Now since the lobster season's conclusion on July first, it can be at least thankfully forgotten along with the vague feelings of hope tinged with guilt that accompanied its final days. The boats presently riding on the Gulf are after a variety of "ground fish," with some few after salmon. They are getting six cents a pound for hake and twelve for cod and no one has seen a haddock for a long, long time. In the cities of Ontario fresh cod sells for $1.65 a pound and the "dried cod" upon which most of us were raised and so heartily despised has become almost a delicacy which sells for $2.15 a pound. "Imagine that," says my grandmother, "who would have ever thought?" Across Cabot Strait in Newfoundland the prices are three to four cents lower and there is talk that the fishermen may strike. All this runs through my mind now although it does not really occupy it. Like the vaguely heard melody of some tuned-down radio station heard softly in the background.

At the outskirts of the village the narrow paved road turns to the left, away from the sea, and begins its journey inland and outward. If followed relentlessly it will take you almost anywhere in North America, perhaps to Central and to South America as well. It will remain narrow and unpretentious and "slow" in the caution that it demands of its drivers for approximately fifty miles. Then it will join the maple-leafed Trans-Canada Highway and together they will boom across the Canso Causeway and off Cape Breton Island and out into the world. As the water of the tributary joins the major river, its traffic and its travellers will blend and mingle within the rushing stream. They will become the camper trailers with their owners' names emblazoned on their sides, and the lumbering high-domed motor homes and the overcrowded station wagons with the dogs forever panting through the rear windows. They will become the high-powered "luxury" products of Detroit, loaded with extras and zooming at eighty miles per hour from service station to service station, as if by speed alone they might somehow outrace the galloping depreciation which even now threatens to overtake and engulf them. They will become the scuttling Volkswagens in the "slow" lanes on the long hills and the grinding trucks with their encased and T-shirted drivers carrying the continent's goods and the weaving, swerving motorcyclists with their helmets reflecting the slanting sun.

By night these travellers will all be miles away, comparing mileages, filling their radiators and looking at their maps. They will be sitting around campfires and sweating in the motels.

Some will be in the havens of their homes while others will follow the probing paths of their bug-spattered headlights deep into the darkened night. Some few will end in the twisted, spectacular wreckages, later moaning incoherently in the unknown hospitals or lying beneath the quiet sheets of death while authorities search through glove compartments and check out licence numbers prior to notifying the next of kin. It is a big, fast, brutal road that leads into the world on this July day and there is no longer any St. Christopher to be the patron saint of travellers.

But for me, in this my twenty-sixth year, it is not into the larger world that I go today. And the road that I follow feeds into no other that will take the traveller to the great adventures of the wild unknown. Instead, at the village's end it veers sharply to the right, leaves the pavement behind and almost immediately begins to climb along the rocky cliffs that hang high above the sea. It winds its tortuous, clinging way for some eight miles before it ends quite abruptly and permanently in my grandmother's yard. There the sea cliff slants down almost vertically and it is as if the road runs into it as it would into a wall. At the wall's base and at the road's end nestles my grandmother's tiny farm: her buildings and her home. Above this last small cultivated outpost and jutting beyond it out to sea is the rocky promontory of Rankin's Point. As one cannot drive beyond it, neither can one see beyond it farther up the coast. It is an end in every way and it is to the beginning of this conclusion that my car now begins its long ascent.

For the first two miles there are still houses strung out along both sides of the road but soon such signs of formal habitation fall behind; and as the road becomes steeper, rockier and more narrow the wildness of the summer's beauty falls and splashes down upon it even to the extent that it is close to lost. The overreaching branches of the silver birch, the maple and the poplar slap across the hood and windshield impeding vision and almost the passage of the road itself. The alders lean and hang from the left bank, their sticky buds smearing the car door's sides and leaving stains that will annoy car washers for a long, long time. The wild flowers burst and hang in all their short-lived, giddy, aromatic profusion. When the tough but delicate red-and-white roses are nudged by the car they cascade and strew their fragile, perfumed petals across its hood even as their thorns scratch the finished lacquer of its sides. *Everything has its price*, they seem to say. The sweet red-and-white clover swarms with bees. The yellow buttercups flutter and the white and gold-green daisies dip and sway. The prickly Scottish thistles are in their lavender bloom and the wild buckwheat and rioting raspberry bushes form netted tapestries of the darkest green. As the road dips and twists around many of its hairpinned turns the icy little streams cascade across it, washing it out in a minor way, the water flowing across the gullied roadbed instead of beneath it through the broken, plugged and unused wooden sluices. At such spots near the fresh water's edge the bluebells cling to the velvet-mossed stones and the blue-and-purple irises march downward to the wetness. The gentle, large-eyed rabbits hop trustingly near the road which is so untravelled that it holds for them neither fear nor any threat of death. The road is now but a minor intrusion that the wildness will reclaim.

Before the final two-mile climb there is one last almost right-angled turn and again the spilling, cascading brook and the washed-over roadbed and the plugged and useless sluice. The road rising from the spot is solid rock and on wet days it is impossible for a car to make the climb. The tires will spin and the rear of the car will slew to the right and hang above the four-hundred-foot drop that falls to the crashing surf which booms and pounds the smooth and rounded boulders far below. Three years ago a lovers' quarrel resulted in a car being stolen from the village below and then pushed over the towering cliff. For weeks the police and the insurance companies and various high-priced towing companies attempted to reach it but with no success. All of the cables and the extended booms and the huge tow trucks that were reared back on their hind and doubled wheels and the men motioning with their gloved hands or hanging on ropes at the sea cliff's wall did nothing to raise the twisted bits of metal that were scattered far below. Finally some men in a small fishing dory were able to get close enough to the cliff's base to wade ashore in water up to their waists and retrieve what remained of the engine. Now if one hangs over the perilous edge the remaining bits of automobile can still be seen strewn along the wet cliff's base. Here the twisted chassis and there the detached body and yards away the steering wheel and the trunk lid and a crumpled, twisted door. The cormorants and the gulls walk carefully amidst the twisted wreckage as if hoping that each day may bring them something that they had previously missed. They peck with curiosity at the gleaming silver knobs and the selector buttons of the once-expensive radio.

The sharp, right-angled turn and its ascending steepness has always been called by us "The Little Turn of Sadness" because it is here that my grandfather died so many years ago on a February night when he somehow fell as he walked or staggered toward his home which was a steep two miles away. He had already covered the six miles from the village when he lost his footing on the ice-covered rock, falling backwards and shattering the rum bottle he carried within his safe back pocket. Now as I feel my own blood, diseased and dying, I think of his, the brightest scarlet, staining the moon-white snow while the joyous rabbits leaped and pirouetted beneath the pale, clear moon. It was a bright and quiet night without a breath of wind, as my grandmother has often told us. All night she kept looking out across the death-white fields for the form of her returning husband. Her eyes became so strained that as the dawn approached the individual spruce trees at the clearing's edge began to take his shape and size and seemed to move toward the house. First one and then another appearing to move and take on human form. Once she was so certain that she went to the door and opened it only to stare again across the whitened, empty stillness of the silent winter snow.

In the morning she sent her oldest son, who was ten at the time, to walk along the frozen cliffs; and when he returned, white and breathless, the news he brought was already expected. Shortly after he left, she has often said, she began to hear the death ring or the sound of the death bell in her right ear. It came from off the frozen Gulf of St. Lawrence borne on the stillness and, no, it was not to be confused with the crying of the white and drifting seals. And then almost in response to the bell she had heard the howls of the three black-and-white border collies that had accompanied her son. Their howls drifted back along the coastline, first the oldest dog and then the second and then the third. She had been able to distinguish each dog's cry and to comprehend the message that their anguished voices bore. At that time and in those sounds she realized that life for her and for her children would never be the same. She was twenty-six and expecting her seventh child.

Later she and her older children hitched the best of their brown-dappled horses to the wood sleigh and went forth to meet their husband and father for the final time. The children cried and the tears froze to their reddened cheeks. The horse began to snort and tremble long before he reached the rigid, log-like figure and then to rear and plunge. Finally he lunged to the side, breaking the shafts of the precious sleigh and adding another stick of destruction to the steadily mounting pile. They had had to abandon the sleigh then and return with the horse and then come back again with the children's coasting sleigh and lengths of rope with which to bind the grizzly burden it was to bear.

The dogs lay restlessly about the stiffened corpse, black against the silent snow. Sometimes they whined softly and licked the frozen opened eyes or the grotesquely parted purple lips with the protruding tongue or nuzzled an out-flung half-curved arm. Then they would flop back again into the snow, covering their noses with their paws while following everything with their deep brown eyes. Sensing too that their lives had changed and not knowing what to do.

Somehow they managed the final two miles though their own feet slipped on the icy rocks and they fell forward several times when the strained rope parted. Because the sleigh was so small there was only room for the upper part of the body, and the legs and heels hung over the end and dragged along the jagged, stony road. Twice it almost slipped off completely and when they reached the house the heels of the rubber boots were worn through to the frozen flesh. The heel of the bottle which had killed him still contained, almost miraculously, a half inch of the dark sweet rum while the neck with its firmly fastened cork was also still intact. Between the perfect top and the perfect bottom all was shattered and splintered and driven deeply into the frozen hip and thigh.

Now this scene of winter death seems strangely out of place

amidst the drunken intensity of the summer's splendor. Like an improbable sequence of old black-and-white pictures taken once in the long ago. Taken of people it is impossible to ever know or to fully understand.

The sun is rising above the mountains and touching the freshly washed earth. The raindrops glisten and sparkle, and the fog and mists that hang above the dirt roads of high places rise and vanish toward the sky. The bobolinks and red-winged blackbirds bounce and sing from the tips of their springing willows. Orange butterflies glide and float on the drafts of air and the chattering squirrels and chipmunks sprint along the fallen logs like busy proprietors doing morning inspection. The earth is alive, refreshed and new.

It does not take long for the rocks above "The Little Turn of Sadness" to dry, and my car in its lowest gear grinds slowly and reluctantly up the steep incline, nearly swinging out and over the hanging ledge, then settling more steadily to the stony and almost familiar roadbed.

For the next two miles the road continues to climb and wind along the cliff's high ledge. In some places erosion has caused the roadside to crumble and fall into the sea. It would be impossible for two vehicles to meet and pass upon such narrowness but there is little likelihood of such an occurrence.

Now and then upon the left I see the remains of the old stone fences and also tiny patches of still cleared land indicating where houses had once stood. The gray granite stones of their foundations are still visible, covered now with green and velvet moss. Now and then a stone flue stands with phallic reality amidst the rubble of the house that has fallen down around it. Only the strength of stone has survived the ravages of time and seasons.

A mile from my grandmother's house her sheep begin to appear, grazing or lying along the roadside and sometimes right in the middle of the road. They are the white-faced Cheviots that she has had for as long as I can remember and there is almost a timelessness about them. Open-faced and independent they do not flock together as do the more conventional Oxfords and Suffolks. As the car approaches, the young lambs bound and scramble out of its way bleating over their shoulders to the

patient, watchful ewes. The thick-shouldered rams, with their
heavy, swinging scrota almost dragging on the ground, move
only at the last minute and then begrudgingly. Their flickering
eyes seem to say they would as soon lower their heads and
charge than relinquish this stony trail which they obviously consider to be theirs.

For decades my grandmother has been concerned about the
purity and well-being of these sheep. She has worried about
strange rams interbreeding and diluting her "stock." And she
has worried about young dogs wild with spring and bloodlust
running them over the cliffs to sea-washed deaths. Now there
is no need to worry. All the other flocks and dogs from the fallen
houses have gone and it is only her sheep whose bleating cries
reverberate across these high cleansed hills.

At the road's end I stop to slide back the poles of the old gate
before the final entrance to her yard. As I bend, the blood bursts
from my nostrils, splashing scarletly upon my shoes, and there
is a dizzying lightness bordering on black within my head. I
straighten and place my hands on the gateposts for steadiness
and lift my face to the sun to reverse the blood's thick flow. I
can feel it coursing sweetly through the back of my mouth and
down the darkened passages of my throat. To avoid further
bending, I slide the bottom pole back by hooking my right foot
underneath it and then stand and wait for the bleeding to cease.
I dab at my nostrils and lips with the pieces of Kleenex that I
now carry in place of standard handkerchiefs.

The car, with its clutch disengaged, rolls easily down the small
incline into the yard. There is no need to even start the motor.
I close the gate, watched with interest by various farm animals
who are not in the least alarmed. Almost all of my grandmother's
animals are descended from livestock that has been here for a
long, long time and over the years they have taken on distinctive
colorings and characteristics that are all their own. They seem
now the same animals that I have always known and heard described, and seen in the faded photographs of the albums of my
mind. The three brown-dappled horses, rolling in the slickness
of their summer fat, have an almost maroon tinge to their coats
when the sun strikes them at certain angles. They have identical

white stars on their foreheads and a solitary white spot the size of a large coin on their barrelled chests. They have always been called either Star or Tena. They have always held their heads high when drawing even the heaviest of loads and have been perfectly in step with each other, their hoofbeats falling in unison through the regulated choreography of their fiercely inbred generations. They have been sure-footed in the snow and long-winded on the hills. They have crossed the drift ice in the blinding blizzards and galloped the cartloads of seaweed ashore across the briny rocks. For years they have refused to eat any hay except that grown upon this hilly farm, as if smelling and tasting within it their own urine, manure and sweat. As if they are part of some great ecological plan, converting themselves into hay and the hay in turn into their wine-dappled sun-strong selves.

Now standing about this yard, whisking their too-long tails and tossing their forelocks out of their eyes, they are idle and at ease. They have felt neither bridle nor harness nor shoes for years and the youngest who is close to ten has never felt them at all. He is so old now, in the years of a horse, that it is unlikely that he ever will.

They have become almost pets waiting for my grandmother to open her door and offer them bits of apple or pieces of stale, dried bread. Yet in their deep, dark eyes and in the muscles that bunch and ripple within their shoulders their power can still be seen. They are like the eyes and muscles of certain animals at the zoo: eyes and muscles that say, *Yes, we are here and we are alive and we eat our food, but we were not bred for this kind of life nor did we come from it nor is this all we are. Look closely at us and you will see.*

The brindled cows with their in-curved horns are busily grazing about the grassy knolls. Because my grandmother no longer tends them as she used to, nor uses their cream-rich milk for her butter and cheese, they too seem wasted and unused. They are followed by overgrown calves who nurse and butt at their swollen and distended udders. Some of their udders are caked and hardened and mastitis has set in. It would be close to impossible to redeem them now and they will nevermore fill to overflow the warm and brimming pails. A black hen with gold flecks around her neck is clucking to her chickens. The chickens are too young for this time of year and will not likely survive the fall.

Entering the porch that leads to my grandmother's house it is necessary to step down. With the passage of the years the house has sunk into the earth. The stone foundation of more than a century has worked itself deep into the soil and now all doors are forced to open inward. The porch is filled with tools and clothes and items from the past. A manual cream separator is on the left, a hand scythe hangs on the wall to the right, and beside it a wire stretcher and a meat grinder. Bits of harness and rope and cans of fence staples, nails, hammers, gunnysacks and fishing rods hang from the spikes driven deep into the wooden beams. Shapeless rain jackets, hats, gloves and worn-out shoes and boots hang and lie cluttered in a corner.

In the kitchen my grandmother sits at her table drinking her morning tea. She has not seen nor heard my arrival and she is staring out the window that looks upon the sea. There the gulls are curving and turning in the sparkling sun. The three black-and-white border collies raise their eyes when I enter but they do not move. They lie about the floor like tossed and familiar rugs. One is under the table, one against the wood box at the stove, and the third beside my grandmother's chair. Unlike my grandmother, they have been aware of my approach for some time. They have recognized the sound of the motor groaning along the cliff's edge and heard the gate poles slide and the opening of the door and the footsteps on the sill. They have heard it all and felt no cause for movement or alarm. I enter now to make my presence fully known and to take my place in time.

Turning from the window with her teacup in her hand, my grandmother is startled to see me and also embarrassed that I have come upon her so silently and unannounced. She is becoming frightened, although she will not admit it, of the loss of her senses, and she fears the silence of the deaf and the darkness of the blind. None of this has happened to her as yet but there are clutching moments seen in her face, as now, that say such thoughts are there.

"Oh, you are here, Calum," she says. "I've been expecting you."

I know that she has as I have been expecting to come, lying in the bed at my parents' house in the village below since 3:00 a.m., listening to the rain upon the roof and thinking of how slippery the rocks of the road might be. Thinking of walking the eight-mile distance in the almost unfathomable rural darkness when the rain clouds blot out the moon and stars and there is only the sound of water: the thunking of the large-dropped rain into the earth and into the splashing, invisible brooks and on the right the lapping and moaning of the sea. Knowing that I will never walk that skin-drenched journey again, any more than will my never-seen grandfather, dead now for seventy years, the biblical life span of three score years and ten.

"I came as soon as I could," I say. "As soon as I thought the cliff would be dry enough for the car to climb."

"Oh yes," she says. "Would you like some tea? The kettle has just finished boiling."

"Yes, all right, I will get it myself," I say as I move about her familiar kitchen, digging into the old square tea can which drifted ashore from one of the long-ago wrecked vessels carrying the precious cargo from Ceylon. I gather the tea into my fist and drop it into the teapot and add the water from the steaming kettle.

"They will not be here for a while," she says. "Not likely until the afternoon."

She seats herself more comfortably at the end of the table.

"Get yourself some biscuits from out of the tin. I made them early this morning. Give some to the dogs."

Obediently I go to another tin and take out four biscuits. They are still warm to the touch. I butter one for myself and toss one to each of the lying, watchful dogs. They catch them while they are still in the air, then flick out their long, pink tongues for any crumbs that may have fallen on the floor. The floor remains as spotless as before, as if the action had never happened. Like footsteps in the water, I think. No trace remains behind.

I sit opposite my grandmother at the other end of the table and look with her out across the azure sea. The sun is higher now and the mists have all burned off. It is the kind of day that at one time would have allowed us to see Prince Edward Island. *On a clear day you can see Prince Edward Island*, we would say. Not "forever," just Prince Edward Island. Now it does not seem to matter.

Today is the first day of the rest of your life, comes to my mind. The slogan from the many "modern" posters, desk mottoes, greeting cards, bookmarks, record jackets, bumper stickers, and graffiti walls. I raise the teacup to my lips, half hopeful it might burn me more fiercely into life.

"Why do you drink your tea like that?" asks my grandmother. "You will burn yourself. One would think you had never drunk tea before."

"It is all right," I say. "I was only trying something."

We sit for a long time, quietly sipping our tea and looking through the window. We do not say what is on our minds nor make inquiries of each other. We are resting and appearing normal, almost as athletes quietly conserving our energy for the game that lies some hours down our road. The bees buzz from the lilacs at the base of the house and bounce drunkenly against the window. The barn swallows with their delicately forked tails flash their orange breasts and dart and swoop after invisible insects. The dogs lie silently, moving only their eyes, conserving their strength as well. We are drowsy and waiting in the summer's heat.

I have come to see my grandmother on this day almost as the double agent of the spy movies. I have come somehow hoping that I might find a way of understanding and of coming to terms with death; yet deep down I know that I will find only the intensity of life and that I am, after all, but twenty-six, and in the eyes of others, in the youngness of my years.

My grandmother gets up and goes for her violin which hangs on a peg inside her bedroom door. It is a very old violin and came from the Scotland of her ancestors, from the crumbled foundations that now dot and haunt Lochaber's shores. She plays two Gaelic airs—*"Gun Bhris Mo Chridh' On Dh'Fhalbh Thu"* ("My Heart Is Broken Since Thy Departure") and *"Cha Till Mi Tuille"* ("Never More Shall I Return" or "MacCrimmon's Lament"). Her hands have suffered stiffness and the lonely laments waver and hesitate as do the trembling fingers upon the four taut strings. She is very moved by the ancient music and there are tears within her eyes.

On the night of this day and on this afternoon as well, two

of her grandchildren and one great-grandchild will gyrate and play the music of their time, the music of the early 1970s. They are at other destinations on that other road that leads into the larger world. One is in Las Vegas and two on Toronto's Yonge Street strip. They swivel and stomp beneath kaleidoscopic lights, stepping nimbly over the cords that bind their instruments to the high-powered amplifiers. Their long hair floats and swirls about their shoulders and their hard-driving booted heels are as insistent as their rhythms. Here in the quietness of Rankin's Point, at another road's end, the body out of which they came and to which they owe their lives has trouble controlling the last quavering notes of "Never More Shall I Return."

"That is the lament of the MacCrimmons," she says when she has finished. "Your grandfather was part MacCrimmon. They were the greatest musicians in the Scottish Highlands. There is a cairn erected to their memory on the Isle of Skye. Your uncles saw it during the war."

"Yes, I know," I say. "You've told me."

"The MacCrimmons were said to be given two gifts," she says, "the gift of music and the gift of foreseeing their own deaths. Those gifts are supposed to follow in all their bloodlines. They are not gifts of the ordinary world."

High on the rafters of the barn that stands outside, my grandfather had written in the blackest of ink the following statement: "We are the children of our own despair, of Skye and Rum and Barra and Tiree." No one knows why he wrote it or when, and even the "how" gives cause for puzzlement. In that time before ballpoint pens or even fountain pens, did he climb such heights holding an ink bottle in one hand and a straight nibbed pen in the other? And what is the significance of ancestral islands long left and never seen? Blown over now by Atlantic winds and touched by scudding foam. What does it mean to all of us that he died as he did? And had he not, how would our grandmother's life have been different and the lives of her children and even mine as I have known it and still feel it as I sit here on this day?

I can know my grandfather only through recreated images of his life and death. Images of the frozen snow and the hot blood turned to crust upon it: blood, hot and sweet with rum and instantly converted like the sweet and boiling maple sap upon the winter's snow.

I would like to realize and understand now my grandmother's perception of death in all its vast diversity. For even the fixedness of death and the accidents that are its agents have changed throughout the years of her many-sequenced life. Three of her brothers, as young men, perished in the accidental ways that grew out of their lives—lives that were as intensely physical as the deaths that marked their end. One as a young man in the summer sun when the brown-dappled horses bolted and he fell into the teeth of a mowing machine. A second in a storm at sea when the vessel sank while plying its way across the straits to Newfoundland. A third frozen upon the lunar ice fields of early March when the sealing ship became separated from its men in a sudden obliterating blizzard.

How lonely now and distant these lives and deaths of my grandmother's early life. And how different from the lives and deaths of the three sons she has outlived. Men who left the crying gulls and hanging cliffs of Rankin's Point to take the road into the larger world and there to fashion careers and lives that would never have been theirs on this tiny sea-washed farm. Careers that were as modern and as affluent as the deaths that marked their termination. Real estate brokers and vice-presidents of grocery chains and buyers for haberdashery firms seldom die in the daily routines of the working lives that they have chosen. The pencil and the telephone replace the broken, dangling reins and the marlinespike and the sealing club; and the adjusted thermostats and the methodic Muzak produce a regulated urban order far removed from the uncertainty of the elements and the unpredictability of suddenly frightened animals.

None of these men died at their work or directly from it, yet die they did in deaths that seem even more bizarre and Grecianly ironic than those of the previous generation. One of them choked on a piece of steak in an expensive Montreal restaurant. A second died at Pompano Beach from too much of the sun he had gone to find. The third died while jogging through the streets of Mississauga at 5:00 a.m. Yet perhaps death by affluence is but the same in the end as that achieved through physical labor and perhaps it is only because I now have no choice of either that first one and then the other seems desperately more frightening.

Outside the window the blackbirds and cowbirds hop with familiarity around the brindle cows. They call out their raucous comments to one another and sometimes perch boldly upon the cattle's spines. A single, white-tailed hawk glides silently back and forth, sometimes above the land and then beyond the cliff's edge out toward the sea. His shadow slides beneath him across the summer grass but is not reflected within the deep, blue water. It is as if the mirror were perhaps too profound. He does not go far out to sea but circles and climbs and returns across the land; silent and graceful, holding his wings with rigid and controlled beauty, he bears with eloquence the message of his gifted life.

Within the house all is silent except for the ticking of the white Westclox on its shelf above the table. The dogs drowse with half-closed eyes. Lost within our own thoughts, we stay, as in a picture, quiet and immobile for a long, long time.

"Well, I suppose I must get ready. They will soon be here," says my grandmother, rising from her seat at the end of the table and seeming to break the spell.

Within her bedroom which opens off the kitchen, I can see or sense the combing of her long, white hair. She leans to one side and combs it away from her body, her left hand running along its electric smoothness ahead of and behind the comb she wields with her right.

Later she emerges, fastening a broach of entwined Scottish thistles to the collar of her recently ironed dress. I recognize both the broach and the dress as gifts that I have purchased for her at earlier times. For an instant I see myself once more in the press of pre-Christmas shoppers in Toronto, jostling and elbowing, moving on and off the crowded elevators and the humming, slanting escalators that stretch between the floors.

I know that in her trunks and scattered jewel boxes there are layers of dresses and mounds of broaches as good as these; yet she has chosen what she has quite consciously. Few of the others, I realize, will recognize what she wears, and there is of course no reason that they should. I am struck once more by the false-ness of the broach, for Scottish thistles do not twine. Perhaps at the time of its purchase I was being more symbolic than I had ever thought.

Returning to her bedroom she emerges once more with a pair of scissors and draws her chair up close to mine. Without saying anything I begin to trim her fingernails. They are long and yellowed and each is bordered by a thin layer of grime.

Trimming the yellowed, unclean fingernails of my grandmother I realize that I am admitted now to the silent, secret communication that the strong have always known in their relationship with the weak. It is the strength and knowledge that my grandmother has previously so fiercely exercised over her own children and in many cases her children's children as well. The strength and knowledge leading into and from the awful privacy of all our secret inadequacies which is the standard that the previous generation waves always over the one that follows. The awareness and memory of dirty diapers and bed-wettings and the first attempts at speech and movement, of the birth and death of Santa Claus and of the myriad childish hopes and fears of the lost time, of the lonely screaming nightmares of childhood terror, of nocturnal emissions and of real and imagined secret sins. The strength and knowledge of actual physical support and the giving and sustaining of such physical life and perhaps even love. I have never thought of my grandmother so much in terms of love as in terms of strength. Perhaps, I think now, because the latter has always been so much more visible.

Down in the village at this time I imagine my own father, now nearing seventy, preparing for his journey here to meet us. Nervously brushing his snow-white hair and slapping his face with talcum powder, still half afraid of his mother's inspection, bound too by those complex cords of strength and knowledge. He cannot, of course, remember ever seeing the father that was his own.

Suddenly my grandmother seizes my right hand and presses it fiercely between both of hers. The scissors that I have held clatter to the floor and I can feel the intensity of her life yearning and pressing outward through the pressure of her palms. "Oh, Calum," she says, "what are you going to do with the rest of your life?"

I do not know whether I am more shocked by the unexpected-ness of the question or by what seems to be its enormity, given the circumstances. The doctor has said that I should try to live "the rest of my life" in as normal a fashion as possible. I have, he has said, "perhaps some months" in which I may continue to live and to appear as normal. I am reminded of the summer chickens outside my grandmother's door, doomed by their time of life to not survive the fall.

"Oh stay with me, Calum," she says, "and I will tell them so when they come. Find yourself a nice girl and get married. You are twenty-six and it is time to be thinking of such things. You have always liked it here and the land and the animals are as good as ever. You can make a good life here for all of us. I have left you everything in my will."

Outside the window I see the piles of roughened field stones picked by the strong, worn fingers of my grandmother's hands in earlier times. I see the falling rail fences and the outbuildings in need of paint and shingles. And the barn that contains my grandfather's only message. This is the "everything" left to me, I am told, by my grandmother's will. Yet no one has ever given me "everything" before and it is true that I have always liked it here amidst the loneliness and the privacy and the crying gulls. And I have thought of it many times during my "absent" years spent teaching the over-urbanized high school students of Burlington and Don Mills in the classrooms that always seemed so overheated. I have returned now, I think, almost as the diseased and polluted salmon, to swim for a brief time in the clear waters of my earlier stream. The returning salmon knows of no "cure" for the termination of his life.

I feel the blackened dizziness as it swirls within my head and clutch the chair's seat for support.

"What is the matter with you?" asks my grandmother. "You look like you are going to faint. Do you want a drink of water?"

"No," I say. "It will soon pass. It will soon be over."

The dogs, as if in concert, lift their heads and cock their ears and rise from their recumbent positions to move toward the door. They have heard the cars grinding along the cliff's edge some miles away. Neither my grandmother nor I can hear anything but we know that we are seeing the coming of sound to finer ears than ours. It is almost as if we can see the sound itself through an exchanging of the senses. Sometimes by looking at the face of the person on the telephone, you can see the nature of the news that is received although your ears hear only the silence that is no sound at all.

"They are coming," says my grandmother, giving a final pat to her hair.

The distant procession consists of members of her family and they are bound on an expedition which might best be entitled "What to do about Grandma?" It is an expedition which has set out with various degrees of optimism for the past fifteen years or so and it has always been launched in the summer when the maximum forces are available. In the summer, numbers of my grandmother's children and grandchildren and great-grandchildren and even great-great-grandchildren return from their scattered destinations on the roads of the larger world. Joining forces with the relatives who are residents of the region, they map and plan strategies which they hope will suit their purpose. Each year in the face of pleas and tears and petitions and almost threats, my grandmother has remained firm in her refusal to be moved from this her home. I see her quietly gathering her inner resources now, preparing her front of strength almost as if she is checking out her equipment.

This year's strategy involves the nursing home in the village below and it is planned as an alternative to last year's failure which was called "living with us" and which was put forth by different people who varied greatly in their enthusiasm and reluctance. The advantages of the nursing home are "privacy" and "being with people near her own age" and "not having to worry about her meals" and receiving what is vaguely described as "care." There are various other "advantages" of the same type. On and on.

My grandmother has visited the nursing home at different times to see certain people who are her friends and she has hated it as much as do the friends she goes to see. Clutching her fingers in parchment hands they whisper to her in Gaelic which most of the staff can no longer understand. They tell her of real and imagined atrocities: that when the visitors leave the staff steal the Kleenex and the chocolates, that poison is being put in the food, that they are strapped to armchairs and wheelchairs for a long time, sitting in their own excrement and urine until their heads flop over onto their shoulders. What does it mean that old women in nursing homes suffer from real and imagined atrocities? And are the imagined ones less terrifying because they are not true?

Perhaps all of us, if we think of it, can see ourselves at some future time unable to use the bedpan in some place called Sunny Brae or Sunny Brook or Sunny Acres or Sunshine Villa; listening while the nurses' aides chew gum and talk about their dates (also real and imagined), "Oh he didn't." "Did he?" "You've got to be kidding!" Having our bodies hosed down by people who know too much about bodies and what they do or fail to do and how they finally end. This now I know is bearing down on me. It is ironically too distant and too close.

Once more I am concerned with my falseness and my cowardice. For I have been sent here on this day even as I have come of my own volition. I have been sent to make the initial request of my grandmother. "Perhaps she will go if Calum asks her," they have said. "If anyone can convince her it will be Calum." But Calum has done nothing but sit here all this morning. He has done nothing because he does not believe in this year's strategy any more than he did in that of the previous year. And in a secret place within his heart he hopes that it will fail.

Now as the cars begin to appear before the pole gate, I see myself as the failed advance rider sent out to scout the territory for the war party that is to follow. Or as an upside-down St. John the Baptist sent to prepare a false way for unlikely prophets. Or as the anguished and befuddled Judas already too close to his halter. At least I will not have to kiss her on the cheek.

After the cars have rolled into the yard, the people spill from them in all their vast variety. I stand at the door as an uncertain welcoming committee of one while my grandmother sits inside as she always does on such occasions. They are almost like a group of brightly colored summer birds, these members of my family, chatting and laughing in plaid pants (with and without cuffs) and floral tops and sport shirts. Slacks, flares, denims, sandals and various "looks" that come from the variety of the worlds they inhabit and the ages that they are going through. Vaguely I think that they do not look much like people who are supposed to have the "gift" of foreseeing their own deaths.

They move into the house, smiling at me and patting me on the shoulder, some of them looking hopefully into my eyes for any message that might be found. Within the house which has not enough chairs, they arrange themselves as best they can, the children sitting on the floor with their arms around their knees. Soon they will run outside to play or be frightened by the animals that are so alien to many of them but for the present they must sit quietly because it is "polite."

Soon they begin to take the pictures. "Here is one of three generations," they say. "And now one of you and Mary and the baby. Four generations." Dutifully my grandmother holds her latest great-grandchild on her lap while her son and his daughter stand on either side of her. The people appear frozen as they look into the camera's lens.

Once as a boy in the summer following the last year of high school, my first cousin and I worked with my uncle on a ship taking barrels of salt fish to the islands of the West Indies and bringing back puncheons of dark and illegal rum. Upon our return we would anchor off the village in the still summer nights while the small local fishing boats plied diligently back and forth without lights and with muffled engines, landing the puncheons on the sandy beaches for the men who waited for them in the darkened pickup trucks.

Once, in Jamaica, my cousin and I were stopped on a street by a boy our own age who showed us a card and asked us to follow him. He took us to a brothel which was so unlike anything we had ever seen that we were actually afraid. When we finally convinced him we did not want "fun" he ushered us into the "picture room" which was only slightly less spectacular. Beautiful girls of all colors and races were being photographed in erotic poses with frightened young men who were about our own age. They undressed the young men and twined their hair about their genitals and brushed their penises with their lips. An energetic little dark-skinned man raced from one posing couple to the next, wheeling a bulky camera before him, shouting directions and asking the first names of the young men. Periodically he would disappear behind a curtain and emerge with the pictures. Across the front of each picture the same hand had written almost identical messages: "To John, my one and only love, Zelda." "To Tim, my one and only love, Tanya." "To George, my one and only love, Goldie."

"Coast Guard, mon!" said our acquaintance. Later we learned that the frightened and virginal-looking young men were members of a group of naval cadets from a Florida-based ship. They would keep the pictures in their wallets and show them secretly to their future friends, saying something like, "That's my girlfriend back home," and wait for the appreciative wows.

I think now that the photographs being taken here today share that same artificiality. In the family groupings in which people are relentlessly encouraged to smile, one cannot always see the desperate hopes and fears that flutter behind the eyes, or fully reach the darkest truth.

Glancing through the window I see my grandmother's maroon-colored horses and darkly brindled cattle moving about the automobiles that seem to fill the yard. Some of the automobiles bear the names of animals: Mustang, Pinto, Maverick. Soon children will have to be dispatched so that the real animals will not scratch or mar their metallized near namesakes.

As the afternoon moves on, the conversation rises and falls. People take flasks of rum from their pockets and pour drinks. My father and my uncles and aunts take the violin from its peg and play the complicated jigs and reels gracefully and without effort. All of them grasp the bow in the same spot and in the same manner and bend their wrists in an identical way. It is a style older than any of our memories and produces what we call "our sound." People remove harmonicas from handbags and pockets and the younger ones bring in guitars. Others rattle the kitchen spoons between their fingers and upon their thighs. My grandmother dances with each of her sons and then with the other men. She swings lightly and easily within my arms. There is no one in the nursing home who has lived as long as she.

The afternoon grows heightened and more animated while

the question hovers like a whining, buzzing insect at the backs of all our minds. No one dares ask it and yet we are afraid to leave. From time to time people look hopefully toward me, raising their eyebrows, looking for a sign. My grandmother continues to dance and swing with easy grace. She is getting through her day. *If I can only hang on for another little while,* her eyes seem to say, *I can win this. I will not be defeated.* I think of her at twenty-six, pregnant and surrounded by weeping children, pulling home the frozen corpse of her husband on a children's sleigh. Perhaps saying the same thing. I cannot fathom how many times she must have said it in the seventy years between.

Too well I know all of the reasons put forth against her staying here. That it is lonely and isolated. That the house is old and heated only by stoves and illuminated but dimly by kerosene lamps. That there is no telephone. That in the winter members of her family must bring up her few groceries on snowmobiles when they can get through and that they are uncertain of what they then might find. That the animals are awkward and expensive and that she might fall and stumble while moving about them within their winter barns.

But I know also, as do most of us here, those other aspects of her life. Her dislike of institutions and her scorn of the "ease" associated with them. After her husband's death it was suggested by "authorities" from Halifax that she could never survive here and that it would "be better for everyone" if she were to move or put some of her children up for adoption or even in an orphanage. It would be "easier," they said. All of us here in this overcrowded room in the early 1970s with our rum and with our music are in some ways the result of her contradiction of such suggestions. Seventy years later. "I would never have my children taken from me to be scattered about like the down of a dead thistle," she has often said. "I would not be that dead. It does not matter that some things are difficult. No one has ever said that life is to be easy. Only that it is to be lived." I have come today, partially at least, hoping to find such strength for the living of my life and the meeting of my death.

The music stops and the sun moves westward. Younger children begin to whisper in their parents' ears that they are hungry and that they would like to leave. The tension seems to mount and crackle. We are waiting for the lightning that will provide us with release, looking at the balancing stone and waiting for its fall.

Suddenly and unexpectedly my grandmother says, "I hope none of you are worrying about me. Calum has said that he is going to stay here with me and now everything will be just fine."

There is a period of unbelieved silence followed by a great gush of relief. As if the plug of a bathtub or the valve of a tire has suddenly set free the contents that had been so controlled and well contained. People look at one another and at me in stunned amazement. The solution seems so perfect that it is almost impossible to comprehend. Much too good really to be true. My parents look at me in wonder that is mingled with relief. They have been uncertain concerning my unexpected return here from Ontario with what seems like no thought of ever going back. "Perhaps he will teach in the high school here," I have heard them say to one another. "Perhaps he is tired and needs a rest." I have not told them or anyone else that I have returned because I know I am to die and do not know where else to do it.

Now it seems that their questions have been temporarily answered and they are glad to know that I have had some plan during the days of this past time. They nod their heads and smile across the room, though still in wonder. My grandmother smiles as if she has just played her great trump card and looks about her in temporary triumph. I have not the courage to destroy the lie she so wishes to be true.

Almost immediately there is a great movement toward departure. It is as if they are afraid that their unexpected and magical gift might suddenly vanish should they stay too long within its presence. "Good-bye for now," they say. "See you later." "So long." "Take care."

The car doors slam, the motors start and the tires turn. The poles of the gate are slid back and then replaced by my father who is the last to leave. He waves to my grandmother and to me as we remain standing in the doorway. He is the middle link of our three generations. Then he too gets into his car beside my mother and drives away. We are left all alone.

Going back into the kitchen my grandmother busies herself

in setting out the supper dishes. She takes the plates from the shelves and the knives and forks from the sliding drawers. The dogs who have been outside for most of the afternoon now return to flop upon the floor and resume their roles of quiet watchfulness. The sun is moving toward the sea.

"It is no good, Grandma," I say finally. "It is not going to work."

"What?" she says, keeping her back to me and reaching for the cups and saucers.

"What you told them. That I will stay here. It is not going to work." For a moment I teeter in hesitation but it seems that now I must go on. "It is not going to work," I say, "because I am going to die."

She turns and looks at me sharply and there is a flicker of fear upon her face which she banishes quickly. "Yes, I know," she laughs. "We all are. Sometime."

"It is no longer sometime," I say. "It is very soon. Only months. I am not going to see another spring. I will be of no use to you here nor any to myself. The doctors have said so."

"Don't be silly," she says. "You are only twenty-six. Your life is just beginning."

She looks at me with almost an indulgent tolerance for the silliness of my ideas and for my distortion of reality. Like the fond mother who is told by her imaginative child that he has seen a giraffe and an elephant upstairs in his bedroom. *I feel great affection for you*, the look says, *even though you do not know what you are talking about.*

For an instant I wish that it were so. To be as silly as she thinks I am and to be back in the time when bruises could be washed away by kisses and for her to be right and me thankfully wrong.

"No," I say. "It is true. Really true."

"What do you mean?" she asks, and now the true note of fear begins to sound in her voice. I wonder if it matches my own.

We sit at opposite ends of the kitchen table and look across at each other, across what seems the vast difference of our separated years. We make some attempts at conversation but they are not very successful.

Suddenly my grandmother leans across the table and grasps my hand in hers. "Oh Calum, Calum," she says. "What are we going to do? What are we going to do? What is to become of us?"

The gesture is almost a replica of the one from the earlier afternoon. In looking at her hands I notice that I have never finished trimming her fingernails. I do not know what to say. She holds my hand so fiercely as if I might pull her from the dark waters of a dream. I try to respond to the pressure with my own hands for I too had somehow hoped I might be saved. Suddenly both of us burst into tears. We are weeping for each other and for ourselves. We two who had hoped to find strength in each other meet now instead in only this display of weeping weakness. The dogs cock their ears and whine softly. Moving from one of us to the other they rest their trusting heads upon our laps and look into our eyes.

Sometimes in the darkness of our fear it is difficult to distinguish the dream from the truth. Sometimes we wake from the dream beyond the midnight hour and it is so much better than the world to which we wake that we would will ourselves back into its soothing comfort. Sometimes the reverse is true and we would pinch ourselves or scrape our knuckles against the bed frame's steel. Sometimes the nightmare knows no lines.

Lying rigid now in this bed of my parents' house all the images and emotions of the past day meet and swirl in the outer and inner darkness. The hopes and fears of my past and present jostle and intertwine. Sometimes when seeing the end of our present our past looms ever larger because it is all we have or think we know. I feel myself falling back into the past now, hoping to have more and more past as I have less and less future. My twenty-six years are not enough and I would want to go farther and farther back through previous generations so that I might have more of what now seems so little. I would go back through the superstitions and the herbal remedies and the fatalistic war cries and the haunting violins and the cancer cures of cobwebs. Back through the knowledge of being and its end as understood through second sight and spectral visions and the intuitive dog and the sea bird's cry. I would go back to the priest with the magic hands. Back to the faith healer if only I had more faith. Back to anything rather than to die at the objective hands of mute, cold science.

I see that old but young MacCrimmon quietly composing the music of his own death before leaving permanently the darkened shores of his misty Skye. I hear the music now and it is almost like a bell even as I see him falling silently through the dark. How strange, I think, that anyone should even consider a violin as sounding like a bell.

I get up from my bed and put on my clothes and walk silently and carefully through the sleeping house. Outside it is very quiet. There is no industry in this region and late at night the silence is profound. The music seems to come from the ocean, from off the quiet Gulf, and, no, it is not to be confused with anything else. It is not a bird or a radio or a shunting train or a passing car. It is not coming from anyone's party. It is only itself, strangely familiar in its unfamiliar way.

And then almost in response to the bell I hear the howls of the three black-and-white border collies. They come borne on the night's stillness drifting along the lonely coastline that leads from Rankin's Point. First the oldest dog and then the second and then the third. I can distinguish each dog's cry and I can comprehend the message that their anguished voices bear. I will not be able to save my grandmother now, I know, any more than I was able to save her in the earlier afternoon.

My car follows its probing headlights up and down and around the hairpinned darkness of the road to Rankin's Point. Some of the turns are so extreme that it is easy to overdrive the headlights. Sometimes the lights shine straight ahead into the darkness of the green foliage even as the road cuts unexpectedly to the right or to the left and becomes at least temporarily invisible. I follow it easily as if guided through a dream.

At "The Little Turn of Sadness" my headlights pick up the eyes of the waiting dogs. They are lying in different positions in the middle of the road and their eyes glow out of the darkness like the highlighted points of a waiting triangle. Red and gleaming they serve as markers and as warnings, somewhat, I think, like the signal buoys of the harbor or the lights along an airstrip's edge.

When I leave the car they are glad to see me. *He will know what to do*, they seem to say. They are dogs who for centuries have been bred for the guiding and guarding of life. They are not the guardians of junkyards or used-car lots or closed-down supermarkets. Not the guardians of steel and stone but of lives as fragile and as uncertain as their own. Running silently to protect the sheep from the crumbling cliff or crouched beside the lamb with the broken leg, they have always worked closely with their human masters and have waited for them when faced with problems beyond their strength. Now they are glad that I have come and move toward me.

My grandmother lies in the middle of the road at the spot where the little brook washes over the roadbed before the steepness of the final climb. I kneel beside her and take her hands into mine. They are still warm to the touch and the fingernails are still untrimmed. No need for that now. There are no marks visible upon her body and her eyes are open and stare upwards into the darkness of the sky. The twining Scottish thistles are still pinned to the collar of her dress. This is the ending that we have.

I rise and climb the steep road until I am standing at the cliff's edge which faces out to sea. I turn my head to the left and try to look up the coast to the home and buildings of Rankin's Point, but I cannot see in the darkness. For the first time in the centuries since the Scottish emigrations there is no human life at the end of this dark road. I turn again to the open sea and concentrate very hard on seeing something but it is no use. My grandmother cannot see Prince Edward Island now nor ever will again. I look down into the darkness beneath my feet but there too there is only a darkened void although I can hear the water lapping gently on the boulders far below.

The music that my grandmother played in the long-ago morning of this day moves slowly through my mind. I cannot tell if it comes from without or from within and then it does not seem to matter. The darkness rises within me in dizzying swirls and seems to yearn for that other darkness that lies without. I reach for the steadying gate post or the chair's firm seat but there is nothing for the hand to touch. And then as with the music, the internal and the external darkness reach to become as one. Flowing toward one another they become enjoined and indistinct and as single as perfection. Without a seam, without a sound, they meet and unite all.

The Closing Down
of Summer

I T IS AUGUST NOW, towards the end, and the weather can no longer be trusted. All summer it has been very hot. So hot that the gardens have died and the hay has not grown and the surface wells have dried to dampened mud. The brooks that flow to the sea have dried to trickles and the trout that inhabit them and the inland lakes are soft and sluggish and gasping for life. Sometimes they are seen floating dead in the over-warm water, their bodies covered with fat gray parasites. They are very unlike the leaping, spirited trout of spring, battling and alive in the rushing, clear, cold water; so electrically filled with movement that it seems no parasite could ever lodge within their flesh.

The heat has been bad for fish and wells and the growth of green but for those who choose to lie on the beaches of the summer sun the weather has been ideal. This is a record year for tourists in Nova Scotia, we are constantly being told. More motorists have crossed the border at Amherst than ever before. More cars have landed at the ferry docks in Yarmouth. Motels and campsites have been filled to capacity. The highways are heavy with touring buses and camper trailers and cars with the inevitable lobster traps fastened to their roofs. Tourism is booming as never before.

Here on this beach, on Cape Breton's west coast, there are no tourists. Only ourselves. We have been here for most of the summer. Surprised at the endurance and consistency of the heat. Waiting for it to break and perhaps to change the spell. At the end of July we said to ourselves and to each other, "The August gale will come and shatter all of this." The August gale is the traditional storm that comes each August, the forerunner of the hurricanes that will sweep up from the Caribbean and beat and lash this coast in the months of autumn. The August gale with its shrieking winds and crashing muddied waves has generally signalled the unofficial end of summer and it may come in August's very early days. But this year, as yet, it has not come and there are only a few days left. Still we know that the weather cannot last much longer and in another week the tourists will be gone and the schools will reopen and the pace of life will change. We will have to gather ourselves together then in some way and make the decisions that we have been postponing in the back of our minds. We are perhaps the best crew of shaft and development miners in the world and we were due in South Africa on the seventh of July.

But as yet we have not gone and the telegrams from Renco Development in Toronto have lain unanswered and the telephone calls have been unreturned. We are waiting for the change in the weather that will make it impossible for us to lie longer on the beach and then we will walk, for the final time, the steep and winding zigzagged trail that climbs the rocky face of Cameron's Point. When we reach the top of the cliff we will all be breathing heavily and then we will follow the little path that winds northward along the cliff's edge to the small field where our cars are parked, their hoods facing out to sea and their front tires scant feet from the cliffside's edge. The climb will take us some twenty minutes but we are all still in good shape after a summer of idleness.

The golden little beach upon which we lie curves in a crescent for approximately three-quarters of a mile and then terminates at either end in looming cliffs. The north cliff is called Cameron's Point after the family that once owned the land, but the south cliff has no name. Both cliffs protect the beach, slowing the winds from both north and south and preserving its tranquility.

At the south cliff a little brook ends its journey and plummets almost vertically some fifty feet into the sea. Sometimes after our swims or after lying too long in the sand we stand underneath its fall as we would a shower, feeling the fresh water fall upon our heads and necks and shoulders and running down our bodies' lengths to our feet which stand within the sea.

All of us have stood and turned our naked bodies unknown, unaccountable times beneath the spraying shower nozzles of the world's mining developments. Bodies that when free of mud and grime and the singed-hair smell of blasting powder are white almost to the color of milk or ivory. Perhaps of leprosy. Too white to be quite healthy, for when we work we are often twelve hours in the shaft's bottom or in the development drifts and we do not often feel the sun. All summer we have watched our bodies change their color and seen our hair grow bleached and ever lighter. Only the scars that all of us bear fail to respond to the healing power of the sun's heat. They seem to stand out even more vividly now, long running pink welts that course down our inner forearms or jagged saw-tooth ridges on the taut calves of our legs.

Many of us carry one shoulder permanently lower than the other where we have been hit by rock falls or the lip of the giant clam that swings down upon us in the narrow closeness of the shaft's bottom. And we have arms that we cannot raise above our heads and touches of arthritis in our backs and in our shoulders, magnified by the water that chills and falls upon us in our work. Few of us have all our fingers and some have lost either eyes or ears from falling tools or discharged blasting caps or flying stone or splintering timbers. Yet it is damage to our feet that we fear most of all. For loss of toes or damage to the intricate bones of heel or ankle means that we cannot support our bodies for the gruelling twelve-hour stand-up shifts. And injury to one foot means that the other must bear double its weight, which it can do for only a short time before poor circulation sets in to numb the leg and make it too inoperative. All of us are big men, over six feet tall and near two hundred pounds, and our feet have at the best of times a great deal of pressure bearing down upon them.

We are always intensely aware of our bodies and the pains

that course and twinge through them. Even late at night when we would sleep they jolt us unexpectedly as if from an electric current, bringing tears to our eyes and causing our fists to clench in the whiteness of knuckles and the biting of nails into palms. At such times we desperately shift our positions or numb ourselves from the tumblers of alcohol we keep close by our sides.

Lying now upon the beach we see the external scars on ourselves and on each other and are stirred to the memories of how they occurred. When we are clothed the price we pay for what we do is not so visible as it is now.

Beside us on the beach lie the white Javex containers filled with alcohol. It is the purest of moonshine made by our relatives back in the hills and is impossible to buy. It comes to us only as a gift or in exchange for long-past favors: bringing home of bodies, small loans of forgotten dollars, kindnesses to now-dead grandmothers. It is as clear as water, and a teaspoonful of it when touched by a match will burn with the low blue flame of a votive candle until it is completely consumed, leaving the teaspoon hot and totally dry. When we are finished here we will pour what remains into forty-ounce vodka bottles and take it with us on the long drive to Toronto. For when we decide to go we will be driving hard and fast and all of our cars are big: Cadillacs with banged-in fenders and Lincolns and Oldsmobiles. We are often stopped for speeding on the stretch outside Mt. Thom, or going through the Wentworth Valley, or on the narrow road to Fredericton, or on the fast straight road that leads from Rivière du Loup to Lévis, sometimes even on the 401. When we say that we must leave for Africa within hours we are seldom fined or in odd instances allowed to pay our speeding fines upon the spot. We do not wish to get into the entanglement of moonshine brought across provincial lines and the tedium that accompanies it. The fine for open commercial liquor is under fifteen dollars in most places and the transparent vodka bottles both show and keep their simple secret.

But we are not yet ready to leave and in the sun we pour the clear white fluid into styrofoam cups and drink it in long burning swallows, sometimes following such swallows with mouthfuls of Teem or Sprite or Seven-Up. No one bothers us here because we are so inaccessible. We can see any figure that would approach us from more than a mile away, silhouetted on the lonely cliff and the rocky and treacherous little footpath that is the only route to where we are. None of the RCMP who police this region are in any way local and it is unlikely that they even know this beach exists. And in the legal sense there is no public road that leads to the cliff where our cars now stand. Only vague paths and sheep trails through the burnt-out grass and around the clumps of alders and blueberry bushes and protruding stones and rotted stumps. The resilient young spruce trees scrape against the mufflers and oil pans of our cars and scratch against the doors. Hundreds of miles hence when we stop by the roadsides in Quebec and Ontario we will find small sprigs of this same spruce still wedged within the grillwork of our cars or stuck beneath the headlight bulbs. We will remove them and take them with us to Africa as mementos or talismans or symbols of identity. Much as our Highland ancestors, for centuries, fashioned crude badges of heather or of whortleberries to accompany them on the battlefields of the world. Perhaps so that in the closeness of their work with death they might find nearness to their homes and an intensified realization of themselves. We are lying now in the ember of summer's heat and in the stillness of its time.

Out on the flatness of the sea we can see the fishermen going about their work. They do not make much money anymore and few of them take it seriously. They say that the grounds have been over-fished by the huge factory fleets from Russia, Spain and Portugal. And it is true that on the still warm nights we can see the lights of such floating factories shining brightly off the coast. They appear as strange, moveable, brilliant cities and when they are far out their blazing lights seem to mingle with those of the stars. The fishermen before us are older men or young boys. Grandfathers with their grandsons acting out their ancient rituals. At noon or at one or two before they start for home they will run their little boats into our quiet cove until their bows are almost touching the sand. They will toss us the gleaming blue-black mackerel and the silver herring and the brown-and-white-striped cod and talk to us for a while, telling us anything that they think we should know. In return we toss them the whitened Javex bottles so that they may drink the pure clear contents. Sometimes the older men miss the toss and the white cylindrical bottles fall into the sea where they bob and toss like marker buoys or a child's duck in the bathtub until they are gaffed by someone in the boat or washed back in to shore. Later we cook the fish over small, crackling driftwood fires. This, we know too, cannot go on much longer.

In the quiet graveyards that lie inland the dead are buried. Behind the small white wooden churches and beneath the monuments of polished black granite they take their silent rest. Before we leave we will visit them to pray and take our last farewell. We will perhaps be afraid then, reading the dates of our brothers and uncles and cousins, recalling their youth and laughter and the place and manner of each death.

Death in the shafts and in the drifts is always violent and very often the body is so crushed or so blown apart that it cannot be reassembled properly for exposure in the coffin. Most of us have accompanied the grisly remains of such bodies trussed up in plastic bags on trains and planes and automobiles and delivered them up to the local undertaker. During the two or three days of the final wake and through the lonely all-night vigils kept in living rooms and old-fashioned parlors only memories and youthful photographs recall the physical reality that lies so dismembered and disturbed within each gray, sealed coffin. The most flattering photograph is placed upon the coffin's lid in an attempt to remind us of what was. I am thinking of this now, of the many youthful deaths I have been part of, and of the long homeward journeys in other seasons of other years. The digging of graves in the bitterness of February's cold, the shovelling of drifts of snow from the barren earth, and then the banging of the pick into the frozen ground, the striking of sparks from steel on stone and the scraping of shovels on earth and rock.

Some twenty years ago when first I went to the uranium shafts of Ontario's Elliot Lake and short-lived Bancroft we would have trouble getting our dead the final few miles to their high white houses. Often, in winter, we would have to use horses and sleighs to get them up the final hills, standing in chest-high snow, taking out window casings so that we might pass the coffin in and then out again for the last time. Or sometimes in the early spring we would again have to resort to horses when the leaving of the frost and the melting of the winter snow turned the brooks into red and roiling rivers and caused the dirt roads that led into the hills to become greasy and impassable. Sometimes in such seasons the underground springs beneath such roads erupt into tiny geysers, shooting their water upward and changing the roadbeds around them into quivering bogs that bury vehicles up to their hubs and axles.

And in November the rain is chill and cold at the graveside's edge. It falls upon our necks and splatters the red mud upon our gleaming shoes and on the pantlegs of our expensive suits. The bagpiper plays "Flowers of the Forest," as the violinist earlier played his haunting laments from the high choir loft. The music causes the hair to bristle on the backs of our necks and brings out the wildness of our grief and dredges the depths of our dense dark sorrow. At the graveside people sometimes shout farewells in Gaelic or throw themselves into the mud or upon the coffin as it is being lowered on its straps into the gaping earth.

Fifteen years ago when the timbers gave way in Springdale, Newfoundland, my younger brother died, crushed and broken amidst the constant tinkle of the dripping water and lying upon a bed of tumbled stone. We could not get him up from the bottom in time, as his eyes bulged from his head and the fluids of his body seeped quietly onto the glistening rock. Yet even as we tried we realized our task was hopeless and that he would not last, even on the surface. Would not last long enough for any kind of medical salvation. And even as the strength of his once-powerful grip began to loosen on my hand and his breath to rattle in his throat, we could see the earthly road that stretched before us as the witnesses and survivors of his death: the report to the local authorities, the statements to the company, to the police, to the coroner and then the difficult phone calls made on badly connected party lines or failing those the more efficient and more impersonal yellow telegrams. The darkness of the midnight phone call seems somehow to fade with the passing of time, or to change and be recreated like the ballads and folktales of the distant lonely past. Changing with each new telling as the tellers of the tales change, as they become different, older, more bitter or more serene. It is possible to hear descriptions of phone calls that you yourself have made some ten or fifteen years ago and to recognize very little about them except the undeniable kernel of truth that was at the center of the messages they contained. But the yellow telegram is more blunt and more permanent in the starkness of its message and it is never, ever thrown away. It is kept in vases and in Bibles and in dresser drawers beneath white shirts and it is stumbled upon sometimes unexpectedly, years later, sometimes by other hands, in little sandalwood boxes containing locks of the baby's hair or tucked inside the small shoes in which he learned to walk. A simple obituary of a formal kind.

When my brother died in Springdale, Newfoundland, it was the twenty-first of October and when we brought his body home we were already deep into fall. On the high hardwood hills the mountain ash and the aspen and the scarlet maple were ablaze with color beneath the weakened rays of the autumn sun. On alternate days the rain fell, sometimes becoming sleet or small hard hailstones. Sometimes the sun would shine in the morning, giving way to the vagaries of precipitation in the afternoon. And sometimes the cloud cover would float over the land even as the sun shone, blocking the sun out temporarily and casting shadows as if a giant bird were passing overhead. Standing beneath such a gliding cloud and feeling its occasional rain we could see the sun shining clearly at a distance of only a mile away. Seeing warmth so reachably near while feeling only the cold of the icy rain. But at the digging of his grave there was no sun at all. Only the rain falling relentlessly down upon us. It turned the crumbling clay to the slickest of mud, as slippery and glistening as that of the potter's wheel but many times more difficult to control. When we had dug some four feet down, the earthen walls began to slide and crumble and to give way around us and to fall upon our rubber boots and to press against the soaking pant legs that clung so clammily to our blue-veined legs. The deeper we dug the more intensely the rain fell, the drops dripping from our eyebrows and from our noses and the icy trickles running down the backs of our necks and down our spines and legs and into our squishing and sucking boots. When we had almost reached the required depth one of the walls that had been continuously crumbling and falling suddenly collapsed and with a great whoosh rolled down upon us. We were digging in our traditional family plot and when the wall gave way it sent the box that contained my father's coffin rolling down upon us. He had been dead for five years then, blown apart in Kirkland Lake, and at the time of his burial his coffin had been sealed. We were wildly and irrationally frightened by the slide and braced our backs against the splintered and disintegrating box, fearful lest it should tip and fall upon us and spill and throw whatever rotting relics remained of that past portion of our lives. Of little flesh but maybe green decaying bones or strands of silver matted hair.

We had held it there, braced by our backs in the pouring rain, until timbers were brought to shore up the new grave's side and to keep the past dead resting quietly. I had been very frightened then, holding the old dead in the quaking mud so that we might make room for the new in that same narrow cell of sliding earth and cracking wood. The next day at his funeral the rain continued to fall and in the grave that received him the unsteady timbers and the ground they held so temporarily back seemed but an extension of those that had caused his life to cease.

Lying now in the precarious heat of this still and burning summer I would wish that such thoughts and scenes of death might rise like the mists from the new day's ocean and leave me dry and somehow emptied on this scorching fine-grained sand.

In Africa it will be hot too, in spite of the coming rainy season, and on the veldt the heat will shimmer and the strange, fine-limbed animals will move across it in patterns older than memory. The nomads will follow their flocks of bleating goats in their constant search for grass and moisture and the women will carry earthen jars of water on their heads or baskets of clothes to slap against the rocks where the water is found.

In my own white house my wife does her declining wash among an increasingly bewildering battery of appliances. Her kitchen and her laundry room and her entire house gleam with porcelain and enamel and an ordered cleanliness that I can no longer comprehend. Little about me or about my work is clean or orderly and I am always mildly amazed to find the earnings of the violence and dirt in which I make my living converted into such meticulous brightness. The lightness of white and yellow curtains rustling crisply in the breeze. For us, most of our working lives is spent in rough, crude bunkhouses thrown up at the shafthead's site. Our bunks are made of two-by-fours sometimes roughly hammered together by ourselves and we sleep two men to a room or sometimes four or sometimes in the development's early stages in the vast "ram pastures" of twenty or thirty or perhaps even forty men crowded together in one vast, rectangular, unpartitioned room. Such rooms are like hospital wards without the privacy of the dividing curtains and they are filled, constantly, day and night, with the sounds of men snoring and coughing or spitting into cans by their bedsides, the incoherent moans and mumbles of uneasy sleepers and the thuds of half-conscious men making groaning love to their passive pillows. In Africa we will sleep, mostly naked, under incongruous structures of mosquito netting, hearing the sometimes rain on the roofs of corrugated iron. In the near 24-hour winter darkness of the Yukon, we have slept in sleeping bags, weighted down with blankets and surrounded by various heaters, still to wake to our breath as vapor in the coldness of the flashlight's gleam.

It is difficult to explain to my wife such things and we have grown more and more apart with the passage of the years. Meeting infrequently now almost as shy strangers, communicating mostly over vast distances through ineffectual say-nothing letters or checks that substitute money for what once was conceived as love. Sometimes the checks do not even come from me for in the developing African nations the political situation is often uncertain and North American money is sometimes suddenly and almost whimsically "frozen" or "nationalized," making it impossible to withdraw or remove. In times and places of such uneasiness, shaft crews such as ours often receive little or no actual money, only slips of paper to show our earnings, which are deposited in the metropolitan banks of New York or Toronto or London and from which our families are issued monthly checks.

I would regain what was once real or imagined with my wife. The long nights of passionate lovemaking that seemed so short, the creating and birth of our seven children. Yet I was never home for the birth of any of my children, only for their fathering. I was not home when two of them died so shortly after birth and I have not been home to participate or to share in many of the youthful accomplishments of the other five. I have attended few parents' nights or eighth-grade graduations or father-and-son hockey banquets, and broken tricycle wheels and dolls with crippled limbs have been mended by other hands than mine.

Now my wife seems to have gone permanently into a world of avocado appliances and household cleanliness and the vicarious experiences provided by the interminable soap operas that fill her television afternoons. She has perhaps gone as deeply into that life as I have into the life of the shafts, seeming to tunnel ever downward and outward through unknown depths and distances and to become lost and separated and unavailable for communication. Yet we are not surprised or critical of each other for she too is from a mining family and grew up largely on funds sent home by an absentee father. Perhaps we are but becoming our previous generation.

And yet there are times, even now, when I can almost physically feel the summer of our marriage and of our honeymoon and of her singing the words of the current popular songs into my then-attentive ears. I had been working as part of a crew in Uranium City all winter and had been so long without proper radio reception that I knew nothing of the music of that time's hit parade. There was always a feeling of mild panic then, on hearing whole dance floors of people singing aloud songs that had come and flourished since my departure and which I had never heard. As if I had been on a journey to the land of the dead.

It would be of little use now to whisper popular lyrics into my ears for I have become partially deaf from the years of the jackleg drill's relentless pounding into walls of constant stone. I cannot hear much of what my wife and children say to me and communicate with the men about me through nods and gestures and the reading of familiar lips. Musically, most of us have long abandoned the modern hit parades and have gone, instead, back to the Gaelic songs remembered from our early youth. It is these songs that we hum now on the hotness of this beach and which we will take with us on our journey when we go.

We have perhaps gone back to the Gaelic songs because they are so constant and unchanging and speak to us as the privately familiar. As a youth and as a young man I did not even realize that I could understand or speak Gaelic and entertained a rather casual disdain for those who did. It was not until the isolation of the shafts began that it started to bubble up somehow within me, causing a feeling of unexpected surprise at finding it there at all. As if it had sunk in unconsciously through some strange osmotic process while I had been unwittingly growing up. Growing up without fully realizing the language of the conversations that swirled around me. Now in the shafts and on the beach we speak it almost constantly though it is no longer spoken in our homes. There is a "Celtic Revival" in the area now, fostered largely by government grants, and the younger children are taught individual Gaelic words in the classrooms for a few brief periods during each month. It is a revival that is very different from our own and it seems, like so much else, to have little relevance for us and to have largely passed us by. Once, it is true, we went up to sing our Gaelic songs at the various Celtic concerts which have become so much a part of the summer culture and we were billed by the bright young schoolteachers who run such things as MacKinnon's Miners' Chorus; but that too seemed as lonely and irrelevant as it was meaningless. It was as if we were parodies of ourselves, standing in rows, wearing our miners' gear, or being asked to shave and wear suits, being plied with rum while waiting for our turn on the program, only then to mouth our songs to batteries of tape recorders and to people who did not understand them. It was as if it were everything that song should not be, contrived and artificial and non-spontaneous and lacking in communication.

I have heard and seen the Zulus dance until they shook the earth. I have seen large splendid men leap and twist and bend their bodies to the hard-baked flatness of the reddened soil. And I have followed their gestures and listened to their shouts and looked into their eyes in the hope that I might understand the meaning of their art. Hoping to find there a message that is recognizable only to primitive men. Yet, though I think I have caught glimpses of their joy, despair or disdain, it seems that in the end they must dance mainly for themselves. Their dancing speaks a language whose true meaning will elude me forever; I will never grasp the full impact of the subtleties and nuances that are spoken by the small head gesture or the flashing fleck of muscle.

I would like to understand more deeply what they have to say in the vague hope that it might be in some way akin to what is expressed in our own singing. That there might be some message that we share. But I can never enter deeply enough into their experience, can never penetrate behind the private mysteries of their eyes. Perhaps, I think sometimes, I am expecting too much. Yet on those occasions when we did sing at the concerts, I would have liked to reach beyond the tape recorders and the faces of the uninvolved to something that might prove to be more substantial and enduring. Yet in the end it seemed we too were only singing to ourselves. Singing songs in an archaic language as we too became more archaic and recognizing the nods of acknowledgement and shouted responses as coming only from our own friends and relatives. In many cases the same individuals from whom we had first learned our songs. Songs that are for the most part local and private and capable of losing almost all of their substance in translation. Yet in the introduction to the literature text that my eldest daughter brings home from the university it states that "the private experience, if articulated with skill, may communicate an appeal that is universal beyond the limitations of time or landscape." I have read that over several times and thought about its meaning in relation to myself.

When I was a boy my father told me that I would never understand the nature of sex until I had participated in it in some worthwhile way, and that there was little point in trying to grasp its meaning through erotic reading or looking at graphic pictures or listening to the real or imagined experiences of older men. As if the written or the spoken word or the mildly pornographic picture were capable of reaching only a small portion of the distance it might hope to journey on the road to understanding. In the early days of such wistful and exploratory reading the sexual act seemed most frequently to be described as "like flying." A boggling comparison at the time to virginal young men who had never been airborne. In the future numbness of our flight to Africa we will find little that is sexual if it is to be like our other flights to such distant destinations.

We will not have much to say about our flight to those we leave behind and little about our destinations when we land. Sending only the almost obligatory postcards that talk about the weather continents and oceans away. Saying that "things are going as expected," "going well." Postcards that have as their most exciting feature the exotic postage stamps sought after by the younger children for games of show and tell.

I have long since abandoned any hope of describing the sexual act or having it described to me. Perhaps it is enough to know that it is not at all like flying, though I do not know what it is really like. I have never been told, nor can I, in my turn, tell. But I would like somehow to show and tell the nature of my work and perhaps some of my entombed feelings to those that I would love, if they would care to listen.

I would like to tell my wife and children something of the way my years pass by on the route to my inevitable death. I would like to explain somehow what it is like to be a gladiator who fights always the impassiveness of water as it drips on darkened stone. And what it is like to work one's life in the tightness of confined space. I would like somehow to say how I felt when I lost my father in Kirkland Lake or my younger brother in Springdale, Newfoundland. I would like to say how frightened I am sometimes of what I do. And of how I lie awake at night aware of my own decline and of the diminishing of the men around me. For all of us know we will not last much longer and that it is unlikely we will be replaced in the shaft's bottom by members of our own flesh and bone. For such replacement, like our Gaelic, seems to be of the past and now largely over.

Our sons will go to the universities to study dentistry or law and to become fatly affluent before they are thirty. Men who will stand over six feet tall and who will move their fat, pudgy fingers over the limited possibilities to be found in other people's mouths. Or men who sit behind desks shuffling papers relating to divorce or theft or assault or the taking of life. To grow prosperous from pain and sorrow and the desolation of human failure. They will be far removed from the physical life and will seek it out only through jogging or golf or games of handball with friendly colleagues. They will join expensive private clubs for the pleasures of perspiration and they will not die in falling stone or chilling water or thousands of miles from those they love. They will not die in any such manner, partially at least because we have told them not to and have encouraged them to seek out other ways of life which lead, we hope, to gentler deaths. And yet because it seems they will follow our advice instead of our lives, we will experience, in any future that is ours, only an increased sense of anguished isolation and an ironic feeling of confused bereavement. Perhaps it is always so for parents who give the young advice and find that it is followed. And who find that those who follow such advice must inevitably journey far from those who give it to distant lonely worlds which are forever unknowable to those who wait behind. Yet perhaps those who go find in the regions to which they travel but another kind of inarticulate loneliness. Perhaps the dentist feels mute anguish as he circles his chair, and the lawyer who lives in a world of words finds little relationship between professional talk and what he would hope to be true expression. Perhaps he too in his quiet heart sings something akin to Gaelic songs, sings in an old archaic language private words that reach to no one. And perhaps both lawyer and dentist journey down into an Africa as deep and dark and distant as ours. I can but vaguely imagine what I will never know.

I have always wished that my children could see me at my work. That they might journey down with me in the dripping cage to the shaft's bottom or walk the eerie tunnels of the drifts that end in walls of staring stone. And that they might see how articulate we are in the accomplishment of what we do. That they might appreciate the perfection of our drilling and the calculation of our angles and the measuring of our powder, and that they might understand that what we know through eye and ear and touch is of a finer quality than any information garnered by the most sophisticated of mining engineers with all their elaborate equipment.

I would like to show them how professional we are and how, in spite of the chill and the water and the dark and the danger, there is perhaps a certain eloquent beauty to be found in what we do. Not the beauty of stillness to be found in gleaming crystal or in the polished hardwood floors to which my wife devotes such care but rather the beauty of motion on the edge of violence, which by its very nature can never long endure. It is perhaps akin to the violent motion of the huge professional athletes on the given days or nights of their many games. Men as huge and physical as are we, polished and eloquent in the propelling of their bodies towards their desired goals and in their relationships and dependencies on one another but often numb and silent before the microphones of sedentary interviewers. Few of us get to show our children what we do on national television; we offer only the numbness and silence by itself. Unable either to show or tell.

I have always wished to be better than the merely mediocre and I have always wanted to use the power of my body in the fulfilling of such a wish. Perhaps that is why I left the university after only one year. A year which was spent mainly as an athlete and as a casual reader of English literature. I could not release myself enough physically and seemed always to be constricted and confined. In sleeping rooms that were too low, by toilet stalls that were too narrow, in lecture halls that were too hot, even by the desks in those lecture halls, which I found always so difficult to get in and out of. Confined too by bells and buzzers and curfews and deadlines, which for me had little meaning. I wanted to burst out, to use my strength in some demanding task that would allow me somehow to feel that I was breaking free. And I could not find enough release in the muddy wars on the football field or in the thudding contact of the enclosed and boarded rink. I suppose I was drawn too by the apparent glamor of the men who followed the shafts. Impressed by their returning here in summer with their fast cars and expensive clothes, also by the fact that I was from a mining family that has given itself for generations to the darkened earth.

I was aware even then of the ultimate irony of my choice. Aware of how contradictory it seemed that someone who was bothered by confinement should choose to spend his working days in the most confined of spaces. Yet the difference seems to be that when we work we are never still. Never merely entombed like the prisoner in the passive darkness of his solitary confinement. For we are always expanding the perimeters of our seeming incarceration. We are always moving downward or inward or forward or in the driving of our raises even upward. We are big men engaged in perhaps the most violent of occupations and we have chosen as our adversary walls and faces of massive stone. It is as if the stone of the spherical earth has challenged us to move its weight and find its treasure and we have accepted the challenge and responded with drill and steel and powder and strength and all our ingenuity. In the chill and damp we have given ourselves to the breaking down of walls and barriers. We have sentenced ourselves to enclosures so that we might taste the giddy joy of breaking through. Always hopeful of breaking through though we know we never will break free.

Drilling and hammering our way to the world's resources, we have left them when found and moved on. Left them for others to expand or to exploit and to make room for the often stable communities that come in our wake: the sewer lines and the fire hydrants and the neat rows of company houses, the over-organized athletic leagues and the ever-hopeful schools, the Junior Chambers of Commerce. We have moved about the world, liberating resources, largely untouched by political uncertainties and upheavals, seldom harmed by the midnight plots, the surprising coups and the fast assassinations. We were in Haiti with Duvalier in 1960 and in Chile before Allende and in the Congo before it became associated with Zaire. In Bolivia and Guatemala and in Mexico and in a Jamaica that the tourists never see. Each segment of the world aspires to the treasure, real or imagined, that lies encased in its vaults of stone, and those who would find such booty are readily admitted and handsomely paid, be they employed by dictator or budding democracy or capitalists expanding their holdings and their wealth. Renco Development on Bay Street will wait for us. They will endure our summer on the beach and our lack of response to their seemingly urgent messages. They will endure our Toronto drunkenness and pay our bail and advance us personal loans. And when we go they will pay us thousands of dollars for our work, optimistically hoping that they may make millions in their turn. They will wait for us because they know from years of many contracts that we are the best bet to deliver for them in the end.

There are two other crews in Canada as strong, perhaps even stronger than we are. They are in Rouyn-Noranda; and as our crew is known as MacKinnon, theirs are known by the names of Lafrenière and Picard. We have worked beside them at various times, competed with them and brawled with them in the hall-like beer parlors of Malartic and Temiskaming, and occasionally we have saved one another's lives. They will not go to Africa for Renco Development because they are imprisoned in the depths of their language. And because they speak no English they will not move out of Quebec or out of northern or northeastern Ontario. Once there was also the O'Leary crew, who were Irish Newfoundlanders. But many of them were lost in a cave-in in India, and of those who remained most have gone to work with their relatives on high-steel construction in New York. We see them sometimes, now, in the bars of Brooklyn or sometimes in the summers at the ferry terminal in North Sydney before they cross to Port-aux-Basques. Iron work, they say, also pays highly for the risk to life; and the long fall from the towering, swaying skyscrapers can occur for any man but once. It seems, for them, that they have exchanged the possibility of being fallen upon for that of falling itself. And that after years of dodging and fearing falling objects from above, they have become such potential objects themselves. Their loss diminishes us too because we know how good they were at what they did, and know too that the mangled remnants of their dead were flown from India in sealed containers to lie on such summer days as these beneath the nodding wild flowers that grow on outport graves.

I must not think too much of death and loss, I tell myself repeatedly. For if I am to survive I must be as careful and calculating with my thoughts as I am with my tools when working so far beneath the earth's surface. I must always be careful of sloppiness and self-indulgence lest they cost me dearly in the end.

Out on the ocean now it is beginning to roughen and the southwest wind is blowing the smallish waves into larger versions of themselves. They are beginning to break upon the beach with curling whitecaps at their crests and the water that they consist of seems no longer blue but rather a dull and somber gray. There are no longer boats visible on the once-flat sea, neither near at hand nor on the horizon's distant line. The sun no longer shines with the fierceness of the earlier day and the sky has begun to cloud over. Evening is approaching. The sand is whipped by the wind and blows into our faces and stings our bodies as might a thousand pinpricks or the tiny tips of many scorching needles. We flinch and shake ourselves and reach for our protective shirts. We leave our prone positions and come restlessly to our feet, coughing and spitting and moving uneasily like nervous animals anticipating a storm. In the sand we trace erratic designs and patterns with impatient toes. We look at one another, arching our eyebrows like bushy question marks. Perhaps this is what we have been waiting for? Perhaps this is the end and the beginning?

And now I can feel the eyes of the men upon me. They are waiting for me to give interpretations of the signals, waiting for my sign. I hesitate for a moment, running my eyes along the beach, watching water touching sand. And then I nod my head. There is almost a collective sigh that is more sensed than really heard. Almost like distant wind in far-off trees. Then suddenly they begin to move. Rapidly they gather their clothes and other belongings, shaking out the sand, folding and packing. Moving swiftly and with certainty they are closing down their summer even as it is closing down on them. MacKinnon's miners are finished now and moving out. We are leaving the beach of the summer sun and perhaps some of us will not see it anymore. For some of us may not return alive from the Africa for which we leave.

We begin to walk. First along the beach towards the north cliff of Cameron's Point, and then up the steep and winding zigzagged trail that climbs its face. When I am halfway up I stop and look back at the men strung out in single file behind me. We are mountain climbers in our way though bound together by no physical ropes of any kind. They stop and look back too, back and down to the beach we have so recently vacated. The waves are higher now and are breaking and cresting and rolling farther in. They have obliterated the outlines of our bodies in the sand and our footprints of brief moments before already have been washed away. There remains no evidence that we have ever been. It is as if we have never lain, nor ever walked nor ever thought what thoughts we had. We leave no art or mark behind. The sea has washed its sand slate clean.

And then the rain begins to fall. Not heavily but almost hesitantly. It is as if it has been hot and dry for so long that the act of raining has almost been forgotten and has now to be slowly and almost painfully relearned.

We reach the summit of the cliff and walk along the little path that leads us to our cars. The cars are dusty and their metal is still hot from the earlier sun. We lean across their hoods to lift the windshield wipers from the glass. The rubber of the wiper blades has almost melted into the windshields because of heat and long disuse, and when we lift them slender slivers of rubber remain behind. These blades will have to be replaced.

The isolated raindrops fall alike on windshield and on roof, on hood and trunk. They trace individual rivulets through the layers of grime and then trickle down to the parched and waiting earth.

And now it is two days later. The rain has continued to fall and in it we have gone about preparing and completing our rituals of farewell. We have visited the banks and checked out all the dates on our insurance policies. And we have gathered our working clothes, which when worn continents hence will make us loom even larger than we are in actual life. As if we are Greek actors or mastodons of an earlier time. Soon to be replaced or else perhaps to be extinct.

We have stood bareheaded by the graves and knelt in the mud by the black granite stones. And we have visited privately and in tiny self-conscious groups the small white churches which we may not see again. As we have become older it seems we have become strangely more religious in ways that border close on superstition. We will take with us worn family rosaries and faded charms and loop ancestral medals and crosses of delicate worn fragility around our scar-lashed necks and about the thickness of our wrists, seemingly unaware of whatever irony they might project. This too seems but a further longing for the past, far removed from the "rational" approaches to religion that we sometimes encounter in our children.

We have said farewells to our children too and to our wives and I have offered kisses and looked into their eyes and wept outwardly and inwardly for all I have not said or done and for my own clumsy failure at communication. I have not been able, as the young say, "to tell it like it is," and perhaps now I never shall.

By four o'clock we are ready to go. Our cars are gathered with their motors running and we will drive them hard and fast and be in Toronto tomorrow afternoon. We will not stop all night except for a few brief moments at the gleaming service stations and we will keep one sober and alert driver at the wheel of each of our speeding cars. Many of the rest of us will numb ourselves with moonshine for our own complex and diverse reasons: perhaps to loosen our thoughts and tongues or perhaps to deaden and hold them down, perhaps to be as the patient who takes an anaesthetic to avoid operational pain. We will hurtle in a dark night convoy across the landscapes and the borders of four waiting provinces.

As we move out, I feel myself a figure in some medieval ballad who has completed his formal farewells and goes now to meet his fatalistic future. I do not particularly wish to feel this way and again would shake myself free from thoughts of death and self-indulgence.

As we gather speed the land of the seacoast flashes by. I am in the front seat of the lead car, on the passenger side next to the window. In the side mirror I can see the other cars stretched out behind us. We go by the scarred and abandoned coal workings of our previous generations and drive swiftly westward into the declining day. The men in the back seat begin to pass around their moonshine and attempt to adjust their long legs within the constricted space. After a while they begin to sing in Gaelic, singing almost unconsciously the old words that are so worn and so familiar. They seem to handle them almost as they would familiar tools. I know that in the other cars they are doing the same even as I begin to silently mouth the words myself. There is no word in Gaelic for good-bye, only for farewell.

More than a quarter of a century ago in my single year at the university, I stumbled across an anonymous lyric from the fifteenth century. Last night while packing my clothes I encountered it again, this time in the literature text of my eldest daughter. The book was very different from the one that I had so casually used, as different perhaps as is my daughter from me. Yet the lyric was exactly the same. It had not changed at all. It comes to me now in this speeding car as the Gaelic choruses rise around me. I do not particularly welcome it or want it and indeed I had almost forgotten it. Yet it enters now regardless of my wants or wishes, much as one might see out of the corner of the eye an old acquaintance one has no wish to see at all. It comes again, unbidden and unexpected and imperfectly remembered. It seems borne up by the mounting, surging Gaelic voices like the flecked white foam on the surge of the towering, breaking wave. Different yet similar, and similar yet different, and in its time unable to deny:

> *I wend to death, knight stith in stour;*
> *Through fight in field I won the flower;*
> *No fights me taught the death to quell—*
> *I wend to death, sooth I you tell.*
>
> *I wend to death, a king iwis;*
> *What helpes honour or worlde's bliss?*
> *Death is to man the final way—*
> *I wende to be clad in clay.*

ABOUT THE AUTHOR

ALISTAIR MACLEOD is a native of Nova Scotia's Inverness County. He has worked as a school teacher, miner, and logger, and is currently a professor of English and creative writing at the University of Windsor in Ontario. His stories have appeared in *The Southern Review, Tamarack Review, The Massachusetts Review*, and many other distinguished North American journals; and have been reprinted in *Best American Short Stories, Best Canadian Short Stories*, and *Selected Stories from The Southern Review, 1965–1985*. His two collections of short fiction are *The Lost Salt Gift of Blood* and *As Birds Bring Forth the Sun*, both published by McClelland and Stewart in Canada.